REFUGE COVE

Don't miss any of Janet Dailey's bestsellers

JANET DAILEY

REFUGE COVE

KENSINGTON BOOKS
http://www.kensingtonbooks.com

KENSINGTON BOOKS are published by

Kensington Publishing Corp.
119 West 40th Street
New York, NY 10018

All Kensington titles, imprints, and distributed lines are available at special quantity discounts for bulk purchases for sales promotion, premiums, fund-raising, educational, or institutional use.

Special book excerpts or customized printings can also be created to fit specific needs. For details, write or phone the office of the Kensington Special Sales Manager: Attn. Special Sales Department. Kensington Publishing Corp, 119 West 40th Street, New York, NY 10018. Phone: 1-800-221-2647.

Library of Congress Card Catalogue Number: 2017951248

ISBN-13: 978-1-4967-1193-9
ISBN-10: 1-4967-1193-9
First Kensington Hardcover Edition: December 2017

10 9 8 7 6 5 4 3 2

Printed in the United States of America

As always, I am deeply grateful to Elizabeth Lane,
without whom this book would not have been possible.

REFUGE
COVE

CHAPTER 1

Southeast Alaska
Early autumn

Along the Tongass Narrows, the cruise ships that plied Alaska's Inside Passage and spilled tourists onto the docks at Ketchikan were gone with the season. The harbor was quiet, the fishing boats at rest in the Basin. The souvenir shops on the boardwalk were closing their doors.

Dead salmon carpeted the shallow streams, their bodies spent in the grueling race to reach home and spawn. White flocks of seagulls gorged on the remains.

Behind the town, and the highway leading up the coast, evergreen-cloaked mountains towered against the sky. On the narrow lowland that skirted the water, clumps of cottonwood and willow blazed with autumn gold. Alder, dogwood, and mountain ash lent the scene rich hues of bronze and crimson.

Fall in Alaska was a time of fleeting beauty. But that beauty was lost on Emma Hunter. As she fled in terror through the deep-shadowed forest, only one thing mattered—staying alive.

Run! The word shrilled in Emma's mind as she fought her way through the maze of thorny undergrowth, rotting stumps, and fallen trees. Low-hanging limbs whipped her face. Tangled roots snagged her feet.

Run!

Again and again, she'd tripped and fallen. Her hands were scratched and bleeding, her jeans ripped, her thin sneakers soaked. Her breath came in gasps. But she mustn't stop, not even to catch her breath or to ease the ripping pain in her side.

If Boone caught her, he would kill her—or make her wish he had.

When Boone Swenson had proposed, two weeks after meeting her at a church dance in Salt Lake City, Emma had felt like the heroine of a romantic novel. The prospect of a life in wild Alaska with the rugged man of her dreams had swept away a lifetime of caution. By the time she'd discovered the truth, it was too late. She was trapped in a nightmare of her own making.

Through the trees behind her, she could hear the hellish baying of Boone's dogs as they followed her scent. The two surly wolf hybrids were probably on leashes. Otherwise, by now, they would've raced ahead of their master and caught her.

If—or *when*—they found her, would Boone turn them loose on his bride, or would he call them off and drag her back to the trailer for his version of a honeymoon?

Boone was unpredictable. She'd already learned that. But one thing was certain. Given what she now knew about him, he would never let her go free.

Her ankle twisted on a root. A hot pain flashed up her leg. Teeth clenched, she ran on, dodging through the shadowy undergrowth. Giant spruces and hemlocks towered above her. A squirrel scolded from a high branch. A jay screeched an alarm, startling a flock of small birds to flight—all signs of her presence that Boone would recognize.

Why go on, you fool? The voice in her head seemed to

mock her. *You're miles from the coast, with no place to go—no road, no neighbors, no food, water, or shelter. You haven't got a chance.*

Refusing to listen, Emma struggled on. Her lungs were burning. Her legs quivered with every step.

The sinking sun cast fingers of light through the treetops. Somewhere to the west lay the highway, her best hope of finding help. But something told Emma she'd never make it that far. Between the coming darkness, her waning strength, and the dogs, there was only one way this chase could end.

It's over, the silent voice argued. *Boone doesn't want you dead. He wants a wife. Give up and go back with him. You can always escape later.*

But giving up was not an option, Emma resolved. Whatever happened, she would keep going. She would run until she dropped. And when she could run no more, she would fight.

The trees were thinning now, giving way to brambles and stands of devil's club, a leggy weed with sharp-edged leaves and spines that burned like fire to the touch. Beyond the trees, she could see an open bog, dotted with pools of dark water. *Muskeg*—that was what Alaskans called places like this, where layers of rotted vegetation, laid down over decades and centuries, clogged the growth of everything but sickly-looking moss, yellowed marsh grass, and a few twisted trees that would never grow tall.

The bog was about half the size of a football field. Going around it, or veering off in another direction, might be safer. But if there was any chance of reaching the road, a straight westward dash across the muskeg would be the shortest way.

She could hear the dogs getting closer. Fueled by terror, Emma gathered the last of her strength and burst into a headlong sprint.

The outer edge of the muskeg was firm enough to support her. But within a few yards, murky water began welling around her sneakers. With every step, the muck grew deeper. Soon it was closing over her ankles, making a sucking sound as she freed each foot. By now, she'd gone too far to turn around. As her feet sank deeper, the effort drained her strength, slowing her progress to a crawl.

When her bare foot came up without the shoe, Emma knew she'd made a fatal mistake. Unfamiliar with muskeg, she hadn't realized how unstable the ground could be. Now she was stuck halfway to her knees, and too exhausted to go on.

She was trapped.

John Wolf slowed the vintage de Havilland Beaver to 75 mph and lowered the flaps for the descent into Refuge Cove. The mail run to the scattered villages up the coast had taken most of the day. Tonight he looked forward to a meal in his cabin, a hot shower, and a good book by the fire.

Through the windscreen of the sixty-year-old single-engine prop plane, he checked the landscape below. Like a yellow stain against the dark green forest, a familiar patch of muskeg lay directly under the flight path. Using it as a marker, he knew he could make a turn there and line up his bearings for a perfect landing in the cove.

He was banking for the turn when he glimpsed something out of place. In the middle of the muskeg, a living creature was struggling to get free. A young deer or bear cub—that was John's first impression. But as he corrected the turn and leveled out to a full view of the muskeg, he realized that it was a woman, caught in the treacherous muck.

What would a lone woman be doing out here? Whatever her story, she was in one hell of a bad spot.

John put the plane into a shallow dive and zoomed in low. There was no place to land here, but he wanted the woman to know she'd been seen and that help would be coming. She waved frantically as he passed overhead. He glimpsed long chestnut hair and a plaid shirt before he climbed again and circled back.

Now what? He could—and would—radio for rescue. But it would soon be dark, and the night would be cold. Even with a helicopter, a rescue team might not be able to reach her before hypothermia set in. And there was another danger. Trapped as she was, the woman would be easy prey for the black bears that roamed the forest and had little fear of humans.

A hard-core loner, John made it a habit to keep to himself. Other people's problems were none of his damned business. The last thing he wanted was to be somebody's hero. But even he couldn't leave a helpless fool woman out here alone.

The Beaver's floats would only allow the small plane to land on water. The soupy surface of a muskeg might do in an emergency, but this open patch, surrounded by dense forest, was way too small. His best bet, a quarter mile from the muskeg, was a place where a creek had eroded its banks to form a shallow lake. From the air, the lake hadn't looked much bigger than a puddle. But he remembered estimating its length to be a little over a thousand feet— barely enough distance to land and take off again. The width was maybe a third of that distance. The landing would be hairy as hell, the takeoff even riskier. But it was his best chance of reaching the woman. Maybe the only chance.

He took a moment to radio his position and pass on what was happening. Then he banked, made one more low pass over the woman, then headed for the lake.

* * *

Emma's flash of hope faded as the plane vanished over the trees. She was sure the pilot had seen her. But now he'd gone.

Was he looking for a place to land, or had he simply radioed her position and left her to wait for rescue?

But what difference would it make? She'd already run out of time.

The drone of the plane faded with distance. Then, abruptly, it stopped, leaving an eerie silence in its wake. It took a moment for Emma to realize that she could no longer hear the dogs.

Her mind scrambled to piece together what was happening. Boone would've been aware of the plane—and it made sense that he wouldn't want the pilot, or any other witness, to see him. He must've silenced the dogs and pulled back into the forest to wait until the coast was clear.

Boone wouldn't wait long. As soon as he could be sure the pilot wasn't coming back, the chase would be over. She would be at his mercy.

But the plane's arrival had bought her time and given her hope. She couldn't give up now.

Dropping forward and sprawling belly down to even out her weight, she dragged herself ahead. One foot pulled free of the muck, then the other. Both shoes were gone now. Even if she made it onto solid ground, her tender feet wouldn't get her very far. But she couldn't stop—not as long as there was any chance of rescue.

As she crawled toward the far side of the muskeg, she focused her thoughts on the plane and the unseen pilot.

Come back . . . she begged silently. *Please, come back . . .*

* * *

The landing had been tight, leaving only a few feet of water between the floats and the bank. John took a long breath, then reached back for the coiled rope he kept in the plane. His Smith & Wesson .44 magnum revolver, which he carried as a precaution against bears, was tucked under the seat. He took it out and buckled on the shoulder holster before climbing out the door, stepping onto the float, and wading through shallow water to reach the bank.

By his reckoning, the muskeg would be about ten minutes due south. There was no trail, but he'd flown over this stretch of forest countless times going in and out of the cove. The map was fixed in his mind.

With the rope slung over his shoulder, he set off at a ground-eating stride. The lady wasn't going anywhere fast, but his danger instincts were prickling. There was only one reason a woman would get herself stranded in the middle of a muskeg. Something—or more likely, someone—was after her.

Whoever that someone might be, it wouldn't hurt to let them know he was on his way, and that he was armed. He paused long enough to draw the .44 and fire two shots in the air. As the echo died away, he broke into a run.

Emma heard the shots. But with her head down, there was no way to tell which direction they were coming from or who was firing. All she could do was stay low and keep moving.

She was nearing the edge of the muskeg. The going was easier here, the ground firmer beneath her weight. But she was wet and shivering with exhaustion. Beyond the ring of scraggly brush and devil's club, the evergreen forest lay deep in twilight shadows. She might be able to hide among the trees, but with the dogs on her trail, how far could she run without shoes?

There was no sign of Boone, but that didn't mean he'd given up and left. Emma knew he'd be just out of sight, waiting for the best chance to rush her. As for the pilot—

She gasped as a man stepped out from among the trees. He was tall and dark, dressed in khakis and a heavy shirt. A rope was coiled over one shoulder. The opposite hand gripped a heavy revolver.

"You're the pilot?" Her teeth were chattering.

"Let's get you out of here."

He slid the gun into its holster, then paused as if deciding on a course of action. He'd brought a rope, but by now she was only a few feet from firm ground. Stepping past the edge of the bog, he planted his work boots for balance, reached down, and caught her bleeding hands. There was no gentleness in his clasp. If anything, his manner suggested that having to rescue her was nothing but an inconvenience.

Emma bit back a whimper as he dragged her off the muskeg. He had just pulled her to her feet when a shot rang out from the forest on the far side of the bog. Missing by inches, the bullet slammed into a tree behind them.

"Get down!" He shoved her to the ground as another bullet whined past. "Sounds like a damned bear rifle," he muttered. "And the bastard's a good shot. I'm guessing it's somebody you know."

"Yes." Emma forced the words through chattering teeth. "My husband."

His stony expression didn't even flicker. "So why would your husband want you dead?"

"It's a long story."

"Come on. And keep low." Crouching, he yanked her along with him into the safety of the trees. Dry pine needles jabbed her feet. She willed herself not to cry out.

"He's got dogs," she said.

"Stay here." Leaving Emma huddled at the base of a stump, he drew his pistol and moved like a shadow to the edge of the clearing. The sound of the pistol, as he fired across the distance, made her ears ring.

Seconds later he was back, offering an impersonal hand to pull her to her feet.

"Why did you shoot?" she asked him. "You couldn't have hit anything in the dark."

"You said he had dogs. Now that he knows I could shoot them, he'll be less likely to send them after us." He gripped her arm above the elbow. "Let's go. The plane isn't far."

She took a step. A sharp pine cone jabbed her foot. Emma yelped.

"What now?" He scowled down at her.

"My shoes. I lost them."

"Hang on." He adjusted the coil of rope. Scooping her up, he slung her over his shoulder like a fireman carrying an unconscious victim out of a burning house. Her hair dangled down his back. Her hips rode his shoulder. The hand that balanced her rested on the backs of her thighs, just below her rump.

"Comfortable?"

"Don't even ask."

"It won't be for long," he said, striding out. "Let me know if you hear anybody behind us."

"What if it's a bear? Will you drop me and run?"

"Don't tempt me, lady."

"My name is Emma."

"Pleased to meet you, Emma," he muttered. "Now let's get the hell out of here."

At least the woman wasn't hard to carry. She was a delicate thing, her bones almost weightless, like a bird's. And she lay over his shoulder like a trusting child. John was painfully aware of his hand, resting across the backs of her legs in a way that was almost intimate. The thin, wet fabric of her jeans clung to her thighs. He could feel her shivering as the chilly darkness of night crept around them.

Emma. A prim, old-fashioned kind of name. For some reason it seemed to suit her.

What kind of man would chase a woman—especially a fragile little thing like her—through the forest with dogs and a gun? She'd said it was a long story. He wouldn't mind hearing it. But she could tell it to the police in Ketchikan. Her troubles were none of his business.

Besides, a woman didn't have to be big and strong to destroy a man. John knew that all too well.

A rising moon crept over the high peaks above the tree line. In the glow of its light he could see the plane, where he'd left it at the end of the small lake. He lengthened his stride, waded to the plane, and set her down with her bare feet on the float. "Climb aboard," he said, opening the passenger door.

When she hesitated, he clasped her waist and boosted her up to the seat. Her teeth were chattering. "My coat's on the seatback behind you," he said. "Put it on and fasten your belt. It's liable to be a bumpy ride out of here."

After closing the door he went around the plane, buckled himself into the pilot's seat, put on his headphones, and started the engine. He only hoped he could manage to be in the air before the woman's crazy husband showed up with his bear rifle and dogs. Maybe they'd just had a lover's spat. Maybe if he hadn't interfered, they would have patched things up and walked home hand in hand. But what was done was done. He was in this mess for the duration.

After turning the plane around, he aligned it to take off

into the wind. He glanced at his passenger to make sure she was securely belted. Wrapped in his old sheepskin flight jacket, she was gazing straight ahead, her hands clasped tightly in her lap. The roar of the engine drowned out anything they might have said to each other.

The short takeoff distance was a worry. But the wind that swept in across the narrows was strong and steady. Setting his jaw, he opened the throttle, revved the engine to 2100 rpm, and pulled back on the yoke. The Beaver shot across the water, lifting off just short of the tall spruces. The floats grazed the treetops as the plane soared skyward.

Emma had forgotten to breathe. As the plane leveled off, she exhaled and tried to relax. She was cold, muddy, scared, and exhausted, and she had no idea where this grim, impersonal man was taking her. But anyplace would be better than where she'd been.

Her nervous hands twisted her plain, gold wedding band. The first moment she'd felt it slide onto her finger, her whole being had flooded with joy. What a trusting, innocent fool she'd been. If she'd known the truth, she would have flung the ring on the ground and run for her life. Now, as she huddled on the narrow passenger seat, she sensed that her nightmare was far from over. Boone was still out there somewhere—and escaping him would not be as simple as flying away in a stranger's airplane.

This was her first flight in anything smaller than an airline jet. The cockpit looked like something out of a World War II movie. The dashboard—or whatever it was called—was a maze of dials, gauges, buttons, and levers. It looked devilishly complicated, but the man at the controls made flying the plane look as easy as driving a car.

The fuselage quivered and rattled with every gust of

wind. The engine roared in her ears. Looking out the side window, she glimpsed trees like dark velvet—and then, in the distance a glimmer of electric lights.

Her stomach lurched as the plane made a rapid descent and zoomed over what appeared to be scattered buildings edging dark water. A forested island flashed past her view as the engine slowed. The floats skimmed the water as the plane settled like a seabird onto the lapping waves.

Revving the engine slightly, the pilot turned the plane around and taxied back toward the lights on shore. He hadn't said a word to her—but even if he had, she wouldn't have been able to hear him over the engine. Once they could talk to each other, he'd be asking plenty of questions.

After winding through channels, the plane stopped alongside a long, narrow floating dock. When the pilot cut the engine, the silence was almost startling.

Emma held her tongue until he'd removed his headphones. "So, what is this place?" she asked. "Where are we?"

A ghost of a smile tightened his lips. "Welcome to Refuge Cove," he said.

CHAPTER 2

John climbed out of the Beaver and left Emma in the cockpit while he secured the plane to the dock and lifted out the mail pouch for delivery to the post office in nearby Ward Cove. His ten-year-old Jeep Wrangler was on the far side of the graveled parking lot. He started it up, parked near the end of the floating dock, and walked back down to help Emma out of the plane.

"Hello, John Wolf," she said as he opened the passenger door. "Since you didn't introduce yourself, I did some snooping. I found your name on the plane's registration."

"You could've asked." He held out his hand.

"When?" She let him guide her onto the float and support her step to the dock. "Should I have asked you while we were ducking bullets, or maybe while you had me slung over your back like a sack of coal?"

"Well, since you know it now, I guess that doesn't matter. That's my Jeep next to the dock. You can thank me for sparing your feet from the parking lot."

"Thanks." She fell silent beside him, taking careful steps on the damp surface.

What now? John asked himself. He hadn't invited this helpless woman into his life, and he had no obligation to keep her. Common sense dictated that he drive her into Ketchikan, drop her off at the police station, and forget he ever saw her. No complications, just an interesting memory.

But she was cold, muddy, barefoot, and probably still scared half to death. Unless there was something in the pocket of her jeans, she appeared to have no money and no identification. Dumping her at the police station would be like leaving a storm-soaked kitten on the front step of the animal pound.

Besides, against his better judgment, he'd become curious. She'd mentioned a husband, and he'd noticed that she was wearing a gold wedding band. What was her story? What kind of bastard would chase his wife into the forest with dogs and a rifle?

Or maybe the question should be what kind of woman would drive her husband to that kind of rage in the first place?

The engine was already running in the Jeep, the heater roaring full blast. Emma sank into the leather seat, savoring the heavenly warmth.

"I don't believe I thanked you," she said. "You literally saved my life."

"I did what anybody would do." He seemed uncomfortable with her gratitude.

"Where are you taking me?" she asked as he shifted into reverse and backed the Jeep away from the dock.

"Up to you," he said. "After I drop off the mail, I can leave you at the police station in Ketchikan, or you can come home with me for the night."

She looked slightly startled. "Would that be all right with your wife?"

"No wife. Just me. But I've got a spare room, a shower, and a washer and dryer for your clothes. You can talk to the police in the morning. Your choice. I'm not trying to talk you into anything."

Emma studied his clean-chiseled profile in the faint light. Could she trust him? Maybe she was being too cautious. After all, the man had saved her life. But given what had happened the last time she'd trusted a man, she had every right to be suspicious.

"Where do you live?" she asked.

"Not that you're familiar with the area, but my cabin's a couple of miles off Revilla Road, past Talbot Lake, on an old logging road. If you're not comfortable with that, I can leave you at a hotel in town. Think it over."

Emma weighed her new reality. She wasn't ready to talk to the police, especially since Boone had bragged about being friends with some of the officers. She didn't have money for a hotel. She didn't even have shoes or a change of clothes. She was filthy, exhausted, and scared that Boone would still come after her. Whether she liked the idea or not, this wasn't a good time to be on her own. And this taciturn stranger was the only refuge she had.

"I'll take you up on your offer," she said. "Thanks— and I'll try not to be any trouble."

"Fine. For what it's worth, you're already trouble. I've had a few house guests over the years, but never a runaway wife."

A knot tightened in Emma's stomach. He had thrown down the challenge, and she owed him the truth. It was time to come clean.

"You said it was a long story," he prompted her. "I'm listening."

"I'm not sure where to begin."

"For starters, you can tell me the name of your husband. Maybe I know him."

She stared down at her hands. "His name is Boone Swenson."

"Good God!"

The Jeep swerved slightly before he corrected his jerk of the wheel. "You're married to Boone Swenson?"

"I take it you know him."

He touched the brake as a deer bounded into the headlights and disappeared on the far side of the road. The release of his breath was slow and controlled. "I do know him," he said. "And if you don't mind saving your story until I've dropped off the mail, I'll listen to every word."

John checked in the mail pouch. Then, leaving Ward Cove, he turned onto Revilla Road and headed the Jeep toward home. He kept his eyes on the road as she began. She was brutally honest, sparing herself nothing.

A lonely, naïve woman, past thirty, desperately wanting love and a family, she'd gone to a singles dance at her church in Salt Lake City. There she'd met a man who'd swept her off her feet—tall, blond, rugged—a bearded Viking warrior in a Pendleton shirt.

That would be Boone all right. Handsome and charming as the devil. Back in high school he'd boasted that he could get any girl he wanted—and did. Evidently he hadn't changed.

"I thought he was the answer to my prayers," she said. "He showed me photos of this beautiful log house and told me he needed a wife and children to make it a home. But he didn't have time for a long courtship because he had to fly back to get his house and boat ready for winter. He could meet me in Ketchikan, he said, and we'd be married there before we left for his home in the bush."

She fell silent as John made a left turn onto the road that led through the forest to his cabin. He could imagine the rest of the story. Boone was a natural-born con artist.

He'd hooked this innocent woman and reeled her in like a fish on a line.

But that didn't mean he should start feeling sorry for her, John reminded himself. There was no way he'd want to get involved in this mess. He was putting her up for the night. That was all. Tomorrow her problems would be just that—*her* problems.

"Within two weeks, I'd quit my job as a first grade teacher," she said, continuing her story. "I moved out of my apartment, bought a ticket on Alaska Airlines, and cashed out the seventeen thousand dollars in my savings account. Boone said I should bring cash, because there weren't any banks where we were going." She shook her head. "Like the fool I was, I took him at his word."

"We're here." John pulled up to the log cabin he'd inherited from his grandfather. It was a solid home, not large but comfortable. The old man had built it two generations ago, when his family was young. John had added a garage for storing his Jeep and snowmobile and the freezer for his winter meat supply. He'd also paid for a top-of-the-line power generator. A high water tank had a line to the kitchen and bath area.

He parked and went around the Jeep to open the door for Emma. She slid off the seat, easing her weight onto her lacerated feet. He offered an arm to help her onto the porch. The hand that gripped his sleeve was small and cold.

"The rest of the story can wait till you're warmed up," he said. "Come on."

Clouds had rolled in across the darkening sky. The wind had freshened, smelling of rain. John could hear Emma's shallow, rapid breathing as he opened the door. She sounded scared, but he could understand that. The woman had been through hell. But that didn't make him her knight in shining armor. He would keep her for one night. Tomorrow he would drop her off someplace where she could get help.

"It's all right," he assured her. "You'll be safe here. Come on in."

Inside the dark cabin, Emma waited while John stepped away to turn on a lamp. What she saw was a long room with log walls and open rafters. At one end was a rudimentary kitchen with shelves above a counter and an ancient-looking fridge and gas stove. At the other end was a tall river stone fireplace faced by a well-worn overstuffed love seat with a woolen blanket in a colorful Native American pattern hung over the back. A stack of books rested on a side table, next to a reading lamp. There was no TV.

A hallway led off one side of the living room to what must've been an added wing. Old photographs, in hand-made wooden frames, hung on the walls.

Rustic and *cozy* were words that came to mind. But the room was also chilly. Shivering, Emma pulled the sheep-skin flight jacket around her. John moved to the fireplace, where he opened a box of matches, and lit the logs and kindling that were already laid for a fire.

Now that he'd turned away from her, in the light, Emma saw that his straight ebony hair was pulled back into a leather-wrapped braid that hung down to the space between his shoulders. He was Native American, she realized. How could she have missed that earlier?

As the flames caught, he disappeared down the hallway and came back with a faded plaid flannel bathrobe. "You'll want a shower. Toss your wet clothes into the hall. I'll put them in the wash. Soap and towels are in the bathroom. The spare bedroom is the door on the right."

John Wolf was a man of few words, Emma reflected as she returned his coat, took the robe, and carried it back down the hall. It went without saying that he wasn't pleased to have her here. Maybe that had something to do with her being married to Boone. She shouldn't have been surprised that the two men knew each other. They appeared to be about the same age, and Ketchikan was a small town.

But were they friends or enemies? Questions twisted the frayed knot of her nerves. After what she'd been through today, she couldn't rule out anything.

Had Boone known whom he was firing at when he'd shot at them in the twilight? Had he shot to kill, or had the near-misses been deliberate?

If Boone knew John and had recognized him earlier, he could show up here demanding to claim his wife. Could she count on John to protect her, or would he hand her over to her lawful husband?

For all she knew, the two men could even be friends. John could be planning to call Boone on his cell phone the minute she got into the shower.

Either way, she knew better than to feel safe here. But right now she had nowhere else to go.

The small bedroom was spotless, the twin bed covered with a Native American blanket and made up with military precision. The upper part of a double wall shelf displayed model planes and boats, and beautiful little figures of bears, seals, and walruses, hand-carved from beechwood. The row of well-thumbed books—mostly adventure stories written for young boys, filled the lower shelf. An Alaska travel poster, showing an eagle in flight, was thumbtacked to one wall. An ancient-looking black bearskin, laid next to the bed, lent a little warmth to the cold wooden floor.

This was a boy's room, carefully, even lovingly arranged. But Emma had seen no boy.

Standing on the bearskin rug, she laid the robe on the

bed and stripped off her wet, muddy clothes. Even her plain pink cotton bra and panties were soaked. She hesitated. An image flashed through her mind—her intimate garments in John Wolf's hands as he put them in the wash. A warm flush crept up her throat and into her cheeks.

But she was being silly now. Shivering in the cold room, she peeled off the undergarments and wrapped them in her shirt, then slipped on the bathrobe. The worn flannel was soft against her bare skin. The scent that rose from its folds blended clean soap and a hint of male sweat.

Opening the door, she tossed her wet clothes into the hall and found the bathroom. The stacked, apartment-sized washer and dryer sat in a niche outside the bathroom door. The shower was a prefab model. Exposed pipes connected to a small water heater. The arrangement looked primitive, but when she turned it on, the hot water was heavenly. It took all her willpower to turn it off after a couple of minutes to save the precious supply.

With a towel around her wet hair and John's oversized robe wrapping her body, she walked back into the kitchen. Her lacerated feet were sore. They stung with every step.

The table was set with two mismatched plates. A pot of chili simmered on the stove. John turned away from stirring it.

"Sit here," he said, indicating one of the two kitchen chairs. "I want to check your feet."

She sat down, making sure the robe covered her knees. After picking up a jar of salve, a pair of rolled-up tube socks, and a box of bandages from the counter, he pulled out the other chair and took a seat facing her, laying a towel across his knees. "Give me your foot," he said.

Emma raised one foot. Resting the heel on the towel, he opened the jar and began rubbing salve on the fresh scrapes and scratches. At his touch, warmth trickled up her leg. She willed herself to ignore it. In the silence, she could hear the washer running and the night wind whistling through the trees.

"Thanks for the shower," she said, needing to make conversation. "The hot water made me feel like I'd died and gone to heaven."

"You didn't stay in there long."

"Believe me, I was tempted. But I wanted to leave enough water for you."

He glanced up at her with sharp, dark eyes, then lowered his gaze to her foot again, giving Emma her first real chance to study him. His features were angular, almost fierce, with a finely chiseled nose, square chin, and high cheekbones. His skin was a deep golden bronze.

From where she sat, she could see one of the old black and white photos that hung on the wall. She couldn't make out the details, but it appeared to show three people in ceremonial garb, with robes and headdresses, standing at the foot of a totem pole.

"The people in the photos, who are they?"

"My relatives—the Tlingit."

"The pictures look old."

"They are. Those people are mostly gone now." He slipped a white tube sock over her foot and lowered it to the floor. She raised the other foot without being asked.

"And those amazing costumes—do your people still wear them?"

"Only at celebrations." He inspected the sole of her foot. "Most of the time we're just people—teachers, lawyers, laborers, fishermen, artists, even pilots."

"I do believe that's the longest sentence I've heard you speak," she teased, trying to draw him out.

"Most people talk too much." He daubed salve on a long scratch. She winced as he touched a deeper cut.

"That one needs more than salve." He unwrapped a bandage. Taking care to clean around the cut, he applied it and pressed it tight.

Emma unwrapped the towel from her hair and began using it to blot away the water. She wasn't here to make small talk, she reminded herself. This might be her only chance to learn more about the man she'd been foolish enough to marry.

"So how do you know Boone?" she asked.

"We went to school together."

"Were you friends?"

"No."

"And now?"

"No." He slipped the other tube sock onto her foot, rose, gathered the supplies he'd used, and set them aside on the counter. "The chili should be hot. Hungry?"

"Starved."

He set butter and a loaf of store-bought bread on the table, and filled two glasses with milk. "Sorry I can't offer you a beer," he said. "Since I've sworn off alcohol, I don't keep it around."

"It's all right," she said, surprised that this taciturn man would reveal something so personal. "I don't drink either. Not even coffee."

"Salt Lake City. I should've guessed." He spooned steaming chili into two bowls and placed one in front of her.

"It smells wonderful," she said. "Did you make it yourself?"

"Yes. I even shot the moose you're about to eat." He took a seat on the opposite side of the table.

Emma blew on a spoonful of chili and took a cautious taste. "It needs time to cool, but it's good," she said, meaning it. "I've never tasted moose before."

"You were married to Boone, and you've never had moose?"

Emma sighed and put down her spoon. "Is that my cue for the rest of the story?"

"You need to eat. Your story can wait."

She shook her head. "I'll feel more like eating after I've told you. Be warned. It isn't pretty."

He propped the spoon on the edge of his bowl. "I'm listening."

John studied the woman sitting across from him, his bathrobe warming her bare body. Her damp chestnut hair hung past her shoulders, curling around her face in soft tendrils. Even though he knew she was in her thirties, there was a look of almost childlike innocence about her. He found her intelligent hazel eyes, generous mouth, and lightly freckled complexion appealing, but her features came together in a way that fell short of beauty. Such a woman—vulnerable and lacking confidence when it came to men—would be a natural target for a man like Boone. The fact that she had money put away would make her the perfect mark.

Outside, the storm had arrived. Thunder boomed across the sky. Rain battered the windows of the cabin as Emma began her story.

"I flew in last night on Alaska Airlines," she said. "Boone met me at the ferry landing. He said he had a motel room for us, but . . ." She flushed awkwardly. "I didn't want to spend the night with him until we were married, so I paid for a room of my own. Early this morning he gave me the marriage license to sign. A minister friend of Boone's performed the ceremony in a park with totem poles. It was beautiful, with the sun coming up, reflecting on the water. I'd even brought along my mother's wedding dress to wear. I was so happy, so trusting . . ."

Her words trailed off. She was close to tears. It would be a kindness to stop her. But John knew he had to hear the rest of her story. He'd never meant to get involved with this woman and her problems. But whatever ugly truths he might be about to hear, he was too curious to turn his back and walk away.

He waited in silence while she fought to bring her emotions under control. She seemed determined not to cry. John liked her for that. He remembered how he'd found her, struggling through the muskeg with dogs on her heels. She might appear as fragile as a violet, but she was a scrapper.

"I'm sorry, this isn't easy." She took a sip of milk and picked up her story. "I gave Boone all my cash. While I changed clothes, he used some of it to fill his pickup truck with gas and supplies and pocketed the rest. Then we left town and drove most of the day, over old logging roads, into the back country. I'd dozed off, dreaming about the beautiful log home he'd shown me in the photo and how we were going to raise our family there.

"I woke up—literally and figuratively—when he stopped the truck and told me we were home. That was when . . ." She paused, lifting her chin. "That was when I knew I'd been a silly, romantic fool. I was looking at a dilapidated house trailer, surrounded by junk. Two huge dogs were chained by the front wheel—they didn't look like they'd had anything to eat, except this old deer head they were fighting over. Some kind of animal carcass was hanging from a tree. . . ."

She shook her head. "There was more. But you get the idea. It was awful. But worst of all was the change in the man I'd married. It was like he'd been acting in a play, and the play was over.

"Boone ordered me to get out of the truck and help him unload. You can imagine what the inside of the trailer was like. Food wrappers, garbage, even flies." She shuddered.

"On the stove there were some burnt-looking pans. Back home, I'd had a neighbor arrested for cooking meth. I recognized the smell."

She'd begun to tremble. Her fingers twisted the gold ring on her finger. John checked the impulse to get up and comfort her. Hands off the lady—that was the only sensible rule.

"So was that when you ran?"

"Not quite." Her reply was laced with irony. "When we'd finished unloading supplies and were back in the house, Boone announced that he was going to the bathroom. He told me, 'When I open the door, I want to see you undressed and in that bed.'

"By then I was already searching for a way out—any way I could find. When he closed the bathroom door, I saw my chance. I'd noticed a jug of kerosene and some matches next to a lamp on the table. I poured some kerosene into a pan on the stove, lit a couple of matches, and tossed them into it. When the fire blazed up, I ran for my life."

"You set the trailer on fire with Boone in the bathroom?" John was torn between horror and admiration. Damn, the woman had guts. No wonder Boone had come after her with a rifle.

"The fire was in a cast-iron pan, on the stove. And I'd left the trailer door open. Boone wouldn't be trapped—I was sure of that. But he'd have to deal with the fire before he came after me. I was hoping that would give me time to get away." Her gaze dropped to her hands. "I was wrong. I'd been on the run for an hour, maybe, hopelessly lost, when I heard the dogs. You know the rest."

"At least you know you didn't kill him," John said.

"I wouldn't want to kill anybody. Not even Boone. But

he's bound to come after me again. And if he recognized you, he could come here. That's why I have to leave."

John glanced upward, listening to the drumbeat of rain on the roof. Emma could be right. But she wasn't equipped to go anywhere. She'd fled Boone's trailer with no spare clothes, no identification, and no money. Without help, she'd be reduced to begging on the street.

Standing, he took her bowl and scraped the chili back into the pot and turned on the gas flame. "You still need something warm in your belly," he said. "And don't worry about tonight. You'll be safe enough with the storm outside. Tomorrow you'll be rested and have dry clothes to wear. I'll drive into town, buy you some shoes, and we'll take it from there."

The chili hadn't taken long to warm. He ladled it back into the bowl and placed it in front of her. "Eat. That's an order."

She took one spoonful, then another. He could tell she was hungry. "I'm sorry," she said. "I know my being here is an imposition. I'll be out of your way as soon as I can walk through that door on my own two feet."

"And then what? Is there somebody you can call? Your parents? A brother or sister, maybe?"

"My parents are gone, and I was their only child. I'm not used to depending on anybody."

Another reason Boone would've chosen her, he thought. No family to come looking for her. Emma had been the perfect victim. Thinking of what he'd have done to her if she hadn't escaped made John want to crush the bastard with his bare hands.

He checked the rising tide of anger. This woman's troubles were none of his business. But his conscience wouldn't condone his leaving her to the mercy of a ruthless bastard like Boone.

"The only way for you to be safe is to leave Ketchikan," he said. "I could fly you someplace close, like Sitka, and find you a place to stay while you work things out. I know people there who'd take you in."

She finished the chili and pushed the bowl aside. "Thank you for your offer. You know I'd repay you for your trouble. But when I think about Boone and what he did to me, and how he'd probably do the same thing, or worse, to some other poor woman . . ." Her hand clenched into a fist. "How can I just walk away? How could I sleep at night, knowing he'd hurt somebody else and I hadn't done anything to stop him?"

John swore silently. This was a complication he hadn't counted on. "Boone's a dangerous man," he said. "You need to get out of his reach and leave him to the law."

She gave him a steely look, her chin determinedly set. "I know you mean well. But after what that man did to me, I can't just walk away. I need to see this through."

John rose and began clearing away the dishes. "You've been through a lot, and you're tired," he said. "Sleep on it. Tomorrow, with a clear head, you'll see your way to a sensible choice."

"All right, for now at least." She rose wearily. "I'm so tired I can hardly think straight, but that doesn't mean I'll change my mind. Thanks for putting up with me tonight. I'll be out of your way as soon as I can figure out where to go next."

John was tired of arguing with her. "The room will get cold when the fire goes out," he said. "The best thing I can offer you for pajamas is a set of thermal underwear. At least it'll be clean and warm."

"Thanks." She yawned. "I don't suppose you have a spare toothbrush."

"You'll find a new one on the shelf above the towel

rack. It's yours. And you can keep the robe for now. I'll get you the thermals."

While she brushed her teeth, he put her wet laundry in the dryer and fetched a folded set of gray winter underwear—top and bottom—from his dresser. He handed it to her as she came out of the bathroom. "The bedroom will be warmer if you leave the door open," he said.

For the space of a breath she froze, her eyes widening. She'd misread him, John realized. Not that he blamed her. After what she'd been through, he wouldn't blame her if she never trusted a man again.

With a chilly good night, she took the thermals and turned away. John cleaned up in the kitchen and banked the fire for morning. When he stepped into the hall again, he saw that Emma's door was firmly closed.

CHAPTER 3

Too wired to sleep, John sat up, swung his legs off the bed, and pulled on his jeans. A glance at the bedside clock told him it was after midnight. He could no longer hear the wind, but the rain was falling in a steady drizzle that poured off the eaves of the cabin. He didn't expect any trouble on a night like this, but as long as he was awake, it wouldn't hurt to check.

His loaded .44 magnum lay on the bedside table. He usually kept it locked in the Jeep, for easy transfer to the Beaver when he flew. Tonight he'd brought it inside. It didn't make sense that Boone would drive for hours over rough forest trails on a stormy night, not even to find his runaway bride. But John couldn't afford to take that chance. His ex-brother-in-law was as unpredictable as he was dangerous.

He had no doubt that Boone had recognized him. True, it had been almost dusk in the forest when he'd rescued Emma. But the red Beaver, with its serial number stenciled on the underside of the wing, would've been plainly visible when he'd made those two low passes over the muskeg.

He'd had little to do with Marlena's family since their divorce fifteen years ago. But they knew his plane, they knew where he lived, and they hated him for giving their daughter a bad marriage and a half-breed son.

Now they could chalk up one more offense against him.

He shoved his feet into sheepskin slippers, picked up the pistol, and stepped out into the hall. Emma's door was still closed—and probably braced with a chair on the inside. John understood that she didn't trust him, and he knew better than to take it personally. He was a man—in her eyes, that was enough to make him suspect.

He'd held back the truth about his family connection to Boone because he wanted her to feel secure. But he didn't like lying, not even for a good reason. When the time was right, he'd come clean.

Unless he could get her out of here first.

Still holding the pistol, he unlocked the front door, stepped out onto the covered porch, and gazed through the curtain of rain that streamed off the roof. He hadn't expected any cause for alarm, and he didn't find any. All he could see was more rain dripping off the trees and down the sides of the Jeep where he'd parked it. But at least, if Emma asked, he'd be able to tell her that he'd checked.

Damn the woman. If he'd had a lick of sense, he would have dropped her off at the police station and never looked back. Why did she have to show up now, when he finally felt like he had his life under control?

He'd been cold sober for seven years and still attended his AA meetings. But right now, if someone had thrust a flask of whiskey into his hand, he would have guzzled it dry. Any business involving the Swensons tended to push him toward the edge. He'd battled Marlena and her family for years over the right to see David, losing time after bitter time. Only when he'd given up the fight and backed off had he found a measure of peace.

Now he'd be dealing with Boone, who was the worst of the lot—but not by much.

The night was chilly, and he hadn't worn his coat. But he wasn't ready to go back inside. The patter of rain was as soothing as a lullaby. He inhaled the fragrances of evergreen trees and wet ground, letting the sounds and smells of nature calm his troubled spirit. His memory recalled the words of his grandfather, who had built this house and passed away under its sheltering roof.

Look to the earth, my son. She is older and wiser than little people like us. She has seen all things come and go, and she knows that our small trials will pass and fade as if they had never been.

Wise words from a wise old man. But when John's spirit was churning, as it was tonight, it was hard to find much comfort in them.

A cold wind whipped his unbound hair and chilled him through the long-sleeved shirt he'd worn to bed. He'd been outside long enough. After a last check from both ends of the porch, he opened the door and stepped back into the house.

"Stay right where you are!" The voice was Emma's. In the faint light from the dying fire, he saw her to the left of the doorway. She was half-crouched for an attack, her hands gripping the heavy iron poker from the fireplace.

John stifled a curse. "Emma, it's only me! Put that thing down!"

Straightening to her full, diminutive height, she lowered the poker. John turned on the lamp. Still defiant, she stood in the circle of light with his oversized gray thermals drooping around her legs. Her hair was a mass of tangled curls. Her eyes blazed with annoyance.

"Give me that." He laid the gun on the table and yanked

the poker out of her hands. "What did you think you were doing? I had a gun. I could've shot you."

"I heard somebody at the front door. I couldn't be sure it was you. Why did you go outside? Was somebody there?"

"Since I wasn't sleeping, I thought I might as well check around. It was a waste of time. There's nothing out there but rain."

Suspicion flashed in her eyes, as if she sensed that he was holding out. *Guilty as charged,* he thought.

"I wasn't sleeping either," she said, hitching up the drawstring waist of her thermals. "Right now, I couldn't sleep if I had to."

She was shivering, whether from cold or from stress he couldn't be sure. But maybe it was time for a truce.

Without a word, he picked up the blanket that lay on the back of the love seat, wrapped it around her, and guided her to a seat. She curled up in it willingly, snuggling into the blanket while he added a couple of small logs and some kindling to the coals in the fireplace.

"As long as we're awake, we might as well be warm," he said. "I've got the makings for hot chocolate. Say the word if you want some."

"That sounds nice, as long as it's not too much trouble."

"No trouble. It might even make you sleepy."

In the kitchen, he broke the seal on a can of powdered cocoa mix, added it to some milk, and heated it in a pan on the stove. He'd never cared much for hot chocolate. It was too sweet. But he'd bought the mix a few years ago, in the hope of having David over for a weekend visit. He should have known better. The visit had never happened.

When the cocoa was hot, he poured it into mugs and carried them to the fireplace. Giving one to Emma, he settled at the other end of the love seat. By now the wood he'd laid on the coals had begun to burn. A small but cheerful blaze crackled in the fireplace. Stretching his legs, he rested his feet on the hearth.

Emma sipped the cocoa. "This is perfect," she said. "Thanks."

"You're welcome." John didn't feel much like talking. But it was pleasant, sitting here by the fire in the middle of the night, with a pretty woman—and Emma *was* pretty, as pretty as the little brown birds that flashed through sunlit pine branches. There was a liveliness about her, a bright, intelligent spirit that made up for her lack of classic beauty.

Of course, he would never tell her that.

She'd been gazing into the fireplace. Now she turned toward him. "You know I've got some hard decisions to make. It would help if I knew more about Boone. What can you tell me?"

Her question shattered John's brief contentment. "How much do you already know?" he asked, weighing the question of how much to tell her.

"I know that he's handsome and charming, and that he lies through his teeth. I know that he stole my life savings, and that if I'd stayed with him in that awful place, I would've been raped, or worse. How's that for starters?"

"Pretty accurate, I'd say."

"How much do you know about his family—if he even has one?"

"Enough." That much was true. "They're bush people. They've chosen to live off the land, away from civilization, where there's nobody to interfere with them. Where you come from, people would probably call them hillbillies."

"You talk as if you know them."

"Most people around here do, at least by sight. They have a homestead far up one of the canyons. Every few months they come into Ketchikan for supplies. The head of the family is the mother. Her husband, whoever he was, is long gone. He left her to raise three children—two boys . . . and a girl. All of them are grown now. Boone is her second son."

"But you said you knew Boone in school. Did they ever live in town?"

"I was coming to that. When the children were young, their mother decided to leave Boone and his sister in Ketchikan with their grandmother. They lived with the old woman until they were out of high school. She died soon after they finished." John took a gulp of his cocoa. It had gone lukewarm and was so sweet toward the bottom that swallowing it was like punishment for the lie of omission he was about to tell. "The girl—Marlena—stayed in town. She's married now, to a fisherman who has his own boat. She has nothing to do with her mother and brothers. It's as if she's pretending she's from somewhere else. I can't say I blame her."

"It sounds like she did all right for herself," Emma said. "But what about Boone?"

"Boone was always too wild for town life. After high school, he went back to his kinfolk in the bush. I don't know what prompted him to go wife-hunting. Maybe he was just lonesome. Or maybe the family needed a good woman to carry on the line. Whatever the reason, I'm sorry you had to be the one he found."

"If not me, it would've been some other poor girl." She gazed into the crackling flames. "I feel so foolish, now that I know. Why wasn't I smart enough to see through all the sweet talk? Why didn't I at least do some research and check him out before I threw my life away?"

"Because you wanted to believe it. You wanted the life you thought he was offering you. That's nothing to be ashamed of."

"All my friends were married. I went to their weddings. I cuddled their babies. I ached to have what they had."

"You said you were a teacher."

"Yes, and I loved my job. I loved those little kids. But they weren't mine. I wanted a good man to share my life. I wanted my own family. When Boone showed up, I was beyond ready for it to happen." She shook her head. "It was easy for him to reel me in. So very easy."

Her brutal honesty shamed him to the bone. He had fed her evasions sprinkled with half truths, hiding the things he didn't want her to hear. But Emma was as true and real as a flame.

"Let me fly you out of here," he said. "You can go to the state police in Juneau, tell them your story. There'll be agencies there that can help you get some ID and find you a way home."

"Thanks, but I'm not ready to leave," she said. "I need to get an annulment and see that Boone never hurts another trusting woman. The money I gave him is probably gone for good, but I'd like to try and get at least some of it back. I'll have better luck with those things if I stay here."

She was right, John conceded. But staying in Ketchikan would put her in danger. And, whether he liked it or not, he'd become her protector. He couldn't walk away until he knew she was safe.

"Fine," he said. "But if you get careless, you could end up in more trouble. So listen to me. Here's what we'll do. In the morning I'll leave you here, drive into town, and buy you some shoes. Then I'll nose around Boone's old haunts and find out whether anybody's seen him. When I get back, we'll take it from there. All right?"

"Yes," she said. "But I don't plan to impose on you any longer than I have to." Sitting up straight, she twisted off her gold wedding band and thrust it toward him. "Take this. Boone told me it was his mother's, but for all I know, he could've stolen it. See how much a pawnshop will give you for it. With luck it should at least be enough to buy me some cheap sneakers. Whatever it's worth, I never want to see it again."

John took the plain band, feeling its weight in his palm. He was no expert, but it had the look and solid feel of gold. He knew a trustworthy pawnbroker in town who'd be able to tell him what it was worth. At least it would give her a little spending money.

"Don't you have to work tomorrow?" she asked him.

"Not on anybody's timetable," he said. "During the cruise ship season, from May to September, I fly six days a week for Taquan Air, taking tourists on sightseeing jaunts, as well as doing the mail run. Now that the season's over, I'll just be doing the mail contract. But if we get some time, I'll take you up. There are some beautiful places I could show you. Maybe we could even look for Boone's trailer from the air. Then you could tell the police where to find it. What do you think?"

Emma didn't reply. She was fast asleep, her head drooping to one side like a tired bird's. Standing, John dropped the ring into his pocket, fetched a pillow from the bedroom, and worked it behind her shoulders to cushion and support her. She snuggled into it with a little sigh.

He gazed down at her, battling a surge of tenderness he had no right to feel. She looked like an innocent child with her eyes closed, her full lips softly parted, and the firelight dancing on her face. He fought the urge to reach down and brush a fingertip along her cheek.

Mouthing a curse, he stepped away from the love seat. There'd be no going down that road. He admired Emma's honesty and her spunky courage. He even found her attractive. But as far as he was concerned, the woman was nothing but a bundle of trouble. The sooner he got her out of his cabin and out of his life, the better off he'd be.

He took another log from the wood box and laid it on the fire. Then, after turning the reading lamp on low and angling the shade toward him, he sat down on the empty end of the love seat and opened a book.

Emma woke with a jerk. In her dream, she'd been running for what seemed like hours, legs pumping, heart pounding, but no matter how hard she ran, it was as if her feet had been nailed to the ground. And the awful, unseen thing behind her was gaining—never quite catching her, but so close that she could hear the rasp of its breath.

As the nightmare dissolved, she opened her eyes. Morning sunlight poured through a high window. From somewhere outside, she could hear a woodpecker drumming. Only after a moment's panic did she realize that she'd spent the night on a love seat, in the remote cabin of the pilot who'd rescued her.

She could hear him in the kitchen, running water and rattling pans. Her nose caught the aroma of frying bacon. The smell reminded her that she was hungry again. Untangling her legs from the blanket, she managed to stand up.

He glanced around and saw her from the kitchen. His hair, which had been long and loose last night, was neatly braided and bound again. "You were out like a hibernating bear," he said. "Are you all right?"

Emma cleared her throat. "Fine. Just crazy dreams. I must've been exhausted. What time is it?"

"It's almost eight. I've been up for a couple of hours, but I didn't want to wake you."

"Heavens, if I were home, I'd be late for school." She took a step, stumbling over the hems of the long underwear he'd lent her.

"Your clothes are dry," he said. "You'll find them on your bed. By the time you're dressed, I should have breakfast on the table."

"Thanks. I'm actually hungry." Hitching up the thermals, she shuffled back to the bedroom and found her clothes neatly folded on the bed. Her jeans were ripped at the knees, and there were stains from the muskeg that no amount of washing would get out. But at least the clothes were clean. If pawning the ring fetched enough money, maybe she could buy a few simple things, like a change of clothes and underwear.

A groan escaped her lips as another thought crossed her mind. She'd left her purse in Boone's truck. He would have not only her cash but her driver's license, passport, cell phone, and credit cards. Until she could get everything cancelled, he would no doubt make good use of them. What a nightmare! It was even worse than her dream because it was real.

Dressed, and with the tube socks still protecting her sore feet, she returned to the kitchen. John had breakfast on the table. She took a seat and loaded her plate with bacon, scrambled eggs, and buttered toast.

"Thank you," she said. "I really mean it. I wasn't at my best last night, but I wasn't ungrateful."

"Understood." He passed her a glass of orange juice. "I'll be leaving for town when we're done here. The shops open at nine. I should be back by ten with your shoes and some cash. After that, I think it's time you told your story to the police." His eyes narrowed as if he'd noticed her hesitation. "What is it?"

"It's just . . . I'm not sure I can trust the police. Boone bragged to me that he had friends on the force. What's to keep them from letting him know where to find me?"

"Friends?" John shook his head. "There are a couple of

guys on the force who went to school with us. But I don't recall their being friends with Boone. He ran with the rough crowd—booze, weed, bullying the weaker kids . . ." He rose, picking up his plate to take to the sink. "I wouldn't worry about the police if I were you. Besides, you're going to need their help. You can't go after Boone by yourself."

Emma had to concede he was right. "Fine. I'll be ready to go when you get back from town. I wear a size six shoe, by the way. Get me whatever's sturdy and comfortable, and hopefully on sale." She glanced toward the sink, where he was rinsing his plate. "Don't worry about cleaning up. I'll do that while you're gone."

"Thanks. That'll save us some time." He took a quilted vest from a hook behind the door and slipped it on. "I'm leaving the pistol," he said. "You're not likely to need it, but if the bastard shows up and threatens you, don't be afraid to pull the trigger."

If he was joking, she could see no sign of it in his stern expression. "Stay inside and keep the door locked," he said. "Don't go out on the porch or even look out the windows until I come back. If anybody knocks, don't answer."

"I understand." Emma eyed the gun where it lay on the side table by his books. He was worried, she realized—maybe as worried as she was.

She checked the locked door as he drove away. Then she went back to the kitchen and started on the dishes.

John drove the Jeep to the highway, then south another eight miles into Ketchikan. The quiet after the end of the season was almost startling—the long boardwalk with its empty ship berths, the closed tourist office, the fishing boats clustered at anchor in the basin below the floating pier.

From where he stood by the parked Jeep, he could see where the streets climbed the steep slope to an area of newer, nicer homes. In one of them, a two-story white frame house, Marlena lived with her fisherman husband, their two young children, and David. They had decent lives, he imagined. With his own boat and crew, a man could make a lot of money during the salmon run. David, seventeen by now, would soon be old enough to help crew.

John wondered if his son would like that kind of work. But he wouldn't get a chance to ask him. Marlena had done a number on the boy. After the things she'd told him, it was no wonder that David wanted nothing to do with his natural father.

A lone bald eagle circled above the water and flapped away to disappear against the sky. Reminding himself that he'd come into town for a reason, John turned away from his view of the white house, locked the Jeep, and strode up Dock Street toward the business section of town.

The pawnshop, on Main, was just opening for the day. The old man who'd run the place for decades examined the ring with his jeweler's loupe. "It's gold, all right. I'd say maybe eighteen carat," he announced. "But the ring's old. It's had some hard wear. Not good for much now except melting down. I can offer you two hundred for it."

Two hundred dollars wouldn't get Emma very far, and the ring was all she had. John had been hoping for more, but he knew the old man was fair and honest. He walked out of the pawnshop with the cash in his wallet.

The bank was on the next block. John walked in and withdrew an additional two hundred dollars from his own account. He knew that Emma would never accept money from him. But she wouldn't have to know that he'd sweetened the price of the ring.

He returned to the Jeep and spent the next twenty minutes driving the streets, looking for Boone's old camo-painted pickup truck. He saw no sign of it, which didn't mean much. Boone could be anywhere.

John checked the supply and gas place where Boone usually stocked up. The clerk remembered Boone from the day before, when he'd loaded up his truck and paid for the goods by peeling bills off a big wad of cash. But no, the man hadn't been in since then.

With no place else to look, John was on his way to pick up Emma's sneakers and head home when a sudden hunch struck him. He hit the brakes, swung the Jeep around, and headed for the Gateway County building. He might be wasting time, he cautioned himself, but if his instincts were right, he could be returning with a surprise for Emma—one that would be even more welcome than new shoes.

By ten minutes after nine, Emma had finished cleaning the kitchen. In the bathroom, she washed her face, brushed her teeth, and finger-combed her hair. No makeup, but then, she'd never worn much. The way she looked this morning would have to be good enough.

Growing restless, she prowled the cabin. She was tempted to open the front door, just to look around, or at least glance out of a window. But the heavy pistol, lying on the table, was a reminder of the danger that could be lurking outside. A calm, capable man like John Wolf wouldn't be worried without good reason.

She wandered to the floor-to-ceiling bookshelf, built into the wall on one side of the fireplace. Most of John's books appeared to be non-fiction—history, true-life adventure, and how-to volumes that covered everything from cooking to airplane engine repair. There were a few novels—authors like Hemingway, Faulkner, and Steinbeck. But Emma, who loved to read but favored contemporary women's fiction, found little to catch her interest.

Still exploring, she walked back down the hallway. The door to John's room stood ajar. She hesitated; then, feeling vaguely naughty, she opened the door and stepped into the room.

Having met John, she should've guessed what his bedroom would be like. It was spare and plain, the double bed neatly made, the laundry piled in a wicker basket. A large map of Alaska was thumbtacked to one wall. A lamp, a book, and a clock radio rested on a bedside table. The only other ornament in the room was a small, framed photograph that sat atop the bureau opposite the bed. Walking closer, she saw that it was a picture of a much younger John, grinning as he held a squirming black-haired toddler in his arms. Behind them, Emma could just make out the lower part of a totem pole.

Had the other bedroom been meant for this boy—the boy whose absence she'd felt so strongly?

Who was he? What had become of him? She could ask John. But she sensed that the answer to that question was painful and deeply personal. She would be wise not to mention it.

She'd just left the room when she heard it—a bumping, scraping sound coming from the front of the house. She crept forward, her heart pounding. Something—or someone—was on the front porch, not knocking on the door but bumping against it. As the noise continued, she imagined Boone, piling wood onto the porch, preparing to set it on fire and burn down the house.

Her shaking hand found the pistol and thumbed back the hammer. Could she do it? Could she fling open the door and shoot whoever was on the other side? Maybe. But she'd never fired a gun before. What if she missed, or froze and couldn't shoot at all? It might be best to keep quiet and wait.

Crouching behind the love seat, she rested the muzzle on the back, aimed the pistol at the front door, and held it steady. In the silent room, she could hear her own heartbeat and taste her own fear.

CHAPTER 4

Still crouched behind the love seat, with the pistol aimed at the door, Emma heard John's Jeep pull up and stop. Something struck the porch with a sharp thump. She heard shouted curses and a scrambling sound. After a moment that seemed far too long, his key turned in the lock.

She rose, still gripping the gun, as the door opened. John stood on the threshold, a shopping bag slung over his arm. He wasn't smiling. "Put that pistol down before you blow a hole in me," he said.

Knees weakening with relief, Emma lowered the gun.

"Are you all right?" he asked, stepping inside.

"Fine! Just scared out of my wits." She laid the gun on the side table. "What just happened out there?"

"Just a blasted bear on the porch. Probably smelled our bacon from this morning. I threw a chunk of firewood at him, and he took off."

"A *bear?*" Emma's knees gave way. She sank onto the arm of the love seat. "Weren't you in danger?"

"He was just a half-grown youngster. Probably the first time on his own. But I couldn't let him stick around. The sooner he learns that people are bad news, the longer he's likely to survive." He held out the shopping bag. "Here are your shoes. Half price this week at Tongass Trading Company. Try them on."

"Thanks." Emma had already resolved not to tell him what she'd imagined happening on the porch. He'd only think she was being flighty.

She took the bag and opened it. The blue and white running shoes were a quality brand. They looked well-made and comfortable. There were three pairs of good wool socks in the bag as well.

"Here's your change." He handed her a thick fold of bills.

"Thanks again." She glanced at the bills, then slipped them into her hip pocket. She could count them later, but there appeared to be several hundred dollars. "That ring must've been real gold," she said.

"It was." He walked to the window while Emma tried on the socks and shoes. "I checked around for Boone. There was no sign of him. But the sooner we get the police on his trail, the safer you'll be. I have one question to ask you."

Emma had laced up the shoes. Standing, she took a few steps in them. They felt fine. "What kind of question?" she asked.

"At your wedding, what do you remember about the preacher? Do you recall his name?"

Puzzled, Emma searched her memory. "Boone introduced us, but I was too excited to pay much attention. It was Reverend Philpot, or Phillips, or something like that. He was tall and thin, with red hair in a braid down his back, and he was wearing this long black coat with a white collar. He did seem a bit strange, but—what? Why are you looking at me like that?"

"Because I know that man. He's an old drinking buddy of Boone's and he's no more a reverend than I am. And that isn't all. This morning I did some checking at the county records office. Emma, there's no legal evidence of your marriage anywhere. As far as I can tell, you aren't married. You had a fake wedding with a fake preacher."

The shock sent Emma staggering backward onto the love seat. She huddled there, her hands pressed to her face as the news sank in—welcome news, to be sure. Her desperate situation had just become simpler. No divorce. No annulment. She was free. But the shame was there, too. She'd been so blind, so hopeful, and so dizzy with love and dreams of the future. But Boone hadn't even cared enough to give her a real wedding.

John watched her take the news, surprised at her reaction. He'd expected nothing from her but happy relief— smiles and laughter, maybe even a little dance of joy. Only now, as she lowered her hands to reveal a glimmer of tears, did he realize how deeply invested she'd been in her dream of a happy marriage and a family.

Boone hadn't just stolen her money and forced her to run for her life. He had made a mockery of everything she held dear. He had humiliated her, destroyed her trust, and shattered her pride.

As he waited by the window, knowing better than to speak, a subtle change came over her. She blinked away her tears, straightened her spine, and lifted her head. When she rose and turned toward him, her expression was one of wounded rage.

"You can drive me to the police station now." Her voice was icily calm. "Whatever it takes, I'm going to see that Boone Swenson never hurts another woman for as long as he lives!"

*   *   *

Detective Sam Traverton was gruff and middle-aged, with a thatch of iron gray hair, an expanding beltline, and a manner that suggested he'd seen everything there was to see in his long career. He listened as Emma told her story, jotting a few notes on a yellow pad.

"We can't charge Boone with a crime until he's caught," he said. "We can pick him up if he comes into town. Otherwise it'll be up to the state troopers to haul him in.

"After he's booked, he'll be charged by the county prosecutor." He gave Emma a knowing look. "Now I know you want this fellow hung out to dry. But you can only get a conviction with a charge that'll stick. In this case, my money's on fraud—or maybe theft by deception. Boone lured you up here under false pretenses and stole your money."

"But what about the rest?" Emma demanded. "Boone would've raped me, maybe even killed me, if I hadn't escaped. At the very least, he should be guilty of kidnapping. And what about the drugs?"

Traverton gave her a wearied look. "A good defense attorney would argue that he didn't kidnap you because you went with him willingly. He might have meant to rape you, but he didn't get the chance because you ran away. And when he chased you, it was because you'd set his trailer on fire. As for the meth—knowing Boone, that doesn't surprise me. But you'd have to catch him with the goods to justify an arrest."

Emma's heart sank. She'd hoped for so much more. "What about the gunshots?" she asked. "He almost hit us."

Traverton shook his head. "Again, unless you can find the bullets and match them to his gun, there's no evidence that he was even the one shooting. If he uses your credit cards, we can get him for identity theft. But he'd be more likely to sell them for cash than use them—especially the passport. Those are worth serious money on the black market." He reached into a drawer and took out a business card. "Here's the contact information for a retired judge who doesn't mind helping folks out with a little pro bono work. She might be willing give you a hand with the credit card companies and the passport office."

He stood, a signal that the interview was over. "Since the wedding and your handing over the money occurred here in Ketchikan, that makes it my case. We'll talk to Philpot and give the state troopers a heads-up to watch for Boone's truck. For now, that's about the best we can do."

Emma accepted the business card and put it in her pocket. She was fuming as they walked outside to John's Jeep. "Theft by deception! What's that worth, about two years behind bars? Boone could've killed me, John! Maybe he was even planning to. That's why he wouldn't bother with a real wedding. For all I know he's done this before, and the other women never got away! What if he's got a whole graveyard out behind that trailer?"

"Whoa, there." John stopped her at the curb, his hand just brushing her elbow. "Let's take this one step at a time. Right now you need to stop Boone from using your passport and credit cards. Here's my phone. You've got the card. Give that retired judge a call."

Stop doing my thinking for me! She bit back the words, knowing they would sound petulant and ungrateful. She already owed this man more than she could ever repay. With a sigh, she fished the card out of her pocket, took the phone, noted the number and the name—Vera Falconi. Turning away from John, she made the call.

"Vera here." The throaty voice was roughened by age, but the ring of authority was unmistakable.

"Judge Falconi, my name is Emma Hunter." At least she didn't have to say that she was Emma Swenson.

"Oh, yes." The voice warmed. "Sam just called me about you. I'd be glad to help, dear, but I'm busy for the rest of the day. Could you come by first thing tomorrow, say, around eight-thirty? Is that all right?"

The thought crossed Emma's mind that she should ask John whether he could drive her in the morning. But given what seemed to be the judge's busy schedule, it seemed best to just accept and work out the details later. "Eight-thirty would be fine, thank you," she said.

"My pleasure, dear. Tomorrow, then."

The call ended. That was when she turned and saw John's rigidly controlled expression. His narrowed eyes and the straight line of his mouth reminded her of a dam holding back a flood of dark emotion.

"Is something wrong?" she asked. "Is there a problem with your driving me tomorrow morning?"

"No. It's fine." He opened the door of the Jeep. Emma climbed inside. Something was bothering him. But she knew better than to pry. She'd already learned that John Wolf was a very private person.

"The judge sounds like an interesting woman. Do you know her?" she asked as he settled in the driver's seat.

"I know her. Everybody around here does."

"Why do I get the feeling she's not your favorite person?"

"As long as she's willing to help you, it doesn't matter." He started the engine. "What do you want to do with the rest of your day?"

"I hadn't planned beyond the visit to the police. I suppose I could buy a change of clothes and a disposable phone. But surely you've got more important things to do than baby-sit me. Just let me out and point me in the right direction. I can meet you somewhere later. Or did you have a different idea?"

"Not different. Just something more." He turned the Jeep onto the main road that led along the docks. "Once your shopping's done, we could take the plane up and look for Boone's trailer. If we can map the coordinates and give them to the state troopers, they could take a chopper in there and check it out."

"That sounds like the best plan I've heard all day," Emma said. "Let's do it."

Emma was an efficient shopper. It took her less than forty minutes to pick out a new pair of jeans and two shirts, some spare underclothes, and a light rainproof jacket on sale at Tongass Trading Company next to the docks. While she was buying clothes, John bought her a disposal phone, which she insisted on paying for. Her cash was dwindling faster than she'd hoped, but that couldn't be helped. If she stayed here more than a few days, she would have to look for a job.

With her purchases stowed in the Jeep, they drove back through the short tunnel toward Refuge Cove, where John had left the Beaver last night. Now that there was a plan in place, his dark mood seemed to have lifted. He was almost cheerful.

Businesses, docks, and warehouses were strung along the highway, which ran parallel to the long, blue stretch of water. John pointed out the airport, located on the shore of Gravina Island, across the narrows. A ferry shuttled vehicles and passengers back and forth from Ketchikan.

Emma gazed across the water as a commuter plane landed on the runway and taxied to the small terminal. How could it be that only yesterday, a naïve woman, brimming with hopes and dreams, had stepped onto Alaskan earth, eager to marry the man she loved and start a new life?

That woman was a different person now. Stripped of her dreams and hopes, she had just two goals—to survive, and to bring the man who'd crushed them to justice.

A few miles beyond Ketchikan, the road looped around Ward Cove, with its deep harbor and surrounding town. Next to the water, on the north side, a complex of docks, sheds, and open space sprawled along the waterline. A few raft-style log platforms floated offshore, some with small structures on them. "That used to be the world's largest pulp mill," John said. "From the late fifties on, it processed logs into pulp. The place supported Ward Cove and Ketchikan with factory jobs as well as a major logging operation— that's why you see so many logging roads in the forest."

"What happened?" Emma asked.

"In 1997 the government shut it down because of environmental issues, and because the lumbering contract ran out. Seven hundred people lost their jobs. Times were pretty tough around here for a while. A lot of the old structures have been cleared away. I've heard talk of converting the property to an industrial park, but that's mostly about money, or the lack of it.

"I was a teenager when it closed. After it shut down, we used to break into the place and play crazy games like paintball, or just hang out and drink. All the kids did, even Boone. The cops chased us out of there a few times, but we always came back. There's not much left of it now, just a few sheds and warehouses that are still good enough to be useful."

"I'd like to have known you then," Emma said.

"No, you wouldn't. I was a mess."

Minutes later, the road turned into Refuge Cove. Separated from Ward Cove by a jutting bight of forest and muskeg, Refuge Cove was small and nestlike in shape, its entrance sheltered by reefs and wooded islands. Seeing it by daylight for the first time, Emma was struck by a sense of coziness. It was the kind of place that made her want to take a deep breath, fill her lungs with clean Alaskan air, and forget the ugliness of the past twenty-four hours.

Narrow floating docks extended over the water, where private boats and sport fishing vessels were moored. There were a few small planes as well, among them the red Beaver she recognized as John's.

Extending northward from the tiny harbor was a stretch of pristine, rocky beach that curved along the water's edge for as far as she could see. John had mentioned that this part of Refuge Cove was a state park, set aside to preserve the natural beauty of the coast. Inland from the beach, a line of tall evergreens sheltered walking paths and picnic tables. But at the water's edge, where waves lapped at the rocks, the shore appeared untouched by time.

While John filled the gas tank and gave the Beaver its preflight check, Emma took a short walk up the beach. The breeze was cool through the light quilted jacket she'd bought. It stirred her hair and teased her nostrils with the smells of saltwater, pine trees, damp earth, and fish. Tiny islands dotted the entrance to the cove, most little more than clumps of rock and tall evergreens.

With the Beaver fueled and checked, it was time to take off. John balanced her while she stepped onto the float and climbed up into the passenger seat. His grip on her arm was light and impersonal, just enough to steady her. But the contact through her sleeve sent a tingle up her arm.

Emma willed herself to ignore the sensation. John Wolf was an attractive man, masculine and mysterious. But he didn't seem the least bit interested in her as a woman. And even if he was, she'd just had her heart crushed by someone she'd thought she loved. She was raw and vulnerable. It could be months, even years before she was ready for a serious relationship. And a brief fling would only burn her again, leaving her even worse off than before.

He climbed into the pilot's seat, put on his headset, and handed her a second set to slip onto her head. "Can you hear me?" His deep voice crackled through the earpieces.

"I can." Emma remembered last night, when they couldn't converse over the roar of the engine. Now that wouldn't be a problem.

"Buckle up. Here we go."

The engine thrummed to life. John turned the plane around, taxied out past the islands into open water, then headed into the wind and opened the throttle. Engine roaring, the Beaver shot forward. Emma's stomach fluttered as the floats skimmed the waves and lifted off. They were airborne and climbing. Wind tore at the wings and fuselage of the sturdy old plane.

"You can unclench your hands now." John's voice crackled through the headset.

Emma glanced down at her white-knuckled fists and forced herself to laugh. Every nerve in her body was taut and quivering. But John seemed as relaxed as she'd ever seen him. Here in the plane, in the air, she realized, was where he felt completely at home.

"Is this your own plane?" she asked, making conversation to calm herself.

"Yes. I bought it six years ago from an old man who couldn't fly anymore. Sold a big share of my Sealaska stock to pay for it—these Beavers are classics. They don't come cheap."

"You say you sold your stock?" Even with the headset, Emma had to speak up. "What's Sealaska? I've never heard of it."

He took a moment to check the radio. "How much do you know about the Trans-Alaska oil pipeline?" he asked.

"I know what it is, and that it was controversial for a long time. That's about all."

"Back when it was being built, in the early seventies, the route lay across land belonging to the Tlingit, Haida, and Tsimshian tribes. The tribal leaders were powerful, they were smart, and I'm guessing they had damn good lawyers. They dug in their heels and said no. After some long and painful negotiations, the tribes settled for a huge trade of stock and valuable land elsewhere. When the deal was done, they formed a corporation to manage their newfound assets—Sealaska—with all the families as stockholders. It's very big and very modern these days. And it uses a share of its profits to help the people and support native traditions."

"I had no idea," Emma said. "So the pipeline actually turned out to be a good thing for the tribes."

"Most people think so."

"But you don't?"

"My father was involved in one of the early protests at the pipeline. A man was killed. My father went to prison for it. He died there. My only memory of him is a sad face behind bars. My mother, who was beautiful, died of grief—which is a polite way of saying she drank herself to death. You might say that my own view of the pipeline, and Sealaska, for all the good it does, is . . . tainted."

He banked the plane into a sharp right turn, pitching the wings so steeply that Emma felt a jolt of terror. Only as the Beaver leveled out did she begin to breathe again. Through the windscreen she could see that now they were headed landward, toward the forested mountains.

"Do you always turn like that?" she asked, still half-breathless.

"You mean did I do it to scare you? No, it's just the

most efficient way to turn. And it's not as dangerous as it looks." He made a slight course correction. "We're going back over the muskeg where I picked you up. From there, with your help, we might be able to find Boone's trailer. If he's there, I'll radio the state troopers. Keep your eyes open. Let me know if you see anything worth mentioning down there."

In other words, he was through talking. It was almost as if she was beginning to understand the man. At least the story about his parents had given her a clue to his brooding, solitary nature. She remembered the photograph she'd seen—John holding the little boy. Was that child his son? What had happened to him?

She turned toward the side window, which gave her the best view of the ground. From the air, the forest was like a thick green carpet. Here and there, small lakes and open patches of muskeg dotted the landscape. Boone's truck, she recalled, had been painted in a camouflage pattern. Even the shell that covered the bed was splotched with tan, green, and brown paint. The trailer, she remembered now, had been painted the same way. But the trash-littered clearing around it, and the well-traveled logging road, should make it easy to spot.

"There's that patch of muskeg," he said. "I spotted you coming out on the west side of it. So I take it you were coming from the east, right?"

Emma struggled to recall the terror-blurred details. "I remember heading toward the sunset. So yes, I was most likely coming from the east. But I was dodging through brush and trees. I changed direction again and again, just to get away."

"But the dogs were behind you. They'd have been coming from the trailer."

"Yes, that does make sense." She studied the vast forest below. "I thought my one hope lay in making it to the highway or the water. But I can see from here that I had miles to go. I never would've made it, would I?"

"No, you wouldn't."

"You saved my life, John. I hope I haven't made you sorry."

His muted laugh crackled through the headphones. "Ask me later," he said.

With the muskeg as a starting point, he flew in a widening spiral, each loop taking the plane farther to the east. Emma did her best to keep her eyes on the forest below, but after a few minutes of circling she began to feel dizzy. She touched John's arm, about to say something, when he spoke.

"Down there. Just ahead. I see something." Breaking pattern, he flew in lower. "I'll be damned," he muttered. "Look at that!"

Emma gasped when she saw it—the blackened metal frame of a trailer, surrounded by ashes and burnt debris.

Mute with shock, she stared down as the plane passed over it. She had done this. The fire she'd started as a delaying tactic had spread to the whole trailer.

She found her voice. "Honest to God, I never meant to do that."

"At least I can understand why Boone was after you," John said. "You're sure this was the place?"

"It's got to be. I can't believe we didn't see the smoke last night."

"You wouldn't have seen it over the trees while you were running. And it would have been behind me when I spotted you from the air. Even if we'd known about it, there's nothing we could've done. At least the forest was too wet to burn. And at least we know Boone didn't die in the fire."

"And he saved the dogs. They were miserable beasts, but I wouldn't have wanted them to die, chained to the wheel like that." Emma pictured Boone chasing her with murder in his heart. She didn't want to think about what he might have done if he'd caught her.

John circled and flew over the spot again. "No sign of the truck. Boone must have moved it away in time to save it."

"He probably didn't have time to save much else," Emma said. "All my packed things were in the trailer, along with the supplies Boone picked up in town. At a minimum we know that he got away with the truck, his rifle, and the dogs. He probably had my cash on him, too. He'd put it in his pocket." As the plane circled and flew on, she took a last look at the burnt remains of the trailer. "Where would he go?"

"Since nobody's seen him in town, I'm betting he went home to his mother," John said. "The family homestead is about fifty miles from here. Boone's brother, Ezra, lives with her. They keep to themselves, run trap lines in the winter for cash. As far as I know, Boone's the only one who's into the drug trade. That's probably why he had that trailer, at a safe distance from the family home. We can fly over, maybe see if Boone's truck's there. Are you up for that?"

"Let's do it."

They fell silent as John banked the plane and flew along the foot of the steep coastal mountain range. Lost in thought, Emma relived last night's escape, remembering how she'd set the fire and fled.

She should have realized how swiftly a blaze could spread through the cheap, lightweight materials that most trailers were made of. What if Boone had died in the fire? She could've been guilty of murder. As it was, could she be arrested for arson? She would have to ask Judge Falconi about that tomorrow.

The plane was climbing, gaining altitude. "What are you doing?" she asked.

"We're getting close to the Swenson place," he said. "I don't want to fly in low and spook them, especially since they'd likely recognize the plane. Keep an eye out. Even from ten thousand feet, you should be able to spot Boone's truck."

Emma's stomach fluttered as the plane climbed and leveled off to a high cruising altitude. From higher up, the trees were a solid green carpet, with small patches of clearing. A blue lake looked like the turquoise stone in a ring. The boat on its surface was no more than a dot.

"It's just ahead," John said. "Look sharp. We'll only be going over the place once."

Emma glued her gaze to the window. Now, below, she saw it—the overgrown sod roof of a lodge-sized cabin, surrounded by small outbuildings and several vehicles and ATV's. These looked ant-sized, but even at a distance, she recognized Boone's camouflage-painted pickup.

"I see it!" she said. "It's parked next to the cabin."

"You're sure it's Boone's truck."

"Unless it's got a twin, I'd know that truck anywhere."

He kept a straight course until the cabin was well out of sight. Then he banked a turn and headed back in the direction of Refuge Cove.

"Are you going to radio the state troopers?" Emma asked.

"I'll let them know where Boone is. But don't expect them to go in after him. That cabin's built like a fortress, and the Swensons have got enough guns and ammo to hold off an army. Bringing in a scumbag who deceived a woman with a fake wedding and took her money isn't worth the risk of a bloodbath."

Emma chewed on his assessment, knowing John was right, and that she mustn't take it personally. "So what do we do now?" she asked.

"I'd say you have a choice," he said. "You could let me fly you out of here, find a way home to Utah, maybe come back for Boone's trial if he's caught, or . . ."

"Or what? You said *if* Boone's caught. What will happen if I leave?"

"Not much. Sooner or later, he's liable to get himself caught. But he could stay holed up with his family for months. If he knows you're gone, and the police are looking for him in town, he'll have no reason to come in."

"And if I choose to stay . . . ?" But he didn't have to draw her a picture. After what she'd done, Boone would be mad enough to kill her—or make her wish he had. If he knew she was in Ketchikan, he wouldn't be able to resist coming after her. She would be bait to trap him.

"You know that I want you to leave." He lowered the flaps, putting the Beaver into its long descent. "Catching Boone isn't worth your life."

"I've already made up my mind. I want to leave Alaska knowing I got the man who wronged me and put him away. I'm staying."

"I wish you'd change your mind."

"I won't. I've got to see this through." She paused in thought. "How will he know I'm still in town?"

"He's got friends. He'll know. But you'll have to be careful. Boone's a dangerous man."

John focused on the controls as the Beaver made its

descent toward Refuge Cove. Emma watched him, her thoughts churning. Something he'd told her sounded out of place, and suddenly she realized what it was.

"One question," she said. "You seem to know a lot about that cabin and Boone's family. Have you been there?"

There was a silent beat while he adjusted the flaps. "Yes, I have," he said. "For now, that's all you need to know."

CHAPTER 5

After leaving the plane and picking up the Jeep in Refuge Cove, they drove back into town for a late lunch of hamburgers, fries, and colas. They were both hungry, and the little burger place just north of the tunnel was one of John's favorites.

From across the table, John studied the woman who'd dropped into his life out of nowhere. He'd tried hard to talk her into leaving Ketchikan. But even in the face of danger, she could be as stubborn as hard-set concrete.

How could he make her understand what she was dealing with? Boone had a crazy vindictive streak—hell, the whole family did. He would do his best to protect her, but given Emma's independent nature, he couldn't be there for her all the time.

The more she understood about her situation, the safer she would be. She might even decide to be sensible and leave. Either way, there was no getting around it—it was time for him to come clean about his relationship to the Swenson family.

"If I'm going to stay here, I'll need a job and a safe place to live," she said. "I can't expect to be your uninvited house-guest forever. And I can't expect you to chauffeur me into town every day."

"You might be safer with me," he said.

"Maybe. But I'd be putting you in danger, as well as imposing on your privacy. Lend me a pocket-sized pistol and teach me to shoot it. I'm a big girl. I can take care of myself."

Brave talk, he thought. But she *wasn't* a big girl, and her spunk, even with a gun, wouldn't be enough to fend off a man like Boone—especially if his mother and brother were to get involved.

"Let's take it slow for now," he said. "Twenty-four hours ago you were still with Boone. Things have changed a lot since then. You'll need time to settle in and learn your way around. For starters, since we've both finished eating, let's go for a walk. Come on."

Since downtown Ketchikan was small enough to explore on foot, they'd parked in the lot by the empty cruise docks on Front Street. He guided her up the slope to the Creek Street Historic District, with its colorful Gold Rush era shops, restaurants, boardwalks, and bridges that crisscrossed the rushing water. With the cruise season over, the crowds were gone, and some businesses were already closed. It was a peaceful place now, perfect for a quiet walk.

John played tour guide while he wrestled with the hard truths he needed to tell her. "This was a wild neighborhood back in the day," he said. "Especially during Prohibition—gambling, liquor, sporting ladies, you name it. There's a hidden path off to your left, over that bridge." He pointed. "It's called Married Man's Trail. The men used it to cut through the woods from their homes so they wouldn't be caught going back and forth."

"For shame!" Her laugh was warm and real. John liked the sound of it. He wouldn't have minded hearing it again. But she wouldn't be laughing when she heard what he had to say.

They came to a sheltered spot at the back of a shop, where a bridge overlooked a tumbling waterfall. A bench stood next to the wooden railing. "Sit down," he said. "I've got something to tell you. Something you need to know before you make plans to stay in Ketchikan."

"What is it?" She lowered herself to the end of the bench, a puzzled expression on her pert face. "Is something wrong?"

"That depends on you. Just hear me out." He sat on the other end of the bench, leaving a polite distance between them.

"Earlier, in the plane, you asked me if I'd ever been to the Swenson place. I told you I had."

"Yes, and you were very mysterious about it."

"What I didn't tell you was that, at the time I was there, I was married to Boone's sister."

He watched the shock sink in. Her face paled. Her lips parted. Although she hadn't moved, it was as if she'd shrunk away from him. "Tell me the rest," she said in a small, cold voice. "All of it."

"We were in high school. Boone and I were seniors. Marlena was a year younger, prettiest girl in the whole school. I was one of a dozen boys who had a crush on her. But I was one of the quiet kids who didn't get noticed much. When she asked me to the Spring Social I was stupefied—didn't even have a suit to wear. But we managed to have a good time. I had a bottle of whiskey in the car— I'd started drinking before my mother died, and was hitting it pretty heavy by then. To cut to the chase, we both got drunk, and I got her pregnant.

"Boone beat me up pretty bad when he found out. I didn't even fight back. Figured I deserved it. After that we had a shotgun wedding and went to live with her mother and Ezra in the bush. Boone came home, too. They all hated me—not only for what I'd done to Marlena, but just because I was Tlingit. As soon as I could, I left and got a job in town, crewing on a fishing boat.

"After I found a place to live, Marlena came too, and brought our baby boy. But things were never good between us, with me drinking and her climbing the walls because we didn't have enough money to go out and have fun. We lasted for a couple of years. Then she left me to marry the man I was working for—the man who owned the boat. She took the boy and got full custody. I went off the deep end for a few years, finally started with AA, pulled myself together, got my pilot's license and bought the Beaver. . . ."

John's voice trailed off. He had never told the full story to anyone. Now that he'd done it, he felt physically drained. He'd been looking out at the waterfall and the flock of small brown birds that dipped and darted in the spray. Now he forced himself to turn and look at Emma.

She sat absolutely still, her hands folded in her lap. In her calm expression, he caught glimpses of shock, sympathy, and wounded anger.

"Why didn't you tell me sooner?" she asked.

"Because I didn't expect it to matter. I thought I could talk you into leaving. You can still leave. Let me fly you out of here. I can deal with Boone when he shows up."

"And if I choose to stay?"

"Then you'll need to know what you're dealing with. I'll do my best to keep you safe, but I can't do that unless you trust me."

Her tightly masked emotions flared to the surface. "Why should I trust you? For heaven's sake, the man who hurt me is your ex-brother-in-law! He's your son's uncle! He's family—and you've only known me for a day!"

John turned to face her directly. "Look at me while I say this, Emma. These people aren't my friends. I know Boone and what he's capable of. If it would keep him from hurting other women the way he hurt you, I'd turn him over to the law in a heartbeat, the consequences be damned. If you don't believe me—and if you can't trust me to stand up for you, then you should leave—because right now, I'm all you've got. And there's one thing we both know for certain—you can't fight Boone alone."

Standing, she tore her gaze from his and walked away, across the bridge to the other side of the creek. John didn't try to follow her. She had no place to go, no option except to come back to him. He kept an eye on her as she stood looking down into a quiet pool below the falls, where the bodies of salmon, their lives given up for the next generation, gleamed like tarnished silver in the depths.

After several minutes she walked back to face him. "I've thought about what you told me," she said. "Your story has raised some doubts about my staying. But I'll sleep on it and give you my decision tomorrow, after I've seen the judge."

"That sounds reasonable enough." They walked back along the boardwalk toward Dolly's House, a former brothel, now a museum and tourist attraction. John lapsed back into the role of guide, trying to ignore the tension that hung between them. They needed a break from each other, some time apart to breathe and think.

"You're a teacher," he said. "Does that mean you like to read?"

She gave him a strained smile. "Not necessarily. But yes, I love to read. I browsed through your bookshelf while you left me to go to town, but I didn't see much to catch my interest."

"We can fix that," he said. "Ketchikan has a first-rate bookstore. I'll treat you to a couple of paperbacks, your choice."

"Thanks. I'll take you up on that." She seemed genuinely pleased, he thought as they walked the short distance downhill to the bookstore. He was finding that he enjoyed pleasing her. But if the woman had any common sense, she'd allow him to fly her to Sitka. She'd be out of danger and out of his life. Wasn't that what he really wanted?

In the bookstore, Emma chose a couple of juicy-looking bestsellers by women authors. John paid for them at the checkout counter. She might not have accepted even this small gift, but she knew he was buying her books to ensure himself some peace in the cabin. She meant to give him just that. The long day had worn her out. Curling up by the fire with a good book sounded like a delicious idea.

They walked back to the Jeep and took the road out of town. The sun was already low in the sky. Boone had mentioned to her that, in Alaska, darkness moved in early. In midwinter, he'd said, the daylight was so brief and the nights so long that people tended to get blue and surly from so much darkness. But for lovers, he'd said with a smile, the nights were never too long.

Boone.

Heaven help her, she'd been so love starved that she'd clung to his every word. He'd fed her a line of pretty words. She'd swallowed it whole and nearly paid a terrible price.

She'd been a naïve, gullible fool. But she'd learned her lesson. Men lied to get what they wanted—and when they thought they had it, they could change without warning. Never again, for as long as she lived, would she put blind trust in any man, including the dark, intriguing pilot who sat beside her now.

This afternoon John Wolf had revealed a part of his past—not an easy thing for such a private man. What he'd told her, she sensed, was true. But what had he left out? How many dangerous secrets was he still hiding?

Right now, she had no choice except to trust him with her safety. But she would keep her guard up. She would never let need make her vulnerable.

They stopped for a few groceries in Ward Cove. Emma waited in the locked Jeep while John went into the store and came out with a tall paper bag. He had asked her if she wanted anything special, but she'd answered with a shake of her head. She'd had a long, emotional twenty-four hours. Thinking about groceries was more than her wearied brain could manage.

But she didn't like the idea of being dead weight. It was time she started helping out around the cabin. She would start by offering to make supper tonight, even if it turned out to be warmed-over chili.

By the time they arrived at the cabin, it was almost dark. Emma stayed locked in the Jeep while John, with a flashlight in one hand and his pistol in the other, circled the cabin. Only after he'd checked inside and turned on the porch light, did he come back for the groceries and Emma. Given how well he knew Boone, his caution confirmed that the danger was worth taking seriously.

The cabin was cold. While John made the fire, Emma unpacked the groceries—mostly basics like coffee, bacon, eggs, milk, and bread. No fresh vegetables. Didn't the man eat salad?

The only surprise was a half gallon of double-fudge chocolate ice cream and a plastic squeeze bottle of chocolate syrup in the bottom of the bag. She stared at it, shaking her head.

"What?" With the fire flickering to a blaze, John had wandered into the kitchen area. "Is something wrong?"

"What were you thinking?" She shook her head again.

"This junk food will give you a heart attack by the time you're fifty!"

He raised one black eyebrow. "Maybe I won't live that long. And tonight, it isn't junk food, it's supper. Join me."

"I was about to warm up the last of the chili. At least it's nourishing."

"Come on." He lifted two good-sized bowls off the shelf and began scooping chocolate ice cream into them. "You haven't lived until you've spent an evening in a forest cabin, eating chocolate ice cream and reading a good book in front of a crackling fire. Live a little, Emma Hunter."

"Oh, all right." She watched as he stowed the carton in the freezer, drenched the mounds of ice cream in chocolate syrup, added spoons, and handed her one bowl to carry.

She followed him toward the overstuffed love seat that faced the fire. John was right, she told herself. An evening of relaxing self-indulgence might be just what she needed. But something, she sensed, was off. He was too artificially cheerful, too set on getting her to do what he wanted.

Should she confront him and demand to know what was going on? But no, that would only raise the tension between them. They both needed a break tonight.

The paperbacks she'd chosen were stacked on the side table. Emma settled on the love seat where she'd slept last night, kicked off her new sneakers, and rested her stocking-clad feet on the hearth. The fire was deliciously warm, the chocolate ice cream a decadent treat. She spooned it slowly into her mouth, savoring the cold, creamy sweetness.

She could tell that John didn't want to talk. Resolving to leave him in peace, she finished the ice cream, set the bowl and spoon on the side table, and opened one of the books. The story was well-written, but Emma was worn-out. She'd barely made it through fifty pages before she began to nod off.

"Hey, sleepyhead." John's touch on her shoulder startled her awake. "You're not spending another night out
here," he said. "I'd say it's about your bedtime."

Emma yawned, put the book on the table, and staggered
to her feet. "Can I wear your thermals again tonight? I did-
n't buy pajamas."

"They're all yours. I may be up for a while. Don't worry
if you hear me go out. I'll just be checking the place."

"Are you concerned?" She remembered how he'd
checked the perimeter of the house before letting her out
of the Jeep.

"I'm just being careful—making sure that bear doesn't
pay us another visit."

"Then I'll try not to worry." She yawned again. "I don't
know if I've thanked you for all you've done. Please know
that I'm grateful."

He raised a mocking eyebrow. "You know I'd do the
same for a lost puppy, don't you? Now get some rest."

Emma tottered down the hall, brushed her teeth, and got
undressed. The bedroom was cold, the bed even colder. But
little by little the sheets and blankets warmed to her body.
Lulled by the wind in the trees outside her high window,
she sank into sleep.

The moon had risen above the mountaintops, its cold
gleam casting a moiré of light and shadow over the forest.
The sky was clear, but the breeze off the narrows carried
the sound of distant thunder and the scent of rain.

Armed with his pistol, John waited in the darkness next
to the Jeep. He hadn't wanted to alarm Emma by telling
her about the tire tracks he'd seen earlier. But he'd gotten
their message. Boone had stopped by while they were gone.
And he'd be back.

After making sure Emma was asleep, he'd turned off the

cabin lights, locked the door, and settled next to the Jeep to wait. His ex-brother-in-law was bound to show up. It was just a question of when.

He'd been outside for about twenty minutes when he heard the snap of a twig. The hair rose on the back of his neck. It wasn't a bear—that much he knew. A bear's approach would have been absolutely silent.

He raised the .44 and pulled back the hammer as a tall, pale form stepped out of the trees at the edge of the clearing. It was Boone, all right, wearing a fringed buckskin jacket with a slouched hat, and carrying a high-powered rifle. He would've parked some distance away, probably driving a vehicle borrowed from his mother's homestead.

"Put the gun on the ground, Boone." John stepped into the light. "Nice and easy. No court would convict me for shooting an armed man on my property."

Boone laughed as he lowered the weapon. "Hell, John, I should've known I couldn't sneak up on a goddamned Injun. But I didn't come to pick a fight with you. I just came to fetch my wife. I know you've got her. Hand her over and we won't have any problem."

"Slide that gun in my direction, and we'll talk."

Boone gave the rifle a shove with the toe of his boot. Keeping a careful eye on the man, John picked it up, removed the shells, and tossed the empty gun behind him on the ground.

"In the first place, she's not your wife," he said. "We found out about the fake wedding."

Boone grinned. "Reckon she was pissed about that. Most women would give their teeth to be Mrs. Boone Swenson."

"She's pissed about more than that, like the money you stole from her."

"Stole? Hell, she gave me that cash with her own sweet little hand. It was a gift. It's mine. Now hand her over before things get ugly."

John took a moment to weigh his options. True, he had the drop on Boone. If he thought he could do it, it would make sense to restrain him and turn him over to the police. But with no outside communication except the radio in the Jeep, he was on his own. And Boone, a tough, dirty brawler who outweighed him by thirty pounds, was bound to put up a fight. If the fight ended the wrong way, Emma would be left alone, without protection. He couldn't take that chance. Short of shooting the bastard, which would be murder now that the man was unarmed, his safest bet would be to talk Boone into leaving.

"What you did is called theft by deception," John said. "Emma's already talked to the police. If they catch you, you'll be in for some serious jail time. But if you'd give back her cash and promise to leave her alone, chances are we could talk the little lady into dropping the charges."

Boone's response was part guffaw, part snarl. "*Charges?* That's a friggin' joke. The bitch set my trailer on fire and burned it to the ground. She owes me!"

"You can tell that to the judge," John said. "But there's one more thing—something even more important to Emma than the money. You played on her trust and betrayed her. What she really wants is to make sure you never hurt another woman that way again."

"Well, you can tell the friggin' little bitch she already got her wish." Raising a bandaged right hand, Boone swept away his hat. Moonlight gleamed on the burned and blistered streak that ran down the side of his head, from the crown of his scalp to his fire-maimed ear and down to his jaw. "No woman's ever goin' to want me again—not unless she's as blind as a bat!"

John willed himself not to stare as the realization sank in. Emma's escape had scarred this man for life. His thirst for revenge wouldn't be satisfied until he'd made her suffer.

Stepping back, he used his foot to shove the empty rifle

back within Boone's reach. "Emma didn't do that to you, Boone," he said. "You brought it on yourself when you set out to cheat her. Now put your hat on, take your gun, and go. If you ever try to come near her again, so help me, I'll shoot you where it'll hurt the worst!"

Boone slapped the hat back on his head and bent down to hook his hand around the rifle. As he straightened, his face wore a smirking grin. "I'll be damned," he said. "You've fallen head over heels for the little bitch, haven't you? Well, good luck with her, my Injun brother. Don't get burned like I did." With that, he turned, strode away, and vanished into the trees.

John stood in place, pistol at the ready, until he heard the distant rumble of a truck pulling away through the trees. Even then he waited in the silence, alert for any sign that Boone hadn't really left.

He took a few minutes to climb into the Jeep and radio the state troopers. But even if they came rushing right out, by the time they got here, Boone would be long gone. Boone knew the back country trails and logging roads like the palm of his hand. He could come and go at will without being seen. And sooner or later, he would be back, looking for Emma.

Knowing he wouldn't sleep, John sank onto the porch steps and watched the cloud bank roll in from the west. Sheet lightning danced across the dark sky. Thunder growled a muted warning.

You've fallen head over heels . . .

Boone's taunting words played like a loop in his head. Why couldn't he just dismiss them? Was it because they'd struck a note of truth?

John muttered a curse. He was too old and cynical for a teenage crush. True, he liked Emma. He admired her spunk and courage. And she'd become important to him. Keeping her safe had become an urgent priority. But falling? That would be crazy. Boone's words were nothing more than an attempt to rattle him.

Emma would need to know that Boone had been here. He didn't want to terrify her, but she had to understand that she was no longer safe in this remote cabin. Not even with him. For now he would let her rest while he kept watch. He could tell her first thing in the morning.

By the time he went inside, the stars were gone and a soft rain had begun to fall. The gentle sound pattered on the porch roof above his head. Not wanting to wake Emma, he opened the door softly. The room was dark, the fire almost out. As he crossed the floor to the hallway, he saw that the love seat had been turned partway toward the front door. Something stirred against the cushions. It was Emma, huddled in the blanket.

"I hope you aren't going to say there was a bear outside," she said. "I don't want to hear a lie."

John walked toward her, pausing to lay the gun on the side table. "No, it wasn't a bear," he said. "Go back to bed. You're safe. We can talk in the morning."

"We can talk now," she said. "I've been awake since I heard you go outside. I couldn't go back to sleep if I had to."

"Fine." He walked to the fireplace, stirred the glowing coals, and added another log, along with a few sticks of kindling. Then he pushed the love seat back to face the fire and settled on the end opposite Emma.

"I heard voices," she said. "It was Boone, wasn't it?"

"It was. He's gone." John watched the log catch fire.

"You couldn't stop him?"

"I stopped him from coming inside. But no, short of shooting the bastard, there was nothing I could do to stop him from leaving." He turned to face her. "He'll be back,

Emma. And after what I saw and heard tonight, I know he's not going to give up until he punishes you in the worst way."

"What did you see?" Her eyes were large in the firelight.

"You didn't just burn the trailer. Boone was burned, too—right here." He indicated the extent of Boone's burns with his hand. "He says that, given the way he looks, no woman will ever want him again—and he's determined to make you pay for what you did to him."

"Pay?" The quiver in her voice betrayed her fear. "He stole seventeen thousand dollars from me. That old trailer was nothing but junk. What can he be thinking?"

John turned away to gaze into the leaping flames. "Knowing what Boone's capable of, I don't think either of us wants to find out," he said.

In the silence that followed, he sensed that she was breaking under the stress. She'd begun to tremble. A low sob escaped her lips. What he'd just said to her was frightening, but she needed to hear it. Growing up, he'd witnessed Boone's cruelty to small, weak creatures unlucky enough to cross his path. Emma needed to understand that the danger to her was all too real.

"I didn't mean for that to happen." She was crying now, her shoulders heaving with deep, heartfelt sobs. "I didn't want him hurt. I only wanted to get away."

Heartsick, John watched her. Lord, she didn't deserve this. She'd come to Alaska full of hope and trust, eager to begin her own loving family. Instead she found herself stalked and hunted by the revenge-hungry monster she'd chosen to be her husband. It was the ultimate betrayal.

Not knowing what else to do, he reached out and gathered her close, cradling her against him. "I'm sorry," he whispered against her soft hair. "Damn it, girl, I'm sorry."

He felt her quivering as she struggled to control herself.

Little by little her crying eased and her shaking slowed, but she made no move to push away. Instead she clung to him, as if he were the only solid element in her crumbling world. Where his hand rested on her back, John could feel the pounding of her heart. Where her head rested in the hollow of his shoulder, his shirt was damp with her tears. He cradled her gently, his free hand stroking her tangled hair. "It's all right," he murmured. "I'm here. I won't let anything happen to you. . . ."

Only then, when she failed to reply, did John realize that she'd fallen asleep in his arms.

CHAPTER 6

Emma opened her eyes to gray dawn filtering through the windows of the cabin. John was standing over her, his black hair flowing over his shoulders. The barest hint of a smile tugged at his lips. "Good morning," he said.

Stirring, she blinked herself fully awake. Only then did she realize that she was on the love seat, wrapped in the wool blanket with pillows under her head.

"Not again!" She groaned, rolled to one side, and sat up. "Have I been here since last night?"

He nodded. "I'd have hauled you up and walked you to your bed, but you were out like a light. And after Boone's visit, I thought you might be nervous sleeping alone."

"You're right. I would have." She yawned. "I hope you got some sleep, too."

"Enough." Emma knew he was fudging the truth. He would have sat up all night keeping watch while she slept.

"Liar," she said. "I know you better than that."

"I'm fine," he said. "Lucky for us, the rest of the night was quiet."

He sat down next to her on the love seat. "Look at me, Emma. You need to understand something. Now that Boone knows you're here with me, this cabin isn't safe for you anymore. It's too isolated. There isn't even any cell phone service out here, just the radio I have in the Jeep."

"Having me here isn't safe for you, either," she said. "Boone could sneak up in the night, block the door, douse the porch with gasoline, and set the place on fire. The old wood in this cabin would go up like tinder, and us with it."

"Let me fly you out of here," he said. "Tomorrow I'm scheduled for another mail run. I can take you along and drop you off in Sitka with some good people I know."

Emma hesitated. It made sense to say yes right now. But if she left, Boone would have a good chance of going free. The police and troopers had more urgent matters to deal with than an elusive man who'd cheated a woman out of her savings with a pretend wedding. She knew she mustn't stay in the cabin, but there had to be other, safer options.

"Let me think about it." She rose, pulling up the waist of John's oversized thermals. "I said I'd let you know after I talk to the judge—and I will."

"I guess that'll have to do for now." He didn't look pleased. "Go on and get dressed while I rustle us up some breakfast."

Emma went down the hall and, after cleaning up in the bathroom, unfolded her new clothes from the plastic shopping bag, which would have to do as a purse until she could find something better. Maybe there was a thrift shop in Ketchikan where she could buy a few more necessities. She would have to ask John, or perhaps the judge.

By the time she'd dressed in her new jeans and a navy blue cotton turtleneck, she could smell bacon cooking in the kitchen. She was just leaving the bedroom when she happened to glance down the hall. At the far end of it, beyond John's room, was a closed door. Strange, she hadn't noticed it earlier. Was it a back door to the cabin? Curious, she walked down the hall to investigate.

The sturdy wooden door was latched from the inside, but opening it was easy enough. Slowly and cautiously, Emma pulled the door open far enough to step through. She'd expected to walk outside. Instead, she found herself in a shedlike structure built like a lean-to on the rear of the cabin.

The enclosed space was almost dark, the air damp and smelling of old wood. As Emma's eyes adjusted, she could see a massively long, pale shape laid out on sawhorses like a coffin for a giant.

Trembling a little, she walked forward and laid a hand on the object. Her fingertips brushed a surface of intricately carved wood, the contours slightly rough to the touch.

"Emma?" John stood in the open doorway, his hair tied back now. "I was wondering where you'd gone to. What are you doing out here?"

"Just exploring." She turned back to face him. "Did I do something wrong?"

"Why would you think that? Here, I'll give you a better look." Crouching in the darkness, he plugged something into the wall. A naked bulb, rigged on a long cord, came on above her head. Bathed in its harsh light, raw and unfinished but still beautiful, lay a twelve-foot totem pole carved from a massive log of red cedar.

Emma's breath caught as she realized what it was. There'd been totem poles in the park where her so-called wedding had taken place. But in size, design, and sheer magnificence, they couldn't hold a candle to the one she was seeing now.

"This is amazing," she said. "Did you do this?"

John shook his head. "My grandfather was a master carver. He passed away years ago. This was his last piece of work."

"It seems a shame to leave it like this. Isn't there anyone who could finish it?" She gazed at him, the realization dawning. "Could *you?*"

He glanced away, as if avoiding her eyes. "The old man taught me to carve. When I was a boy, I used to help him out here in the carving shed. One of his last wishes was that I finish this totem for him."

"But you haven't. Why not?"

His face assumed its stoic expression, shutting her out. "Your breakfast is getting cold," he said. "Come on, we've got a long day ahead."

On the way to town John talked about totem carving. Emma had come to recognize what she called his tour-guide mode. It was like a mask, or a role in a play, a means to hide whatever he was feeling.

"In the old days, my people, the Tlingit, had no written language," he said. "Our totems were our stories, our messages, our history. But about a hundred years ago, with the coming of so-called white civilization, the totems began to disappear. The old ones lay fallen and rotting. And the carvers, the few that still lived, were old men. In the late 1930s, the WPA started a movement to bring back totem poles. Young artists were trained by the elders—my grandfather was one of them. He was still a boy when he learned to carve.

"They went to the old places, recovered the rotting totem poles, and copied them, down to the last detail. Many of the totems you see now are copies from that time. There's a place I'll show you, called Totem Bight, that has some the best ones on display. Since then, the art of carving has been passed down from fathers to sons and grandsons. I always hoped that my son would help me finish my grandfather's totem. . . ." His voice trailed off. "But my son is half-white, and that's a story for another time."

"Was your father a carver?"

"He might have become a great one. He had the talent. But it wasn't to be."

Now Emma recalled the story of how John's father had killed a man in a protest over the Trans-Alaska pipeline and died in prison. John's tragic family history was still painful. If she wanted a pleasant day, she would be wise to stop prying into his past.

They reached town in time for Emma's appointment with Judge Falconi. John drove her up a winding road to the foot of a wooden stairway. At the top was a blue-gray frame home with a Prairie-style roof and a broad, covered porch overlooking the town and the water.

"I'm sure the judge won't mind if you come with me," Emma said.

John's displeasure showed in his face. "I've got things to do," he said. "Call when you're done. I'll pick you up right here."

As Emma watched him drive away, she remembered yesterday's reaction to the judge's name. John Wolf was a man of raw nerves and dark secrets. Trying to understand him was like walking through a labyrinth, with something new and unexpected at every turn.

She climbed the stairs to the house, which was small but so pleasing to the eye that Emma had to pause near the top of the steps to study it. The side that faced the water was mostly glass. Sliding doors opened onto a sheltered porch, furnished with white Adirondack chairs, bright-colored cushions, and lush potted plants. At the top of the stairs, rhododendrons, past blooming but still green, framed the winding stone pathway that led to the front door.

She hesitated, her finger hovering over the doorbell. It was so early in the day. Maybe she should have called first to remind the judge that she was coming. But it was too late for that now.

Judge Vera Falconi answered the door on the first ring. Not much taller than Emma herself, she was in her sixties, with olive skin, hawkish features, striking black eyes, and a wealth of elegantly coiffed iron gray hair. The black pants ensemble that draped her lean body was accented with a Navajo-style turquoise necklace that looked like the real thing.

"Come in, dear. I was just making tea." She ushered Emma indoors with a welcoming smile. "We can drink it in the kitchen."

The inside of the house was immaculate and as elegant as its owner. Emma followed the judge to the kitchen. "Thank you so much for offering to help me, Judge Falconi," she said, "especially since I'm not able to pay you right now."

"Don't worry about it. I'm happy to help. And please call me Vera. I hope you like chai." After seating Emma, she poured the spicy red tea into cups as delicate as eggshells, and passed Emma a plate of homemade hazelnut cookies. "Detective Traverton told me your story, so you won't have to go through the ordeal of repeating it. My goodness, dear, what an awful time you've been through. Boone Swenson's always had a lawless streak, but even I can't believe he'd go this far."

"You know Boone?"

"Ketchikan's a small town. I was a judge here for almost twenty-five years." Vera offered Emma cream and sugar for her tea, then added it to her own. "Sam mentioned that it was John Wolf who rescued you."

The sound of John's spoken name had touched off a surprising quiver beneath her ribs. She stirred her tea before answering. "Yes. He's taken me under his wing, so to speak, until I decide what to do next. I think he'll be glad to see the last of me."

Vera smiled. "John's a good-hearted man. But I suspect he's never forgiven me for what happened fifteen years ago. Did he tell you about it?"

"No, but I've wondered."

"You know about his divorce?" Vera nibbled a cookie. Her nails were neatly trimmed. She wore a plain gold band on the third finger of her right hand. Emma guessed that she must be a widow.

"I know he was married to Boone's sister, and that they had a little boy," she said.

"Yes. David." Vera sipped her tea. "I was the family court judge who ruled in their custody hearing. It was a heartbreaking case. For John, the sun rose and set with that little boy. He adored David. But he was an alcoholic, and he'd gotten worse, to the point of recklessness, since the separation. He'd even been arrested for DUI. Marlena was about to get remarried to a stable man with a nice home. She'd asked for full custody with no visitation rights."

"And that's what you gave her?" Emma asked.

"I did what any responsible judge would do. I put the child's welfare first. And I don't think John will ever forgive me for that."

"But he's been sober for years—that's what he told me. And I have no reason to doubt him."

"I'm sure you're right," Vera said. "John's done an admirable job of turning his life around. A few years ago, after he'd stopped drinking, he petitioned the court again for the right to see David. I might have ruled in his favor that time. But I'd moved on by then. Another judge heard the case."

"And John lost again."

"Marlena showed up. She convinced the judge that her

son was at a vulnerable age, and being forced to spend time with a man he barely knew, a man known to act rashly, would cause the boy undue distress and possible harm. As far as I know, John hasn't tried again."

So that explained it—the empty bedroom, the photo on John's bureau, the unfinished totem pole, and the melancholy nature of the man who'd taken her in. Little by little, Emma was beginning to understand.

"What do you say we get started with your problem?" Vera opened the laptop she'd set on the table and brought up a file. On the screen, Emma saw a list of government agencies, banks, airlines, insurance companies, and credit card companies, all with their contact information.

"Take this." She passed Emma a yellow pad and a pen. "Write down everything you remember having in your purse—the credit card companies, any part of the numbers you might know, and as much about your driver's license and passport as you can remember. When you're ready we'll start making calls."

John picked Emma up at the bottom of the stairs, where he'd let her off two hours earlier. He could tell she was tired, but relief was written all over her face.

"How did it go?" he asked as she buckled herself into the passenger seat.

"Oh, the judge was fantastic! We managed to call the passport office and all four of my credit card companies. They'll be sending me new cards. It'll take a couple of weeks. Since I don't know where I'll be, Vera—the judge— said they could mail them to her address." She gave him a hesitant glance. "I guess that argues for my staying here in Ketchikan, at least until the cards arrive."

"I see." John had made it clear that he wanted Emma to leave. He had to admit the idea of her staying didn't sound all that unpleasant, but above all, he needed to keep her safe. "I can always pick up the cards from the judge and fly them to you in Sitka on the next mail run," he said.

"Thanks, but I've made up my mind. I already know I can't stay in the cabin with you. Vera offered me her spare room until the cards arrive, but I turned her down. I can't impose on her—or you—any longer. I need my own safe place to stay, and I need a job."

Good luck with that. But before John could voice the thought, a possibility struck him. "You might try the Gateway Hotel," he said. "It's right there on Front Street, across from the docks. Ninety-year-old hotel, rock solid, no elevators, and you need a key to get in at night, so you'd be safe from Boone. There's a good restaurant right downstairs. They even give you free breakfast. Now that the season's over, you should be able to negotiate a good discount. They might even give you a job."

"That's what Vera suggested, too—and I'm going to need a job, even if it's just scrubbing and cleaning. I put myself through college waitressing. Maybe they need somebody to fill in. Can we check it out while we're in town?"

"Sure." Maybe he'd said too much. It would be cruel to get her hopes up, only to have them dashed if things didn't work out.

"She also suggested that I check in with the school district about substitute teaching. But for that, I'd need transportation."

"And you'd be unprotected coming and going. As long as Boone's on the loose, that might not be such a good idea."

"Oh, you're probably right." She was silent a moment. Then she pulled a folded paper out of the shopping bag that served as her purse. "I almost forgot. We need to go to the driver's license office. Vera gave me this note, asking them to give me a temporary license. I'll need some kind of photo ID to apply for a job—and to get on the plane when I leave."

"No problem. That judge is a useful person to know. In this town, all she has to do is say the word."

An edge had crept into John's voice. He hadn't meant for it to happen, but the bitterness over Vera Falconi's decision to bar him from David had never gone away.

"Vera told me about the divorce and your son," Emma said. "If it's any comfort, she said that if she'd been on the bench the second time you went to court, she would have ruled in your favor."

"For whatever that's worth."

"If I understand right, David will be eighteen on his next birthday. Won't he be able to spend time with you then?"

"Maybe. But that doesn't matter. Marlena's done a number on him over the years. My son doesn't want anything to do with me."

"Oh, John . . ." With a murmur of dismay, she laid a hand on his shoulder. John fought the urge to shake off the contact. Emma meant well, but he didn't need her pity. Damn it, he didn't need anything from her.

Still, her touch triggered a memory—holding her in his arms last night, while she clung to him, seeking his strength and comfort. Even after she slept, he had cradled her for a time, feeling her soft, womanly warmth and breathing in the subtle fragrance of her hair. She'd needed him, and it had felt good to be needed by a woman.

But that was all, John told himself. He was a man, and that brief intimacy had put a few ideas into his head. But it meant nothing. If he had any sense, he would forget the whole episode.

It was a relief to pull up to the county building and let

Emma out of the Jeep. "I'll wait out here," he said. "You won't have any trouble finding the right room."

"I'll try not to be too long," she said. "Wish me luck with the long lines."

"This is Ketchikan. You won't have to worry about long lines."

As she hurried into the building, he found a shaded spot near the entrance, parked, and levered back the seat. He'd been awake all night and hadn't slept much the night before. What he needed right now was a nap.

He was just getting comfortable when the front door of the county building opened and three people came out together. John felt the familiar pain, like acid burning his gut, as Marlena, her husband, Carl, and David came down the walk, laughing and talking. Clearly, they hadn't seen him where he was parked under an overhanging tree.

Sinking lower in the seat, John willed himself not to look at them. But he couldn't help noticing the piece of paper David was waving as if it were a trophy. It was his new driver's license, John realized, a rite of passage for any young man. And his family was sharing in the celebration.

John hadn't seen them in a while. Marlena looked good—her tawny hair beauty-parlor fresh, her nails manicured and painted black, her pricy jeans skin tight on her gym-toned body. Even Carl, who'd be into his fifties by now and was putting on weight, looked prosperous and happy.

And David. John's jaw tightened against a pain that was almost physical. Lord, his son had become a man overnight. His still-gangly body had some filling out do to, but he was getting there. Soon he'd be full-grown, out of school, and on his own.

And John would have missed it all.

Marlena and Carl had been decent parents to the boy.

But the fact that he'd been barred from sharing those precious, growing-up years would haunt John forever.

The name on his son's new driver's license would read *David McKenzie*. The boy had been using his stepfather's name since he started school. Years ago, Marlena's lawyer had approached John about allowing Carl to adopt him. John had refused. He was still David's legal father. That, and blood, were the only ties he had left.

The three had turned away now. They were headed across the parking lot, toward Carl's big, shiny Cadillac Escalade. John tore his gaze away as David climbed into the driver's side and, grinning, took his place behind the wheel. It was too late to change the past, he reminded himself. And he had no power to change the present.

Getting a temporary license had taken Emma a little over an hour. There'd been no long lines, but the counter had been short-staffed, with only one clerk. John was waiting when she came out. He started the Jeep without comment.

"Sorry it took me so long," she said.

"It's fine."

"You've been awfully nice about waiting around for me," she said, making conversation. "What did you do while I was at the judge's this morning?"

"Not much." He turned the Jeep back toward Front Street. "I had some coffee. Then I made a call to the state troopers to see if anybody had checked out the burned trailer. They said they'd flown over it in the chopper, but since there wasn't enough open space to land, they'd have to send somebody in by road—when they could spare a team and a vehicle."

"Which means they might not ever get around to it. This is so frustrating, John. If they'd only look, there's no telling what kind of evidence they could find against Boone." Emma leaned forward and slipped the new temporary license into the hip pocket of her jeans. "I asked the judge whether I might be in trouble for setting the trailer on fire."

He pulled into the parking lot by the docks and stopped the Jeep. "I didn't know you were worried about it. What did she say?"

"She said that would depend on whether I truly believed I was in danger."

"You did, right?"

"Of course I did. You saw me. I was terrified. But she said that a sharp lawyer might argue that I was just a new bride who got cold feet about the wedding night—or maybe, when I discovered Boone had lied about his home, I was so angry that I set the place on fire to get even." Her interlaced hands tightened in her lap. "I'm scared, John. I could be in as much trouble as Boone is."

"I'm no legal expert, but it's not too late to leave."

She shook her head. "You're wrong. It's too late now. I need to wait for my credit cards and follow through in case Boone is actually caught. Besides, how would it look to the police if I ran away? They might think I had something to be afraid of."

"Look at me, Emma." He turned in the seat to face her. "You were lied to, robbed, and chased through the forest with dogs. You were wronged. You deserve justice. And I want you to know that, whatever happens, I've got your back."

Whatever happens.

Emma blinked back a tear. She owed everything to this taciturn, solitary man who'd dropped out of the sky to rescue her. But could she believe him? Could she trust him not to walk away if her needs demanded too much of him?

She faked a smile. "I'll try not to make you sorry you said that."

"Don't worry about it. See that building across the street, with the upstairs windows? That's the Gateway. You're going to see them about a room and a job. Should I wait here?"

"Would you mind coming with me? I could use the support."

They walked across Front Street and into the vintage hotel. The reception area was small, with most of the ground floor space taken up by the restaurant through the door to the right. A narrow, walled stairway opposite the desk led to the upper floors.

John stayed back while the perky receptionist greeted Emma. "Oh, yes! Judge Falconi called and said you might be coming by. She said you'd lost everything in a robbery, and that you needed a room and a job."

"Can you help me with either one?" Emma asked. "I've had plenty of waitress experience, or I'd be happy to clean, or paint, or anything else you might need."

The pretty brunette smiled. "It so happens you're in luck. One of our waitresses is getting married, and she wants a couple weeks off for her wedding and honeymoon. Plus another part-time girl just quit to go back to school. If you'll promise to stay and work both shifts for the full two weeks, the job's yours."

"And the room?"

"In the off-season, we've been updating our rooms with new paint, carpet, and furniture. The small rooms on the third floor have yet to be done. If you don't mind some noise and inconvenience, and maybe having to change rooms, you can stay up there for half the fall rate. We could take it out of your salary if you like. My name's

Megan, by the way." She reached into a file drawer and took out a form. "If you're good to go, you can fill in your information here, move in tonight, and start work in the morning."

John couldn't see Emma's face, but he could picture her expression. Neither of them had imagined her problem would be resolved so easily. All it had taken was the right timing and a word from Judge Falconi.

Whenever the judge's name came up, his thoughts flew back to the day when Vera Falconi had looked down at him from the bench and pronounced the words that had broken his heart. Had she made the right decision? Maybe so. He'd been an alcoholic mess back then, and David had grown up fine without him—John had seen that today. But losing his son had left a hole in his heart that had never healed—and never would.

CHAPTER 7

With the employment form on a clipboard, Emma found a chair in the corner of the lobby and began filling in the blanks. She was grateful for Vera's kindness in making the call, and for the judge's discretion. The full story of her fake marriage to Boone and her flight from the burning trailer would have made for some juicy gossip.

John had wandered off after telling her he'd be back to take her to lunch. Emma was handing the completed form back to Megan when he walked in the door carrying a paper take-out bag. "Ready to go?" he asked.

"Almost." Emma turned back to the girl. "Thanks so much. This experience has taught me a lot about the kindness of strangers."

"No problem," the girl said. "Come back after five. We should have your room and a couple of uniforms ready by then. I'm afraid they'll be big on you. You're such a little thing."

"For two weeks, I can make them do. See you then."

She walked out the door with John, who steered her back toward the Jeep. "Is that lunch?" she asked, glancing at the bag.

"It is. I should've asked you if you like fish."

"I love fish."

"Then we're good. The bag's insulated so the food should stay warm until we get to where we're going."

"Where *are* we going?"

"It's a surprise—to celebrate your new job. You'll see."

In the Jeep, he drove back north along the highway and turned off at Refuge Cove. Emma waited while he prechecked the Beaver for flight. Tonight she'd be leaving his cabin to stay at the hotel. Tomorrow he'd be flying the mail run while she started her new job.

Was this outing a farewell gesture? Did it mean he'd be stepping out of her life for good?

By now she was getting accustomed to the routine: buckling into the passenger seat, slipping on her headpiece. She'd learned to anticipate the cough and throb of the starting engine, the subtle quickening of her pulse as John turned the plane and taxied out of the cove, passed the forested islets, and headed into the north wind. Emma felt the sudden rush as the plane roared forward and the floats lifted off the waves. Just north of Refuge Cove, they passed over a small piece of land jutting out into the water. She could see beautiful totem poles and a large, traditionally painted building. That had to be the Totem Bight that John had mentioned to her.

Until now, she hadn't realized how much she would miss this—the sound of the engine, the wind lifting the wings, and John in his element, calm and happy.

"Where are we going? Can you tell me now?" she asked.

His laugh crackled through her headphones. "I told you, it's a surprise. It'll take a while. Just hang on and enjoy the ride."

He banked the plane in a steep turn and headed south. The plane was climbing now, gaining altitude until it leveled off at 11,000 feet. Here, in the vastness of the sky, the

Beaver seemed lost against the limitless blue. The land below was a mosaic of islands, inlets, and steep mountains rising on the left. Emma said little, not wanting to distract John from piloting the plane. The silence between them was comfortable, an easy sharing, like reading together in front of the fire.

The plane made a landward descent. Now they were flying low, through a glistening labyrinth of sheer marbled cliffs rising like towers out of the dark water. Waterfalls cascaded down the cliff faces, falling into clouds of mist. It was beautiful—perhaps the most beautiful place Emma had ever seen.

"Where are we?" Emma asked, half-breathless.

"Officially, it's called Misty Fjords National Monument," John said. "During the cruise season I fly tourists up here almost every day. I wanted to show it to you while we had the chance."

While we had the chance. Emma knew what that meant. This was John's way of saying good-bye. Her time with this compelling, troubled man was almost at an end.

"Thank you," she said. "I'll never forget this." *Or you,* she added silently. What was happening to her? Was she falling in love with this man?

But what a crazy idea. The last time she thought she'd fallen in love had ended in the most miserable experience of her life. Did she even know what love was?

The plane was flying low now, swooping down winding canyons and dipping between high cliffs. At last it glided down to rest like a dragonfly on the surface of a crystalline lake. Barely moving now, it taxied across the water and stopped alongside the narrow strip of shoreline. John cut the engine and lifted off his headset. "Stay here until I come around," he said.

After securing the plane, he opened Emma's door, took

the bagged lunch, and steadied her as she climbed onto the float. The pressure of his hand sent a pleasant tingle up her arm. She was aware of the sun on his hair, the warmth of his skin, and the subtle aroma of freshly cut wood on his clothes.

"Careful now. It's a jump to shore." He took her hand, propelling her leap from the float to the water's edge. His touch lingered on her palm after he let her go.

They sat on the rocks and opened the bag, which held two restaurant take-out boxes and a couple of sodas. John held out the boxes. "One salmon and one halibut, both fresh caught. Take your pick," he said.

Emma chose the salmon, so fresh that its taste was worlds away from anything she'd ever eaten in a restaurant. They ate their fish with fried potatoes and miniature tubs of coleslaw.

"This is so perfect," she said, gazing up at the patch of blue sky above the cliffs. "Perfect day, perfect food, perfect setting . . . " *And an imperfect man who was just as he should be,* she thought.

At a time like this, her troubles seemed far away. But she knew that those troubles would all be waiting, like cats at a mouse hole, when she returned to Ketchikan.

By the time they finished their lunch, black clouds were moving in from the west. Hurrying now, they bagged everything and climbed back into the Beaver. Moments later, after a heart-stopping takeoff, they were soaring over the cliff tops. The plane's shadow passed over a cluster of mountain goats. Then, in the next moment, they were in the open sky, with the clouds rolling in behind them.

"Have you ever flown in a storm?" Emma asked.

"More times than I'd care to remember." John's voice came through her headphones. "But it's not a good idea in a plane this size. The best way to deal with bad weather is to land somewhere safe and wait it out."

A strong wind was blowing in ahead of the storm. It buffeted the wings of the sturdy vintage plane and battered against the fuselage.

Emma did her best to appear calm, but her heart was pounding in her ears. Every plane crash movie scene she'd ever watched replayed on a loop in her mind.

"What if we have to land?" she asked, trying not to sound nervous.

His laugh was edgy. "That isn't going to happen, but we'd be fine. It's not like we'd have to find a runway. We could land on the water and taxi to shore."

The plane lurched as a wind gust rocked the wings. Emma suppressed the urge to grab John's arm. He chuckled. "Relax, we'll be fine," he said. And they were.

By the time they sighted Refuge Cove, the rain had caught up with them. John brought the Beaver in low, its floats skimming the waves as they came to rest. Rain spattered the windows as they taxied past the wooded islands into the little harbor. Emma breathed a silent prayer of thanks. Refuge Cove was well named.

With the plane secured, they raced through the rain to the Jeep. Damp and breathless, they climbed inside. Raindrops glistened on John's black hair. Emma's shirt clung to her skin. She shivered, her teeth chattering.

"Here." John reached behind the seat and pulled out a folded vinyl rain poncho. "It won't be warm, but at least it should keep the chill off."

Emma murmured her thanks and slipped the poncho over her head. The thin plastic was cold, but as she huddled inside, she felt her body begin to warm the small spaces around her.

John glanced at his watch. "It's almost four. We've got a

little time before you're due back at the Gateway. Is there anything you want to do?"

"You've already given me enough of your time," Emma said. "I left a few odds and ends in the cabin. After you take me back to get them, you can drive me into town."

"Fine." He started the engine and drove out of the parking lot, toward the main highway. "I have a couple of things to offer you. I hope you'll take them."

"If one of them is your toothbrush, you can count on it."

"Funny girl." He gave her a rare smile.

They said little on the way back to the cabin, both of them tired and lost in thought. Emma's thoughts returned to Boone. She tried to imagine how he must look after the fire had burned him, and how full of rage he must be. Had he been back to the cabin since last night? Would John be safe there, even with her gone?

A few minutes later they came out of the trees and into the small clearing where John's cabin stood. When John saw the dark shape on the front porch, he touched the brake, muttered a curse, then stepped on the gas and drove forward, honking the horn. The young black bear, about the size of a large dog, ambled off the porch and trotted off through the trees.

"He didn't seem very scared," Emma said. "And he's kind of cute. Maybe you ought to keep him."

"Not a good idea." John climbed out of the Jeep and helped Emma to the ground. They raced through the rain to the porch. "By next year that youngster will be an adult. A full-grown bear can do a lot of damage. And if he loses his fear of people, he's liable to hurt somebody or get himself shot."

"So you're doing him a favor, chasing him away like that?" Emma stood under the overhang on the porch, looking out at the rain.

"That's the idea. If he hasn't learned his lesson this time, I'll have to think of some new way to scare him off." John was scanning the ground, probably looking for any sign that Boone had been here. But if there'd been any new tracks, the rain would have washed them away.

He unlocked the door and they went inside. The cabin was chilly but it wasn't worth making a fire. They wouldn't be here that long. In her room Emma bundled up her old clothes and put them in a paper bag from the grocery store.

"Here's your toothbrush." John stood in the doorway of the bedroom. "And you can have my thermals to sleep in. At least they'll keep you warm at night."

"Thanks." She stuffed them into the bag, leaving his bathrobe on the bed. "I'll return them after I find something that fits me."

Would she get the chance? Would she even see him again after today?

"I said I had something for you. I want you to take it." He handed her a zipped canvas pouch. Emma opened it to find a small handgun and a magazine loaded with ammunition, along with a lightweight shoulder holster. "This is a Kel-Tec PF-9," he said. "Easy to carry, easy to shoot. Keep it with you in your room and whenever you leave the hotel. If Boone shows up and threatens you, don't hesitate to use it."

Emma stared down at the deadly little weapon. "I've never fired a gun in my life," she said.

"I guessed as much. That's why I'm going to give you a quick lesson. Let's go out on the porch."

She followed him outside. The rain was still falling, and water streamed off the edges of the roof. There was no more sign of the bear.

First he showed her how to insert and remove the magazine in the grip. "I'll give it to you with the magazine loaded," he said. "I can't imagine you'll need to load it again."

"With luck I won't need to use it at all. Guns have always made me nervous."

"With Boone around, you'll be a lot safer with protection. Let's take a couple of practice shots."

After showing her how to release the small safety catch, he took his place behind her, reaching around with both arms to show her the proper two-handed grip for aiming and firing the gun. Emma tried to pay full attention, but the awareness of his body pressing against her back, his arms surrounding her, his voice a breath in her ear, kindled a low-burning flame inside her. A shimmering heat rose from the depths of her body to spread into her limbs and her cheeks. Emma struggled to ignore the pounding of her pulse. The gun was cold in her hands. She willed herself to listen to him and follow his instructions.

"Aim and hold it steady . . . that's why you want to use both hands. For a little gun it has a snappy recoil. If you don't have a good grip, it'll give you a kick. You'll see.

"Shoot in the general direction of that dead stump by the road. You don't need to hit it. Just aim and squeeze the trigger—that's it." His hands supported hers as her finger tightened.

She hesitated. "There's no chance I'll hit that bear, is there?"

"Don't worry. The bear went the other way. Just squeeze. Like . . . that."

The gunshot shattered the peaceful murmur of the rain. Startled, Emma flinched, the report ringing in her ears.

"See, nothing to it." He stepped back, letting her go. "If Boone, or anyone else, comes at you, just point the gun at the biggest part of their body and squeeze the trigger."

"I can't imagine shooting anybody, not even Boone," Emma said.

"Let's hope you don't have to. But in case you do, you need to be able to protect yourself. Try it again, on your own this time."

Emma took a deep breath and raised the pistol, gripping two-handed the way John had taught her. Steeling herself against the sound, she aimed at the dead stump and squeezed the trigger.

The shot rang out, less of a surprise this time. She'd missed the stump again, but at least she knew how to fire the gun.

"Do you want more practice?" John asked her. "It can be fun once you get used to it."

"No thanks." Emma handed him the pistol. "I can shoot if I have to. That's enough."

"If you're sure, I'll reload the magazine for you." He took two spare bullets out of his shirt pocket, slipped them into the magazine, and zipped everything back into the canvas pouch. "One more thing," he said. "Follow me."

Leaving the gun pouch on the porch, he led her under the eaves of the house and around the corner of the cabin to what appeared to be a garage attached to the side. After removing the padlock, he opened one of the double doors far enough to let in some light. "Come on in," he said.

Emma stepped inside. As her eyes adjusted to the dimness, she saw a snowmobile with a double seat. Next to the house wall was a good-sized freezer which, she guessed, would be stocked with moose and salmon. Tools of every imaginable kind hung neatly on racks. Spare belts, hoses, and other machine parts, along with cans of motor oil and antifreeze, sat on sturdy shelves.

"Come here, Emma." John was standing next to something in the far corner of the garage. Walking closer, Emma saw that it was a bicycle. Slightly smaller than a full-sized adult bike, it looked expensive and brand-new. Even before John told her, Emma guessed the heartbreaking story behind it.

"I got this for my son when he was twelve," John said. "His mother never let me give it to him. By now, he'd be too big to ride it. But since you're small, it might do for you. Just promise to stay where there are people to keep you safe, and never go off to where you'll be alone."

"Oh, John—" Tears sprang to her eyes. She thought of the love that had gone into buying this gift for the son who would never ride it, or even see it. Now this tender, broken man was entrusting it to her.

He was looking down at her, his eyes in deep shadow. Suddenly this wasn't about the bike anymore. It wasn't about her new job or even about Boone. It was as if the world around them had blurred into mist, leaving nothing but the two of them alone.

He kissed her—his lips brushing hers, then taking possession of her mouth with a sureness that triggered whorls of hungry heat in the depths of her body. Stretching on tiptoe, she wrapped his neck with her arms, letting him lift her off her feet as the kiss deepened.

Need cried out in her. She wanted to feel safe with this man, to stay in his arms, trusting him enough to let her give without holding back.

But even as he held her close, she knew it couldn't happen. She wasn't classy enough, or pretty enough, or seductive enough for a good man to love her. She was only fit to be used. Boone had taught her that lesson. She had learned it well.

He kissed her again, his hands growing bolder on her body. Emma froze. Sensing the change, he let her go and stepped back. "Are you all right?"

"Yes—no—" She shook her head. "It's just too soon, that's all. I'm hurting, I'm angry, I'm a mess. I can't do this now."

"Understood. Sorry if I crossed the line."

"It's not you, John. You're one of the best men I've ever known. You saved my life!"

"Saving your life had nothing to do with why I kissed you."

"So why did you?" Right then, all Emma wanted was to shrink inside herself and crawl away.

"Because you looked like you needed kissing. I guess I was wrong about that." He turned away and changed the subject. "Still want the bike? I'll throw in a backpack to go with it."

"Of course I do. And thank you. I promise to return it in good condition."

"I've got no use for it. Find it a new owner when you leave town—some poor kid who'd be glad to have it."

The tension lay leaden between them as they prepared to go back to town. The backpack was a new brown schoolbag, perfect for Emma's needs. She filled it with the extra clothes she'd stuffed in the paper bag earlier.

"Don't forget this." John handed her the pistol, zipped into the pouch. "If I'm not around when you go, you can leave it at the desk in the Gateway." He paused in the doorway. "I loaded the bike into the back of the Jeep. If the hotel doesn't have a storage place for it, you should be able to keep it in your room. I can carry it up the stairs for you."

She slipped the pouch into the backpack. "Thank you for everything, John. I mean it."

John didn't reply. When Emma glanced around, she saw that he'd already gone outside.

*   *   *

By the time John let Emma off at the Gateway, the rain had slowed to a gloomy drizzle. He'd carried the bike inside, where the receptionist had found space for it in a storage closet. After that, with no chance to say good-bye to Emma alone, he'd left her in the lobby and gone back outside.

Now he sat in the driver's seat with the side window rolled down, listening to the rain and feeling like three-day-old roadkill.

Kissing Emma had been a crazy mistake. He should have known better. But the way she'd stood there in the shadows, looking up at him with tears in her eyes would have tempted a saint—and he was no saint.

He'd wanted her, pure and simple. He'd been wanting to feel that neat little body next to his and taste that luscious mouth from the first night she'd spent in his cabin. But if he'd used his damn fool head, he'd have realized that, after what she'd been through, the last thing Emma would want was some horny male making moves on her. He wouldn't have blamed her if she'd slapped his face.

Would he see her again? Maybe not. And maybe that was for the best. She was on her own now, and taking steps to get her life back. He could only hope that staying in town, with plenty of people around her, would keep her safe from Boone.

It wouldn't hurt to let the police know where Emma was now, so they could be aware of her and keep an eye out for Boone in town. At least stopping by the station would give him something to do.

Sam Traverton was still on duty. John had known the man a long time. They shared a coffee while John brought him up to date.

"You say Boone got burned in that fire she set, and the

trailer went up in smoke, too?" Traverton swore. "Boone must be madder than a branded polecat."

"He's out to get Emma and do God knows what to her. When he showed up at my cabin, I knew she wouldn't be safe there. So now she's at the Gateway. I'd appreciate if you'd keep an eye on her—and nab Boone if he gets within a hundred yards of her."

"I'll pass the word to the officers," Traverton said. "We'll do our best to get Boone off the street. But it won't be easy. The man can move in and out of town like a shadow. He's as sneaky as a damned Injun—no offense, John."

"None taken." John had long since learned to let such comments roll off his back. "If the odds had been in my favor, I'd have brought him in the other night."

"No, you had a woman to protect. You did the right thing." The detective finished his coffee and rose. "Thanks for the update. You'd be smart to watch your own back. The way Boone would see it, you've stolen his woman. He could have it in for you, as well as for her."

"I'll keep that in mind." John left, feeling that he'd done little more than kill time. Traverton had been sympathetic but nothing had changed. The detective had more urgent things on his mind than Boone's threat to Emma's safety. So far, all he'd done was make excuses.

Climbing back into the Jeep, John sat watching the rain stream down the windshield. He remembered Emma's happy excitement today on the flight to Misty Fjords. He remembered their easy companionship, and her blazing response to his kiss—before she'd turned cold and pulled away.

Now she was gone. When he drove home to his dark, chilly cabin, she wouldn't be there to share supper with him, to read with him in front of the fire, or to fall asleep in his arms. She'd been part of his life for just three days, but her absence had already left a void.

Across the street, the neon sign above the door of a tavern glowed through the dark rain, tempting him to come inside and forget his discontent. Just one drink. He'd take it in slow sips, feeling the welcome burn of the alcohol sliding down his throat. Just one drink. When it was gone, he would leave and go home.

But he'd been down that road before, and he knew where it led. Even after seven years of sobriety, the old urge was a devil whispering in his ear. When things were going well, it was easy to say no. But times like tonight, when he felt down and dark, the voice was there, and it never went away. *Just one drink. Just one . . .*

He glanced at his watch. His AA group met in the basement of a local church. A meeting was scheduled for tonight. It was early yet, but there'd be coffee and doughnuts and people he could talk to who were fighting demons of their own.

John started the Jeep, pulled into the street, and drove up the hill to the church. Tomorrow he'd be making the mail run in the Beaver. He'd be fine then, in the open sky. But tonight he could use some help.

The bar section of The Silver Salmon, the restaurant on the ground floor of the Gateway, could have served as a backdrop for an early 1900s gangster movie. There were wooden tables by the window with a view of the docks and more tables around the floor. But the most outstanding feature was the massive, ornately carved wooden bar that took up much of one wall and lent a touch of vintage elegance to the room. Doors on the far side opened into a tastefully remodeled dining room, but now that the cruise

season was over, the locals seemed to prefer the rustic coziness of the bar.

Customers came for the local beers, the steaming chow-
ders served in bread bowls, the salmon and crab, and the
home-style comfort food. Even in the off season, the place
was always busy.

Emma's first shift was to begin at eleven o'clock, from
lunch until closing time. Today she'd agreed to come down
an hour early to learn the ropes. She felt a nervous flutter
in the pit of her stomach as she slipped on the pink poly-
ester waitress dress, which was at least two sizes too big,
and cinched it in at the waist with a white apron. With her
blue and white sneakers and bulky wool socks, it wasn't
exactly a fashion statement, but she could wear anything
for two weeks.

After locking her small, plain room and dodging workmen in the hall, she made her way downstairs. She'd put herself through college working as a waitress, but she hadn't
waited tables for almost nine years. She could only hope
she'd remember what to do.

"Hi, honey. You must be Emma." A friendly voice greeted
her as she walked into the restaurant. Standing next to the
bar was a plump, silver-haired woman in a waitress uniform.
"I'm Pearl." She pointed to her name badge. "Welcome to
The Silver Salmon."

As Pearl showed her around the restaurant and re-
viewed the menus, chatting the whole time, Emma felt her
old confidence returning. Yes, she could do this.

"Remember, The Silver Salmon is a friendly place," Pearl
said. "We get lots of locals, especially now that the cruise
ship crowds are gone. Smile, introduce yourself, and chat
them up. They'll like that, and they'll remember you. If
there's anything you need to know, just ask me. I'll be here
the whole time."

By the time lunch was winding down, Emma was hitting her stride. The forgotten skills had resurfaced, as sharp as ever. She was greeting customers, taking orders, balancing platters of food and dishes, and running credit cards like a pro.

By three o'clock, the flow of lunch customers had dwindled to a trickle. Pearl pulled her aside as she carried a stack of dishes to the kitchen.

"You're doing great, honey," she said. "How are you holding up?"

Emma laughed. "My brain remembers what to do. But my feet and body are feeling the strain. I'll be sore, but don't worry, I'll get used to it."

"You're entitled to a break," Pearl said. "Go on, grab a bite to eat, and get the weight off your feet somewhere. I've asked one of the cooks to bag you a sandwich and a Coke. There's a nice bench on the dock, where you can eat and unwind."

"Thanks so much," Emma said. "Believe me, I won't expect this kind of royal treatment every day."

"Get going, honey. I'll be fine here until you get back."

Emma took the lunch, thanked the cook, and wandered across the street to the dock. John had told her to make sure there were people around when she went out. This afternoon that was no problem. There were plenty of folks outside, shopping, walking their dogs, or just enjoying the weather, which, according to the forecast, was due to turn cold soon.

She finished her sandwich and soda, tossed the can and wrapper into a recycle bin, and crossed the street to the restaurant. Inside, she found Pearl talking to a tall, dark-haired boy, who appeared to be about seventeen.

"Hi, Emma," Pearl greeted her. "You're just in time to meet our new busboy and assistant dishwasher. He'll be working here after school, to save up for a car, at least that's what he tells me. David, this is Emma Hunter, our new temporary waitress."

"Hello, David." Emma managed to get the words out of her tight throat. Looking up at the tall youth, with his black hair and dark eyes and the sharp, emerging planes of his face, one thing was certain.

She was meeting John's son.

CHAPTER 8

The youth gave Emma a questioning look. Then his face lit in a grin. "Hey, I remember you. You were at the driver's license place. I saw you filling out your application."

"It's nice to meet you, David." Still stunned, Emma had to struggle for words. "I don't remember seeing you. I guess I wasn't looking up."

"If I'd known we'd be working together, I'd have come over and said hi." David seemed as open and friendly as his father was taciturn and reserved.

"I would've liked that," Emma said, knowing better than to say more. This was no time to bring up her relationship with David's father.

"So, are you ready to show me the ropes, Aunt Pearl?" David asked.

Aunt?

Emma must have looked startled because Pearl was quick to explain. "David's stepfather, Carl, is my younger brother. I've known this boy since he was just a little sprout."

"I'm not supposed to be working here because I'm under eighteen," David said. "But Aunt Pearl promised to keep an eye on me, so here I am. Don't tell anybody."

"Don't worry. My lips are sealed." Emma gave him a smile as two customers walked in the door. "Meanwhile, it looks like time to get back to work."

Business picked up toward evening. Emma and Pearl were kept busy running orders to the kitchen and back. David had broken a plate early on, but now he was learning fast, clearing the tables as soon as they were empty. Watching the boy, Emma caught glimpses of how John must've looked at that age—tall and gangly, his body still filling out, his hands big and long fingered. David would grow up to be a good man, she thought. A strong man, like his father.

Seen through the window, the last rays of the setting sun brushed the clouds with pewter and violet. Streetlights flickered on, glowing through the light mist that had crept in over the water.

By now, John would be winging home from his mail run. He would fly above the muskeg where he'd first found her, bank over the water, and glide into Refuge Cove. From there he would drive home to his cabin, light a fire, eat supper, and settle in for the night—a night she wouldn't be there to share.

By closing time it was dark outside. Emma was wiping off the last table when a black Cadillac Escalade pulled up to the curb. The woman who climbed out and strode inside was strikingly tall, with a model's figure and long, dark blond hair. She was fashionably dressed in tight jeans, high-heeled boots, and a short lambskin jacket.

Only when Pearl greeted her with "Hello, Marlena," did Emma realize who stood before her. This woman was John's ex-wife, David's mother, and Boone's sister.

It was hard not to stare. Marlena's resemblance to Boone was unmistakable—the chiseled jaw and straight nose, the commanding blue eyes, the golden skin and hair. She had Boone's lanky grace and a cool gaze that seemed to look through Emma without seeing her at all.

"Where's David?" she asked Pearl. "I'm here to drive him home."

"In the kitchen," Pearl said. "He'll be out in a minute. He did fine tonight. You'd have been proud of him."

"I'd be prouder if he'd stay home and work on improving his grades. But now that he has his license, all he cares about is getting his own car. What about his future? I ask you. What about college?"

"You didn't go to college," Pearl said. "Neither did Carl, and he's been a good provider for you and the boys."

Marlena ran a manicured hand through her golden mane of hair. "Oh, I know. But I want something better for David. Maybe I'm afraid that if I don't push him, he'll end up a worthless drunk like his father."

"John's done all right for himself, Marlena. A pilot with his own plane—"

"Maybe so. But I remember how he used to drink when we were married. People don't change. That's why I never want him around David."

The conversation ended abruptly when the kitchen door swung open and David walked out, wiping his hands on a towel. "Hi, Mom," he said.

"It's about time," Marlena said. "Come on, you've got homework."

"Okay," David said. "But remember it's a teacher training day at school tomorrow, so there'll be no classes. Aunt Pearl said I could come in early tomorrow and pick up some extra hours."

Marlena sighed and shook her head. "All right. But I wish you were saving your money for college instead of that blasted car."

She left without saying good-bye, David trailing behind her. An awkward silence hung in the air as the big SUV pulled away. Emma turned back to wiping the table.

"I'm sorry you had to hear that," Pearl said. "I know it was John who helped you and brought you here. Megan told me."

"Do you know John?" Emma asked.

"Not well. But I hear a lot, working in this place. I know that John isn't the man he used to be. He's earned the respect of people in this town."

"I talked to Judge Falconi. She told me how Marlena's kept him from seeing David."

"Marlena's a good mother. But she's very protective of David. I've never believed it was fair for John to be separated from the boy, but I know better than to say it to Marlena's face."

"What can I say? John literally saved my life. He's a good man. And it's plain he's never gotten over losing his son."

Pearl's blue eyes narrowed. She shook her head. "If you're thinking you might be able to change things, forget it, honey. It is what it is. Meddling will only stir up trouble and make things worse."

"I understand." Emma had finished wiping the table. She gathered up the cloth and the bottle of spray cleaner to take back to the kitchen.

"If you speak to John, don't mention that David is here," Pearl said. "Marlena's done a number on the boy. He's convinced that John is a worthless lowlife and will try to take advantage of him if given half a chance. Any meeting between the two would only end up hurting them both."

After what she'd heard from Marlena, Emma could believe that. Pearl was right. Pushing John and his son together would only stir up trouble in the family. If there was a door to be opened, David would have to be the one to open it. Meanwhile, all she could do was wait and hope the right time would come.

Emma finished cleaning up, thanked Pearl again for her help, and went upstairs to her room. Dressed in John's comfy oversized thermals, she crawled into bed and tried to unwind from the day by reading. But her troubled thoughts would not let her focus on her book.

All her life, she'd believed in being open and honest. But now she found herself drowning in secrets. She was keeping secrets from her employer, from Pearl, from Marlena, and from David. And now, she realized, she'd be keeping the most vital secret of all from John.

The mail run had taken longer than usual. Not that it mattered. This was Alaska, where life didn't always run on the clock. Pleasantly tired, John taxied into Refuge Cove, secured the Beaver to the dock, and carried the mail pouch to the Jeep. He'd tried not to think about Emma during the long day. But as he drove to the post office, he couldn't help wondering how she'd managed with her new job, and whether she'd seen or heard any sign of Boone.

After checking the mail pouch into the post office in Ward Cove, he turned the Jeep around and headed back up the highway, toward home. He was tempted to call Emma on her burner phone, before he lost service. But no, he'd already done what he could for her. She had a pistol, a safe place to stay, and plenty of access to help. It was time he stopped hovering over her like an overanxious parent.

A bank of fog had moved in from the narrows, spreading like a misty flood across the highway and into the forest. The night was eerily quiet—maybe too quiet. As he switched the lights to high beam and turned off the highway onto the logging road, John felt the hair prickle on the back of his neck—a sign he knew better than to ignore. Stopping the car, he drew his .44 pistol from the holster, where it lay on the seat beside him. With the heavy pistol cocked, and a round in the chamber, he drove on. If Boone, or anybody else, was waiting for him at the cabin, he would have to be ready.

Nearing the cabin, he switched off the headlights and climbed out of the vehicle. Here the fog was just moving in. Ghostly fingers of mist wove through the trees, but the night was clear enough for John to see his way. He moved like a shadow, gripping the pistol as he slipped from tree to tree.

His ears heard nothing but the familiar sounds of night. But the smell that reached his nostrils, faint but somehow familiar, raised a nauseous sensation in his throat. His gut tightened with a sense of dread.

He had almost reached the clearing when he saw what he'd been meant to see. A pale, lifeless form hung by a rope from the corner of the porch, drooping shoulders, dangling limbs, no visible head.

Driven by a sick panic, he plunged forward. Only then, as he got closer, did he realize what he was seeing.

It was the skinned carcass of the young bear.

The ringing cell phone woke Emma in the night. She grabbed it off the nightstand and took the call.

"Emma?" She could hear the strain in John's voice. "Are you all right?"

"I'm fine. I'm in my room. You woke me up."

"Is your room locked? Both the key and the bolt?"

"Yes. I always do that in hotels. What's wrong?"

"Is the window locked, the shade down?"

"Yes. For heaven's sake, John, what is it? What's happened?"

There was a beat of silence on the line. "Boone was at the cabin today, while I was gone. He wasn't there tonight, but he left me a message."

Emma felt the chill, as if an icy hand had run a finger up her back. She lowered her voice. "What kind of message?"

This time the pause was longer. "It was a dead animal. You don't need to know more. It was pretty sick." He took a breath. "Emma, the man's not just dangerous. He's crazy. Let me fly you out of here tomorrow. It's the only way you'll be safe."

"My job—"

"You don't need the damned job. You can get another one in Sitka. And when your credit cards get here, I can pick them up and drop them off to you on the mail run."

Emma took a moment to think. John was making sense. She might be safer in Sitka. She could find another job. But how could she leave when she'd just met David? How could she abandon the only hope, however dim, of bringing John and his son together?

"What about you?" she asked, stalling for time. "Aren't you in danger, too?"

"If Boone meant to hurt me, he'd have done it by now. What he wants is to get to *you*—and going through me is one way to do it. So what will it be? Will I have to drag you onto the plane to save your life?"

Emma braced for a storm. John wasn't going to like her answer. "If Boone figures out that I'm in Sitka, there's no reason he can't get on a plane or boat and follow me there. I'm safer here, where the police can keep an eye out for him, and I have friends to protect me. Besides, I promised to stay at my job for two weeks. Hopefully, by then, this will all be over. Boone will be in jail, and I'll have enough money for an airline ticket out of here."

He muttered a curse. "Emma, you've got no idea—"

"I'll be careful," she said. "I'll be fine. So let's both get some sleep."

He muttered something she couldn't hear. "I'll talk to you later," he said, and ended the call.

John had driven back to the highway to get cell phone service. After his call to Emma he radioed the dispatchers for the police and state troopers and warned them to be on the lookout for Boone. Not that it would do much good. The bear carcass had been cold. Unless Boone had stayed around to watch John's reaction, the bastard would be long gone by now.

He could only hope that Boone would keep to the family homestead and the backwoods, leaving Emma safe in town. Boone was clever, but John also knew him to be vain. He might not want to show himself in Ketchikan with that ugly burn down his once-handsome face. But there was no way to be sure of that. Boone could be as unpredictable as the path of a lightning bolt.

Still seething with frustration, he drove back up the logging road to the cabin. He'd done his best to talk Emma into leaving. But he might as well have been talking to a brick wall.

Damn the woman! Why couldn't he make her listen?

Maybe he should have told her what Boone had done to the bear—and it had been Boone, all right. He'd seen the fresh tracks around the cabin, and the blood where he'd gunned down that poor dumb bear and skinned it.

John had laid a plastic tarp under the carcass and cut it down from where it hung. When he got back to the cabin, he would drag it off into the trees, wrap it, and bury it. He could leave the job until morning, but he knew he wouldn't rest until it was done.

At the cabin, he strapped on his shoulder holster to keep the pistol handy. There was always a chance that Boone would show up again, or that the scent of blood would draw more bears, or wolves, to investigate.

With the Jeep and cabin secure, he opened the garage, found a shovel and a pair of heavy rubber gloves, and went to work. The task ahead would be grueling and dirty, but it had to be done.

What would've happened if Emma had been here in the cabin, alone? Blocking the question from his mind, John pulled on the gloves, picked up the shovel, and went to work.

Emma had meant to sleep late, but the sounds of workers, revamping the rooms on her floor, woke her early. By the time she'd climbed out of bed, showered, dressed, and gone downstairs for the free breakfast of cereal, fruit, and toast, her shift was still more than two hours away.

John would want her to stay inside the hotel, but she'd spent too much time behind closed doors. She needed fresh air, sunshine, and room to stretch her legs. As long as she stayed in the open, with plenty of people around her, she should be perfectly safe.

Megan had given her the address of a good thrift shop and marked the location on a map of the town. Its distance from the hotel gave Emma a good excuse to try out the new bicycle.

With her money in her jeans, and her jacket, her phone, and the pistol in the backpack, she wheeled the bike out of the storage closet, through the front door, and across the street to the wide boardwalk that ran by the docks. She hadn't ridden a bicycle since she was in college, but how hard could it be?

The bike's smaller size was a perfect fit for her. She straddled the seat, gripped the handlebars, and took off pedaling. For the first few dozen yards her progress was wobbly. But soon her muscle memory took over, and she began to enjoy herself. By the time she headed uphill toward the thrift shop, she was riding like a carefree teenager.

The charity thrift shop had just opened. After an hour of browsing, Emma bought a waterproof down parka, a quilted vest, a pair of stretch pants, two nice sweaters, some socks, and a bra. She was tempted by a pair of barely worn boots, but those could wait for another visit. For now, it was all she could do to stuff all her purchases in her pack. She wouldn't look glamorous like Marlena in her "new" clothes. But at least when the weather changed, as it was bound to, she'd be warm.

As she left the store, she glanced at the clock above the register. It was barely ten o'clock. Her shift didn't start for another hour. Surely it wouldn't hurt to go exploring a little on the bike. As long as she stayed where there was plenty of traffic, she'd be fine.

With the backpack strapped to her shoulders, she climbed on the bike and set off, headed south on the Tongass Highway, past the businesses that were strung along the road.

John was at Refuge Cove, servicing the Beaver after yesterday's mail flight, when his cell phone rang. Hoping it might be Emma, he grabbed for it so fast that he almost dropped it in the water.

"Emma?"

The laugh on the other end chilled his blood. "So how did you like my little present, brother?"

"Can't say I was impressed. That bear wasn't half-grown and no meaner than a dog. It wouldn't have taken much of a man to shoot it."

"That little bearskin will be just right for makin' me a new winter hat. But I'll bet I scared you. I'll bet for the first few seconds you thought it was *her*, hangin' there. Lordy, I wish I could've seen your face."

"You're sick, Boone. I'd say you need help, but something tells me you're long past that."

"Where is she?" Boone's voice had turned hard and mean. "I know she's not with you because of how you answered the phone. But I'll bet you know where she is."

"She's gone. She won't be at the cabin anymore. So you can quit coming around."

"Tell me where she is, and you'll never see my face again."

"Give it up, Boone. She's gone for good. And if you show up looking for her, I'll be seeing your ugly face behind bars."

Boone laughed again. "Hell, I didn't do anything to that little bitch except give her a thrill. And even if I'd committed a crime, you think I'm dumb enough to get caught? I've got eyes all over the place—friends, family, you name it. Any one of them spots her, and she's mine for keeps. Maybe I'll give her a real wedding this time, just to keep things nice and legal."

The call ended with a laugh and a click, leaving John glaring down at the phone in mute fury. Was it true? Did Boone have other people watching for Emma—people who could snatch her off the sidewalk before she even had time to react?

Damn it, why had he assumed Boone would be acting alone in this? If what the bastard had said was true, Emma wouldn't be safe anywhere in town, maybe not even in the hotel.

He needed to warn her. Maybe now she'd listen. Maybe now she'd agree to leave.

He brought up her cell number, called it, and held his breath as it rang. *Pick up, damn it, Emma. Pick up.* . . .

A chilling fear stole over him as the phone rang again, then again and again.

By the time she'd pedaled a mile along the shoulder of the road, Emma's legs were getting tired. A cool wind had sprung up, the traffic had begun to thin out, and she was getting thirsty. The map she'd picked up at the hotel showed the highway going south, rounding a point, and changing to unpaved road that ended thirteen miles out of town. But she was not going to make it anywhere near that distance. It was time to turn around and go back the way she'd come.

A few minutes ago, she'd felt a slight vibration against her back. After the third or fourth time, she'd realized it was her phone, buried in her backpack beneath all the clothes she'd bought at the thrift store.

It was probably John, calling to check on her and lecture her about the need to leave town. Since she could hardly empty the pack on the roadside to get to the phone, there was nothing to do. She would have to call him back from the hotel.

After turning around, she pedaled back toward town. The distance seemed much longer now that she was getting tired. A hundred yards ahead, on the far side of the road, was a business that sold liquid propane, exchanging full tanks for empty ones. Emma had paid it scant attention when she'd passed it going the other way. Now she braked and skidded to a stop, her heart pounding in her throat.

Pulled up next to the door of the business was a camouflage-painted pickup truck. Even without the shell on the back, there could be no mistaking that sloppy spray job. It was Boone's.

Two people, a man and a woman, stood outside the truck. From a distance, Emma could see that the woman was of medium height, stocky build, with gray hair knotted in a bun. The man was tall, even taller than Boone, with long, unkempt blond hair and a long, shaggy beard. Both of them were clad in baggy jeans and plaid lumberjack-style shirts. They had to be Boone's mother and his brother, Ezra, in town from the homestead. So far, she could see no sign of Boone. Maybe he wasn't with them. But he could have gone inside the building.

Emma waited, keeping her distance and wondering what to do next. There was no way she could get back to town without passing them. The sides of the highway were overgrown with thorny scrub. Leaving the road with the bike and cutting around through the trees would be next to impossible.

She could pedal past them, look the other way, and hope she wouldn't be recognized. The pair had never met her. But Boone had probably shown them a photograph of his bride-to-be. She couldn't take that chance, especially if they were looking for her—and especially if Boone happened to be with them, inside the building or even in the truck.

She could always wait for them to finish their business and leave. But if they were headed south, out of town, they would be driving right toward her. There had to be another way.

Suddenly Emma saw her chance. The mother and son were headed into the building, and now that they'd moved, she could see that the cab was empty. It was now or never.

Pumping with all her strength, she sped forward. She would pass the place on the opposite side, but the road was narrow. If seen, she could easily be recognized. How long would it take her to get a safe distance past the truck? Surely no more than seconds, but it was as if everything had fallen into slow motion, like a chase in a dream. *Faster . . .* she urged herself. *Faster . . .*

She was coming even with the truck. So far nobody had come back outside. She was going to make it. She was going to be all right.

Just then two shaggy heads popped up from the bed of the truck, followed at once by a chorus of baying, barking howls.

Boone's dogs. They must've recognized her scent. Or maybe they just didn't like cyclists.

Panic driven, she pumped harder. She could still hear the dogs. Even without looking back, she could tell that they'd jumped out of the truck and were coming after her. If they caught her, she wouldn't have a chance against the big wolf hybrids. They would bring her down like a deer.

Faster . . .

Her legs were getting rubbery, and her side had developed a painful stitch, and the dogs were gaining. The bike wobbled as powerful jaws caught the rear tire. If she threw down her backpack, would they attack it and let her get away? But why even wonder? Before she could get the pack off her shoulders the dogs would be all over her.

She pushed ahead, but the small bike wasn't built for speed. Sharp teeth caught her pants leg—and then, like a miracle, came a sharp whistle and a string of curses from the direction of the truck. Abruptly, the dogs wheeled and trotted back the way they'd come.

Emma rode on, forcing her tired legs to push the pedals. She'd been well past the truck when the dogs caught up with her. With luck, the Swensons wouldn't have seen her face. They wouldn't have realized who she was.

Relief and exhaustion hit her like an earthquake. Too shaky to ride on, she pulled off the shoulder of the road to catch her breath. When she dared to glance behind her, she saw that the camouflaged truck was nowhere in sight.

And coming toward her, at breakneck speed, was a familiar tan Jeep.

CHAPTER 9

Emma waited in the passenger seat while John lifted the bike into the rear of the Jeep. When he climbed back in beside her, his mouth was a grim line.

"John—"

"Don't say a word." He started the engine, turned the vehicle around, and drove back toward town. Emma had seen him angry before, but not like this.

For a few minutes he drove in silence. Then he began to speak, the words coming sharp and hard. "I got a call from Boone this morning. He said his friends and family would be looking for you. I tried to call and warn you. When you didn't answer your damn phone, I called the hotel. They said you'd taken the bike out." He shot her a stormy glance. "Do you have any idea how worried I was? Why didn't you answer your phone?"

"It was buried in the pack. I couldn't get to it. I meant to call you when I got back to the hotel, but then—"

"Never mind. I saw enough to figure out what happened. You're damned lucky to be alive."

Tires squealing, he swung the Jeep onto a narrow, little-used side road that cut through thickets of willow and salmonberry and ended at a dilapidated boat ramp on a narrow stretch of beach. Braking, he switched off the engine, then sat gazing out at the water.

Emma waited in the tension-filled silence until she could stand it no longer. "I'm sorry, John," she said. "I never meant to worry you."

An eternity of seconds seemed to pass before he turned in the seat to face her, another eternity before he spoke. "Damn it, Emma, I never thought I'd say this. But right now I'm almost wishing I'd just flown home and left you to fend for yourself in that muskeg."

Emma gasped as the cold words penetrated. "You can't mean that," she said. "You saved my life."

"And what about *my* life? I was doing fine until you showed up. Now, half the time, it's like I don't know whether I'm coming or going. I can't even sleep for fear that something will happen and I'll lose you."

She stared at him, her heart pounding. "What are you saying?"

"What the hell do you think I'm saying?"

He reached across the seat, caught her in his arms, and jerked her against him. His mouth crushed hers in a forceful kiss that blended fury, desire, and exquisite tenderness.

Emma's pulse rocketed. A throbbing heat surged from the depths of her body. The response to John's kiss was like nothing she'd ever known. She went molten against him, her lips softening, her hands tangling in his hair, her mouth open, tasting him, feeling him. She wanted his hands on her, and more. Heaven help her, she wanted all the things she'd denied herself as a woman.

But it wasn't going to happen here. Their awkward position in the seats, with the gearbox jutting between them, ended their embrace too soon. They broke apart, both of them breathing hard. Emma pulled down her shirt and smoothed back her hair. John was looking at her in a way that—perhaps for the first time in her life—made her feel beautiful.

It was a look that said *to be continued*.

"I think you'd better get me back to the hotel." Her voice had taken on a husky, sensual tone that she barely recognized.

"I think you're right." He started the Jeep and pulled back onto the main road. "Just promise me you won't take any more crazy chances, Emma. And that you'll keep in touch with me. I need to know you're all right."

"I've learned my lesson," Emma said. "I promise."

They drove back into town, both of them striving to come to terms with what had just happened. It was too soon to talk about it, too soon to put a name on it—even if it was love.

"It's not too late to change your mind about Sitka," John said. "I've got another mail run the day after tomorrow. I can take you with me—or even take you sooner, if you want."

"I'll be fine," she said, retrieving her pack from where she'd stowed it by her feet. "If it'll put your mind at ease, I'll even stay inside the hotel while you're gone."

"That would help. I'm learning how stubborn you can be." He pulled up to the curb in front of the hotel and came around to bring the bike. "Are you sure I can trust you with this?"

"Like I said, I've learned my lesson."

"Call me," he said as they stood on the curb. "I mean it. I need to know you're okay."

"I will." And she would. Everything had changed with that soul-searing kiss. For the first time, she felt stirrings of hope, as if her shattered heart was already beginning to heal.

* * *

John left her and drove away, his heart still thudding in his chest. The euphoria from that kiss was mixed with uncertainty. Had he found something real with this tender, brave, impossibly stubborn woman? Or was it just a passing attraction that would fade when she no longer needed a protector?

Emma had believed completely in Boone and the future they would have together. But Boone had crushed her dream and her faith in the cruelest way possible. She would be a long time healing. Meanwhile, she was vulnerable, clinging to any refuge she could find. Right now he was that refuge.

He'd be wise to keep that in mind.

He glanced at his watch. It was barely eleven. He'd been headed back to Refuge Cove, but a sudden thought changed his mind. He had plenty of time. Why not check around town and see if there was any truth to Boone's boast that he had people watching for Emma?

He'd seen Boone's camouflage truck vanishing south down the highway with Lillian driving and Ezra sitting next to her, probably headed back to the homestead. Except for Marlena and David, who wanted nothing to do with him, Boone had no other family in town. But John knew most of Boone's friends and where they hung out. Maybe they'd seen Boone recently. If so, they'd be more apt to talk to him than to the police.

At the top of his mental list was Sherman Philpot, the fake preacher who'd officiated at Emma's so-called wedding.

Philpot lived on the lower floor of a cheap rental house in a part of town that dated back to the gold rush days. The dilapidated structure was peeling blue paint. Two rusted junk cars and a motorcycle were parked in the front yard. A feisty-looking mongrel dog yapped from the front porch but slunk off as John mounted the sagging steps.

The doorbell seemed to be broken. After trying it and hearing nothing, he rapped on the door. There was a scurrying sound from the other side. The door opened a few cautious inches, then more. A girl, slim and doe-eyed, with a face from a milk carton, was gazing up at him. She was dressed in a cut-down muscle shirt and ragged jeans. John couldn't help wondering whose daughter she was and whether her parents were looking for her.

"Hey, John!" Sherman Philpot wandered out of the kitchen smoking a joint. He was wearing stained khakis with suspenders and no shirt. His carrot-colored hair hung down around his skinny shoulders. "What brings you here, old buddy?"

"Just looking for a friend. All right if I come in?"

"Sure, long as you ain't the cops." He opened the door and John stepped inside. He hadn't been in the house before, but it was what he'd expected—mattresses and pillows on the floor, an Indian print cloth over the window, wine bottles, and the odor of weed permeating everything. A woman with a family resemblance to the girl wandered in from the kitchen looking stoned.

Sherman held out the joint, offering to share. John shook his head. Years ago he might have accepted, but not now. "Are you saying you've had trouble with the police?" he asked, knowing Sam Traverton had planned to question him.

"Yeah. Those ball-busters hauled me out an' grilled me up one side and down the other about a joke I helped Boone Swenson play on this woman he'd met. She was one of them Sunday school types who wouldn't go to bed with him lessn' they were married. So I just helped him along a little. Boone paid me a hundred dollars, just like the last time. Hell, it was only a joke. No harm done. But I'll bet those ladies were madder than hell when they found out they weren't really married."

Just like the last time.

John's pulse slammed. Was Philpot saying Boone had done this before?

"How many of these so-called weddings have you done for Boone," he asked, trying to sound casual.

"Just two. This one and one last spring. Boone doesn't usually have trouble gettin' his women in the sack. The last one was a cute little thing. White wedding dress and all. Hell, she was so happy she even cried. The first one was older and as plain as a mud fence. Big thick glasses, had old maid schoolteacher written all over her. I can't figure out for the life of me what Boone saw in her."

"I'm guessing it didn't work out."

"I guess not. Boone never said."

John would have pushed him for more, but he didn't want to set off any alarms. "Speaking of Boone, he and I need to settle some unfinished business. Any idea where I might find him?"

"Not a clue. Haven't seen him since the wedding." Philpot's grin showed a missing incisor. "Far as I know, he's still off on his happy honeymoon."

John thanked him, made his excuses, and left. If Philpot had spoken with Boone since Emma's escape, the man was a damned good liar. But John was inclined to believe him. He didn't seem to be hiding anything.

But the fact that there'd been an earlier wedding cast a whole new light on what Boone had done to Emma. Finding out what had happened to that first bride could make all the difference. He would start with the police.

He drove to the station, only to learn that Sam Traverton was out on a case. "He's due back after lunch," the dispatcher said. I'll let him know you want to see him."

That left John with time to kill. He wolfed down a burger and Coke at the drive-in and drove on up the highway to a seedy bar on the outskirts of town. He didn't like going into bars. They tended to remind him of what his drinking years had cost him. But this place was a hangout for the wild crowd from the old days, including Boone. And John himself was no stranger here.

He stepped inside, keeping to the shadowed entryway as his eyes adjusted to the dim light. He didn't expect Boone to be here, but he scanned every face just to make sure. It didn't take long. The bar wasn't crowded at this time of day.

The air was stale and smoky. The TV above the bar was broadcasting a pro wrestling match. From the pool tables in the rear came the click of colliding balls.

"John Wolf!" Maisy Jo, the tough, fiftyish woman who owned the bar, greeted him with a wave. "It's been a long time. How about a beer on the house?"

John, who'd always liked the woman, gave her a wink. "If anybody could tempt me, it would be you. But you know better than to try. I'm on the wagon."

"Too bad, honey. There's nobody I'd rather tempt." Her outsized breasts jiggled through her black tee when she fluffed her bleached curls. "How about a cold ginger ale?"

"I'll take it, but you've got to let me pay." He laid a five on the bar, knowing she wouldn't give him change. She tucked the bill into her ample cleavage before she opened the chilled bottle and poured it into a glass.

"So, if you're not here to drink, what can I do for you?" she asked.

"Just looking for an old friend. Boone Swenson. Have you seen him around lately?"

"Boone?" She shook her head. "I haven't seen that big galoot in weeks. Why?"

"Let's say it's personal. So he hasn't talked to you?"

"Not since the salmon run ended. But you're welcome to ask around. You know who his friends are."

John did. He left the bar ten minutes later, having learned nothing. Either Boone was bluffing about having eyes everywhere, or he had allies John didn't know about. Either way, he could be lying low to hide his shameful burns.

John glanced at his watch. By now Traverton should be back in his office. He drove back to the police station and found the detective just pulling up in his car. They walked inside together.

"I hear you wanted to see me." Traverton tossed his cigarette into a nearby shrub before stepping through the automatic door. "I heard your report about the bear. Lord, that must've given you a shock. But we can't arrest Boone for killing a bear, especially if he claimed it was threatening him."

"That young bear was no more threat than a dog. Boone killed it to spook me. Not that it would make any difference. This is something else. What did you learn when you talked to Sherman Philpott?"

"Just that he performed the wedding as a joke."

"Did he mention that he'd done the same thing once before?"

"No." Traverton paused with his hand on the doorknob of his office. "When?"

"Last spring. Philpot mentioned that the woman was older and not very good-looking. When I tried to find out what happened to her, he said he'd never heard."

"What you're implying is pretty farfetched," Traverton said. "I've known Boone most of my life. He was always wild. I could believe the part about the fake weddings—but murder? That's a pretty big pill to swallow. The woman probably just got sick of bush life and left."

"Maybe," John said. "But you can't deny that it's possible. At least it would be worth checking around that burned-out trailer."

"It might be. But we're short staffed, and I know the troopers have their hands full, too. You're talking at least a full day for a team of investigators, all based on your say-so. We're dealing with real crimes here. We don't have time to chase after something that probably never happened."

John reined in his frustration. Anger would buy him nothing. "In that case, I don't suppose you'd mind if I checked the place myself," he said.

"Knock yourself out," said Traverton. "If you find anything, take a photo and leave it be. Any evidence that you've disturbed becomes questionable—and worthless in court."

"Understood—but one thing more. You might check the local pawnshops and see if Boone's hocked any expensive jewelry since last spring. I could do it myself but the owners would be more likely to talk you."

The detective sighed. "Fine. I'm not expecting a lot, but I guess I owe you that much."

John thanked Traverton for his time and left. He'd hoped for a very different response from the cynical detective. But at least the door wasn't closed all the way.

If nothing interfered, he could go tomorrow. Driving to the burned trailer wouldn't be easy, but after flying over the spot, he had the position in his mind. All he had to do was find the logging road that cut off from the highway. For that, he could go to the library and use the Internet to look at satellite maps.

He could also ask Emma if she remembered anything about the road when Boone drove her to the trailer. But why force her to relive a bad memory when there were other ways of getting what he needed?

It might even be best not to tell Emma what he knew. Hearing that Boone had "married" another woman a few months earlier, and that his bride had disappeared would only upset her. He would save that story until he had more proof of what had happened. But at least he would need to let her know where he was going tomorrow. He would drop by the restaurant on his way home today and warn her to be extra cautious.

At the library, he spent the next half hour using Google Earth to pinpoint the road. From above, most of it was covered by trees. If it branched and forked, which was likely, he could use his compass to get the bearings for the right way to the trailer.

It would be deeply satisfying to find something that might incriminate Boone, he mused as he drove back to the hotel. The bastard had tormented Emma long enough. The experience would probably give her nightmares for the rest of her life.

John imagined being there to hold and comfort her in the night. He wanted it to happen—wanted *her,* more than any woman he'd ever known. But life could be unpredictable, and Emma had a long journey of healing ahead of her. Only time would tell whether he'd be there at the end of it.

He drove to the Gateway and parked outside. Through the restaurant window, he caught the flash of Emma's pink uniform as she carried a tray full of beer mugs to a table. He was tempted to go in and order something, just so he could sit in a booth and watch her. But he'd already eaten lunch. He also needed to get back to Refuge Cove and finish servicing the Beaver's vintage engine, which would run forever, but only if properly cared for.

Entering through the hotel lobby, he stood in the doorway, waiting to catch her eye. By now the height of the lunch hour had passed. Most of the late customers were getting ready to leave. Emma gave him a quick smile as she ran the bill to a table. He could wait a few minutes to speak to her. It was a pleasure, just watching her walk and interact with the people she served.

He was still waiting when the kitchen door swung open and a tall young man stepped through, wearing a uniform shirt and carrying a tray. John gave him a glance. Then the realization hit him.

It was David.

Emma saw them just before they saw each other. The feeling was like waiting for two trains to collide, with no power to stop them.

They would recognize one another, of course. Ketchikan was a small town. Beyond that, Emma had no idea what was going to happen. Since Pearl was out on break, there was no one to buffer the situation.

For a moment the two of them faced each other. Awkwardness hung in the air. John spoke first.

"Hello, David."

David cleared his throat. "My mom says I'm not supposed to talk to you."

"I know. I didn't expect you to be here."

"I'm working here, to earn money for my own car."

"Good for you. You're growing into a fine young man. I'm proud of you."

David swallowed. "I've got to work."

With that he turned toward a vacated booth and began scrambling to clear the dirty dishes off the table. Plates clattered. A fork fell to the floor. David bent to pick it up. Emma caught the glimmer of a tear in his eye.

"Outside, Emma." John, looking like he'd been gut punched, had stepped back into the lobby. Emma followed him out onto the sidewalk. He turned back to face her, his expression troubled in a way she hadn't seen before.

"Why didn't you tell me David was here?" he demanded. "You certainly had your chance."

"I was told not to—by his aunt Pearl."

"Pearl." He shook his head. "If she was afraid I'd show up and try to talk to the boy, she was wrong. You saw what it was like in there. It was awkward and painful for both of us. And it wouldn't have happened if you'd let me know he was working here."

"I'm sorry," Emma said. "But I'm not a mind reader. How would I have known you'd walk in, or what would happen if you did?"

John's scowl deepened. "Damn it, you should have told me. You should have trusted me enough to know I'd do the right thing and stay away."

Emma looked into his stormy eyes. This wasn't about David, she realized. It was about trust—a trust she'd betrayed by holding back the truth. And everything about John—his gaze, his voice, his posture—told her she'd made a serious mistake. And no amount of apologizing would undo it.

"So why did you come?" she asked.

He took a deep breath, as if silently counting to ten. "I

came to tell you that I won't be around for the next couple of days. Tomorrow I'll be driving to the trailer site to look around for any evidence that might build a case against Boone. Then the next day I'll be flying the mail route."

"Will you let me know when you're back?"

"I guess so. But we could both use a break for a couple of days. I'll let you know if I find anything at the trailer. Meanwhile, don't take any stupid chances."

"Fine," she said. "Don't worry about me."

He left without another word, striding toward the Jeep, climbing in, and driving away without a backward glance.

Heartsick, Emma stood looking after him. Was this their first lover's quarrel, or was it the beginning of the end? She would never have set up a meeting between John and David. But it was almost as if she had. And John, proud man that he was, would not be quick to forgive her.

In his most private heart of hearts, John carried a wound that would never heal. That wound was the loss of his son.

Today had taught her a bitter lesson. John might care for her. He might even come to love her. But that wound in his heart went deeper than even she could ever reach.

By the time John finished changing the Beaver's oil and refilling the fuel tank, the sun was going down. Restless now, and needing to move, he secured the plane, slipped on a fleece jacket against the chilling breeze, and set off up the deserted shore.

The incoming tide lapped at his boots as he strode along the rocky beach. A lone bald eagle soared against the glowing sky. Pausing, John watched its flight until it vanished beyond the trees. As a young boy, he'd wished for wings like a bird so he could fly away from the ugly realities of an incarcerated father and an alcoholic mother. Now he had those wings, and he felt more at home in the air than on the ground. In the air there was no anger, no ugliness, just him, the plane and the sky.

He'd been harder on Emma than she deserved. She should have warned him that she was working with David, but she'd been told not to. How could she have known that he would walk into the restaurant and find himself face to face with his son?

That look of alarm in David's eyes when their gazes met would haunt him for a long time to come. Marlena had done a good job of convincing the boy that his natural father was a drunken, evil monster—and maybe, in part, that's what he had been. But even in the worst times, he'd never laid a hand on his wife or his son. And even when he was drinking, he'd always worked hard to provide for them.

Ketchikan was a small town. He'd had other chances to confront David, but he'd gone out of his way to avoid the boy. It was that look—the surprise that bordered on terror in those dark eyes so like his own—that struck like a bullet to his heart. He didn't want to see that look. He didn't want to lie awake at night, remembering it.

Next spring, David would be eighteen years old and ready to graduate from high school. If Marlena had any say in it, he would go away to college, find a new life far from Ketchikan, and never again set eyes on the man who'd fathered him. The best John could hope for was to be at peace, knowing his son was happy.

And Emma . . . He'd never expected anyone like her to come into his world. Her warmth, her strength and her sweet vulnerability touched him in ways he'd never known before. But how could he expect her to stay and share his life, when he had so little to offer? And a deeper question—

how could he keep his fear of losing her from driving her away, as it likely had today?

The last rays of sunset reflected streaks of mauve and violet in the water. The breeze had turned colder. Turning up his collar, John thrust his hands into his pockets and walked back along the beach to the harbor.

CHAPTER 10

Emma should have known what to expect. She and Pearl were getting ready to open for lunch the next day when a familiar black Escalade pulled up to the curb outside. Marlena, in her designer jeans and stiletto-heeled boots, strode into the hotel lobby and rapped on the glass door of the restaurant.

Pearl unlocked the door and held it open. Ignoring her sister-in-law, Marlena zeroed in on Emma like a heat-seeking missile.

"David told me John came in here last night, and that they spoke to each other. He was very emotional, very upset. John was your friend, he said, so that's why I'm talking to you. Keep him away from my son, missy."

"My name is Emma—right here." Emma pointed to the name badge on her uniform. Marlena was a tall woman, especially in high heels. Groomed to the nines, she loomed over Emma in her ill-fitting uniform and blue and white sneakers. But Emma had made up her mind not to be intimidated.

"Well, *Emma*," Marlena snapped. "I'm here to tell you, I have full legal custody of David, and I won't put up with your meddling. If I hear anything about your inviting John here while David is working, the boy won't be working here anymore. And you'll be facing a lawsuit." She swung to face her husband's sister. "As for you, Pearl—"

"Pearl was on break," Emma said. "And John came in to talk to *me*. He didn't even know David was working here until they saw each other. Even then, they only spoke a few words."

"And you expect me to believe that."

The woman was actually calling her a liar. Emma's temper flared. She held it in check for John's sake and for David's.

"John doesn't want to make trouble for David or you, Marlena," she said. "Neither do I. I won't apologize because I didn't do anything wrong. But I know John won't let it happen again."

"He'd better not, or he'll find himself in court," Marlena said. "He was a bad husband and a bad father. He cared more about the next bottle of booze than he did about his family. Two different judges ruled that he was an unfit parent."

"He's changed, Marlena. Anybody who knows him will tell you that."

"Nobody changes, especially John. He'll always be an alcoholic, and I won't have him trying to influence my son."

"*Influence* him? What are you talking about?" Emma demanded.

"Don't you know anything?" Marlena glared down at Emma as if she were speaking to a backward child. "Alcoholism is a disease. It's passed down in families. John's mother was an alcoholic. So is John. If David inherited the trait, one drink could be enough to tip him over the edge. That's why I can't let him be around John—ever."

"Marlena, John would never—"

"No, that's enough." Marlena cut her off. "You don't even know him. Maybe you think he's wonderful. Maybe you're even in love with him. But you don't know what he can be like." She turned to Pearl. "You promised to look out for David. Do your job."

"He'll be fine, Marlena. I won't take my eyes off him." Pearl spoke calmly, as if she'd long since grown accustomed to her sister-in-law's rants. "Now it's time for us to open these doors for customers. So run along, dear. I'll call you if there's a problem."

"There'd better not be a problem." With those words, Marlena stalked outside and drove away.

Pearl unlocked the doors, and turned over the OPEN sign. But if there'd been any customers waiting for an early lunch, they'd gone elsewhere.

"I think I need to sit down." Emma sank onto a chair, her legs unsteady beneath her.

Pearl gave her a knowing smile. "Don't take it to heart, honey. Marlena's been a drama queen for as long as I've known her. I try to cut her some slack because she came from a pretty tough background. Horrible family. Like something out of that old movie, *Deliverance*. You can't imagine."

Yes, I can, Emma thought, reminding herself that Pearl didn't know about her time with Boone.

"Marlena's fought her way up from her roots, but she's still insecure—the clothes, the car, the manicures, it's all part of what she needs to convince herself she's as good as anybody else. My brother adores her, and she's good with their kids. But she can be pretty . . . intense, for want of a better word."

"And John?" Emma rose and began setting napkins and cutlery on the tables.

"He's part of the past she wants to put behind her. I guess she had a pretty bad time of it with him. I can't say I blame her for leaving. I know John's been sober a long time, and that he'd never influence David to drink. But you won't convince Marlena of that."

"So I guess the best thing to do is just accept the situation for what it is." Emma found herself wishing she could confide in this warm, understanding woman and tell her how John yearned to have his son in his life. But she'd already stepped into enough trouble. Maybe some things were better left unsaid.

The first lunch customers began to trickle in. By noon, every booth and table was full. Emma was constantly busy, bustling between the dining room and the kitchen. Still, her thoughts kept straying to John. She knew he'd planned to drive to Boone's burned-out trailer and look for evidence today, but she had no idea what he was hoping to find. Maybe if they hadn't had the blowup over David, he'd have told her.

Last night he'd said they needed a break. Still, she couldn't help hoping he would change his mind and call her. She missed hearing his voice. She missed knowing he was safe and that he cared about her. But her phone had remained stubbornly silent until she turned the ringer off to go down to work.

Was he all right? Had he forgiven her for not telling him about David?

Stepping into a quiet corner, she slipped her phone out of her pocket and checked for voice and text messages. Nothing.

Stop worrying, she told herself. *The man's been in your life just a few days. And now you're tying yourself in knots because he hasn't called. Grow up and deal with it, Emma Hunter.*

Emma thrust the phone into her pocket and went back to work. But despite her resolve, she couldn't still the echo of Marlena's caustic voice in her memory.

Maybe you're even in love with him. . . .

Once John had found the old logging road, it wasn't hard to follow. The worn ruts, clear of overgrowth, showed signs of regular and recent travel, including food wrappers and beer cans tossed out along the sides.

There was no way to know if Boone had been back to the trailer since the burnout. The absence of fresh tire tracks since the last rain suggested that he wasn't there now. But John knew better than to take anything for granted. The loaded .44 was in his shoulder holster, close at hand. Boone was as wily as a cougar and even more dangerous. He could be anywhere.

Aside from its serious purpose, the drive was a pleasant one. The day was cool but sunny, the air fresh with the fragrance of spruce and hemlock. Squirrels, gathering their winter supply, frisked among the branches. Jays squawked and scolded. A bull moose, with a massive rack, wandered across the road, taking its time. John backed up to give the huge animal plenty of room. With the rut season on, the big boys were known to be ill tempered. They would charge anything that looked like a challenger—even a Jeep.

Given his own frustrations, John couldn't say he blamed them.

The deeply rutted road was slow going. John had plenty of time for his mind to wander. Mostly it wandered to thoughts of Emma.

That kiss yesterday had got him believing they had the start of something good. But they'd both been burned by relationships, and they both had trust issues. All it had taken was a small misunderstanding—like her failure to tell him about David—to set off all the old alarms. Emma was everything he'd ever wanted in a woman. He loved her courage, her tenderness, her quirky sense of humor. And the more time he spent with her, the more beautiful she appeared to him. But unless they could learn to have faith in each other, their relationship was doomed.

Maybe he should have called her this morning. It was too late now. There was no phone service this deep in the bush. Maybe tonight, when he got back to town, he could do some fence mending. But he didn't want to stop by the restaurant if David would be there. And tomorrow he'd be flying the mail run. Most of that time, he'd be out of touch.

Never mind. He'd sort things out when he got back to town. One way or another, he needed to make things right with her.

Three hours after leaving the highway, he sighted the clearing, with the burned frame of the trailer, through the trees. The place appeared quiet, but just to be sure, he parked the Jeep thirty yards away, behind a stand of devil's club, and approached on foot with his pistol drawn.

There were no boot tracks in the bare, wet earth and no other signs that anyone had been here since the last rain. After checking around, John holstered his gun and got out his phone to take photos of anything he found.

He took a few shots of the trailer, a black skeleton with the charred remains of bath fixtures, kitchen appliances, metal pipes, and broken glass inside. The cast-iron pan where Emma had poured kerosene to start the fire lay next to what was left of the stove.

The exploding propane tank behind the trailer had likely done most of the damage. If Boone had been inside when it blew up, he wouldn't have survived.

Reminding himself that he was here to find incriminating evidence against Boone, John moved in closer. Right away, he noticed two metal gasoline cans, barely scorched, lying empty some distance from the trailer. What if Boone had put out Emma's fire, then, after failing to recapture her, gone back and burned the trailer himself? Anything he had to hide from the police would have gone up in flames, and Emma would have been blamed. The delay between the first and second fires would explain why neither he nor Emma had noticed any smoke.

Boone's burns could have been caused by either blaze. Whichever way he might have come by them, he would have blamed Emma.

John photographed the gasoline cans and continued his search. Emma had mentioned that she'd left her luggage inside the trailer. But John could see no remains, such as locks, hinges, or metal framework. And there was no trace of any personal items that might have belonged to her. Again, that argued for the case that Boone had removed them before starting the second fire.

So what was he looking for now? After taking a few more photos, John began walking in a slow, outward spiral around the trailer, his eyes on the ground. He couldn't afford to miss anything—not when the tiniest object could provide a vital clue.

A bobby pin—it didn't mean much by itself, but he took a picture. The metal cap off a lipstick tube—interesting, but no proof of anything.

He had reached the edge of the clearing without finding anything that would've made the long drive worthwhile. He was about to give up when his gaze caught a glint of something under the edge of a blackberry thicket. If the sun hadn't been shining overhead, he would have missed it.

Crouching, he used the barrel of his gun to raise the

prickly branches. What he saw caused his breath to catch. He stared at it as if he'd found the Holy Grail.

It was a pair of glasses—big and round with harlequin frames and thick lenses lying half-buried in the dirt.

. . . plain as a mud fence. Big thick glasses . . .

Sherman Philpot's words shot to the surface of John's memory. Sam Traverton had suggested that Boone's earlier bride might have left on her own. But she wouldn't have left without her glasses.

Knowing he mustn't touch anything, John used a stick to prop the branches out of the way while he photographed the glasses. He took several distance shots to show the location, then close-ups from every possible angle. One lens was cracked, and the frames looked twisted, as if they might have come off in a struggle.

John had little doubt that the woman was dead or that Boone had been responsible. Maybe she'd died accidentally or been killed by an animal—such things happened out here in the bush. Maybe she'd been killed while trying to escape. Or maybe her murder had been planned from the beginning.

So far, there was no way to be sure. But John was already imagining what Emma's fate might have been if he hadn't come to her rescue.

He finished his search, went back to the Jeep, and started the long, slow drive home. He'd found a few odds and ends, but only the glasses stood out as evidence. If Philpot could identify them in the photos, surely that would justify a search of the area and hopefully lead to Boone's arrest.

The question now was, would Philpot cooperate or was the fake reverend a closer friend to Boone than he'd let on?

*   *   *

David had shown up for work at his regular time. He was his usual cheerful, friendly self, leading Emma to suspect that Marlena had exaggerated her son's emotional state. But she knew better than to mention his mother's visit, or to meddle in a volatile situation that was none of her making.

Business had been brisk all day. Pearl had mentioned that this might be the last of the nice weather before the cold autumn storms moved in. Everyone who came by seemed to feel the same urgency to be out and about, getting things done and enjoying a pleasant meal before battening down the hatches for harsh Alaskan weather.

By late afternoon the flow of diners had trickled off. But the restaurant was still busy. Emma was getting tired. She was functioning on autopilot when a new customer, wearing a sweatshirt and a red baseball cap left over from the Trump campaign, came in and sat down at a table with his back toward her.

Pen poised over her order pad, she walked around the table. "Hi," she said. "Welcome to Ara—"

The words died in her throat as the man smiled up at her.

"Well, I'll be damned," the man she'd known as Reverend Sherman Philpot said in a ringing voice. "If it isn't Mrs. Boone Swenson, in the flesh."

Pearl's head swiveled in their direction. Only a quick grab saved her from dropping the tray she was carrying.

Emma's legs had gone wobbly beneath her. Until now she had almost believed that she could move on past that fake wedding and the nightmare that had followed. But the sight of Philpot, grinning up at her with that missing tooth, brought it all back.

"So I take it things didn't work out between you and ol' Boone. Pity. I thought you made a right handsome couple."

A few other people were turning their heads to look.

Emma felt as if an iron band had clamped around her ribs. She could barely breathe. She glanced around to see if David had heard. He was nowhere in sight.

"So are you going to take my order, Mrs. Swenson?" Philpot asked, clearly enjoying her discomfort.

Emma's hands shook, blurring the pad in her vision. The pen clattered to the floor. Nausea crept up her throat. She'd never had a panic attack in her life, but right now she couldn't do this.

"Excuse me, I'm not feeling well," she muttered, and fled the dining room.

Pearl found her a few minutes later in the employee restroom. She was splashing cold water on her face. "Are you all right, honey?" Pearl asked.

At the sound of a friendly voice, Emma shut off the water and turned around. She still felt unsteady, but the worst was over. "Sorry, this isn't like me at all," she said. "I'm so embarrassed."

"Never mind. I know that man. He's a real scumbag. Did he say what it sounded like he said—that you were married to Boone Swenson?"

"I'm afraid so. But it's a lie. It's a long story, Pearl, and you don't have time to hear it. We both need to get back to work."

"It's all right. David's there. He can fill water glasses and bring orders for a few minutes. But I think it might help you to talk—and as your supervisor, it would help me to know what you're dealing with."

Emma gave her the briefest possible version. Even so, her story was longer and more wrenching than she'd expected it to be. By the time she'd finished, she was drained of words and emotion.

Pearl wiped away a sympathetic tear. "You poor baby, you've really been through it."

"The thing is, I mustn't feel sorry for myself," Emma said. "If I do, I'll never be able to move on. I thought I *had* moved on until that horrible man came in today. When he looked up at me and smiled, the whole nightmare came crashing in on me. And when he called me Mrs. Boone Swenson, I wanted to die of shame. The worst of it was, I could tell he was enjoying himself."

"Well, don't worry, dear." Pearl squeezed Emma's shoulders. "Whatever happens out there, I'll have your back. And I'll wait on that slimeball myself—even though I might be tempted to slip a good, strong dose of laxative in his beer."

"Do you think David heard what he said?"

"I'm pretty sure he was in the kitchen. But don't worry. If he did hear, I'll make sure he knows the truth. Now what d'you say we go out there and show 'em what we're made of?"

Heartened by Pearl's support, Emma followed her back to the dining room. After what had just happened, all she could do was hold her head up and go back to work. But a new fear had taken root inside her, and she could feel it growing.

Since Philpot knew she was working here, it would only be a matter of time before word got back to Boone.

She cast a furtive glance toward his table, hoping she wouldn't catch him looking back at her.

The table was empty.

It was late afternoon, the sun already low in the sky, when John arrived back in Ketchikan. He thought about calling Emma, but since he knew she'd be working, he went straight to the police station.

Traverton was just leaving to go home, but when he saw the photos on John's phone, he called his wife and asked her to hold dinner. After they'd transferred the photos to the police database, they brought up the shots of the glasses on Traverton's computer.

"They're just like Philpot described," John said. "Boone's first so-called bride wore big glasses with thick lenses. If they were anything like this pair, she was probably too near-sighted to get by without them. She would never have gone off on her own and left them behind."

"You're saying Boone might have killed her?"

"I didn't say that. But something must've happened to the woman. I hope you'll agree that this justifies a search of the area—maybe with a cadaver dog."

"Yes, but the decision to search would be up to the state troopers. It would involve their men and equipment."

"You could recommend it, based on the evidence."

"True. But before that I'd like to get a positive ID on those glasses. Let's go see Philpot."

Waste of time, John thought as he and Traverton pulled up to the shabby blue house in Traverton's police vehicle. Those glasses hadn't dropped out of the sky and crawled under that blackberry bush by themselves. The only expla-nation for their being there was the obvious one. But Sam Traverton was a methodical man, and this caution was typical of him.

John had hesitated to come along on this errand. The last time he'd spoken with Philpot, he'd come here under the guise of friendship. This time, Philpot would know that he was aligned with the enemy. But that couldn't be helped. John knew he'd be needed to back up the account of where the glasses had been found, and to keep Philpot from denying his earlier story.

Their timing was good. They arrived at the house just as Philpot was pulling up on his motorcycle. The look on his horsey face made words unnecessary.

They stood next to the porch while John showed the pictures on his phone and Traverton asked the questions.

"You told John that Boone's so-called bride was wearing glasses when you performed the ceremony. Are these the glasses you saw?"

Philpot scratched behind his ear. "Can't say for certain. Maybe, maybe not. The woman wasn't much of a looker, that's for sure. As I recollect, her glasses had black frames, or maybe gold. It was a while ago, and my memory isn't as sharp as it used to be."

"I don't suppose you remember her name, do you?"

Philpot shrugged. "Mary Frances or somethin'. Maybe Mary Josephine. Anyway, it sounded Catholic."

"Any last name?"

"Boone never told me that."

"Thanks for your time. If your memory improves, give us a call." Traverton motioned to John, and they walked back toward the car.

"You know he's lying about the glasses, don't you?" John said as they climbed inside and drove away.

"Maybe. But why would he lie?"

"Boone's his friend. He's protecting him—and maybe protecting himself. Glasses like that, with those lenses, there's no way they'd be there unless that poor woman had lost them. You are going to recommend a search, aren't you?"

"Probably. But I want to check the missing persons database first. Narrow the search down to women of a certain age, maybe named Mary, maybe a teacher or librarian, gone missing last spring. She might be there. There might even be a photo of her wearing those glasses."

John suppressed the urge to grind his teeth. It was commonly known that Sam Traverton would rather lose an arm than be proven wrong because he took action before all the facts were in. As Sam himself was fond of saying, he didn't like playing his hand until he knew how the deck was stacked.

"It's possible that no one reported her," John said. "Emma had no family and lived alone. I'm guessing that Boone looked for women who might not be missed."

"Maybe so," Traverton said. "But we'll have time to look. There's a storm moving in tomorrow. Nobody will be going out to search until it clears."

John had checked the forecast for tomorrow's mail run, so he knew about the storm. He'd flown in bad weather plenty of times, and this patch of rain and sleet didn't look serious enough to alter his plans. But Traverton was right. The troopers would need decent weather to search the trailer site.

They drove back to the police station. Traverton let John out at the Jeep with a promise to pass on anything he learned. Alone now, John got out his phone to call Emma. She'd be working now, and might have the ringer on silent. But at least he could leave her a message or send her a text before he went home and lost service.

Damn! John stared at the dead phone. He must've been too distracted to charge it last night. Now it was useless, and the charger was in the cabin.

He didn't want to go into the restaurant with David there. But at least he could drive by and make sure Emma was all right.

He drove down Front Street, parked by the docks, and walked across the street. By now it was almost dark. The wind, blowing in from the west, felt dense and moist, the prelude to a storm.

The lights were on in the restaurant. He could see Emma

carrying a tray of meals to a table—a feat of strength and balance that amazed him. Nearby, David was stacking plates on another table.

From a safe distance on the sidewalk John watched them—the two most precious people in his life. Then, knowing he mustn't stay, he crossed the street again and drove home.

CHAPTER 11

John picked up the mail pouch at the Ward Cove post office, then drove the short distance to Refuge Cove. The wind was brisk and cold. As he climbed out of his Jeep in the parking lot, he paused to turn up the collar of the sheepskin coat.

He'd meant to call Emma this morning. But he'd decided to leave at first light, ahead of the storm. He knew she'd be tired from work, and he didn't want to wake her. Taking his charged phone out of his pocket, he brought up her number and sent her a simple text.

Leaving early. Back tonight. Talk then. Stay safe.

After stowing the mail in the Beaver and doing the customary preflight check, he climbed into the pilot's seat, started the engine, and taxied out of the cove.

The waves were whitecapped in the main channel. The plane pitched slightly as John turned into the wind, set the flaps to takeoff position, and opened the throttle. The Beaver shot forward and roared into the air.

Wind rocked the wings and battered the fuselage as the plane climbed to cruising altitude of ten thousand feet. He'd hoped to fly above the storm, but even here, the air was rough. He might have postponed the mail flight for a day or two, until the weather cleared, but this was the day when many folks in the villages received their assistance and dividend checks. For some, even a short delay would be a hardship.

The main storm front had yet to move in. If it proved to be too dangerous, John knew he could set down on some lake or inlet to wait out the worst of it. But he wasn't worried. The sturdy Beaver was built to take a beating. It had survived plenty of storms. So had he. This one would be no different.

Emma woke to the clatter of hail against the windowpane. According to the bedside clock, it was almost eight. But the room was barely light.

She swung her legs off the bed and pattered barefoot to the window. Roiling soot-black clouds filled the sky outside. The wind howled, blowing the hail in a wild tattoo against the glass. The storm had struck in full fury. She could only hope that John had cancelled his flight. Surely he wouldn't go up in weather like this. But John was a determined man.

Had he left her a message? Rushing back across the room she snatched up her phone. Dread jerked a knot in her stomach as she read his text from earlier this morning. Just as she'd feared, John had taken the plane up in the storm.

There was no TV in her room, but there was one mounted over the bar downstairs. She dressed in jeans and a sweater, splashed her face, finger-combed her hair, and hurried downstairs.

The TV in the bar was already on, tuned to a local news and weather broadcast. A half dozen people were watching it. Most of them appeared to be guests who were worried about their airline flights. Luggage was stacked in the lobby, but clearly no one was going anywhere this morning.

Too nervous to sample the breakfast buffet, Emma pulled out a stool and sat at the bar to watch the images on TV. What she saw only heightened her fear for John. The storm was a big one, with rain, hail, and sleet pounding the Alaskan coast from Ketchikan to Skagway and beyond. Emma saw news shots of flooded streets, highway wrecks, beached fishing boats, and airports with grounded planes and cancelled flights.

Where was John in all this? He must've set down somewhere. What was it he'd said when she'd asked him about flying in bad storms? Something about landing and waiting out the weather. Surely that's what he would do.

Turning away from the TV, she rose, walked to the front of the restaurant, and looked over the low curtain that shielded seated patrons from sidewalk traffic. Beyond the glass, sleet and hail flew past the window, blown almost horizontal by the keening wind. The docks and water were a blur, glimpsed through streaking daggers of icy white. A few vehicles, their drivers accustomed to storms, moved along Front Street at a crawl. Here and there, people, caught unaware or driven by some urgent errand, staggered into the wind, clutching their parkas and ponchos around them.

The tall figure of a man emerged like a wraith from the swirling whiteness. Walking along the docks at a leisurely stroll, almost as if the storm didn't exist, he paused opposite the hotel and stood looking across Front Street, toward the window where Emma stood. Although it didn't make sense that he could see her through the sleet-blasted window, she took an instinctive step back from the glass. A chill passed through her body.

She could still see him, but not his face. He was wearing

a storm poncho over a dark hoodie that was drawn down and over his forehead and cheeks, leaving little more than his eyes and mouth visible.

Even without a clear look at the man, Emma knew it was Boone. No one else could trigger the gut-clenching dread she felt when he stepped into the street, walking at an even pace toward the window, as if he wanted to prolong her fear. Emma knew she should get away and hide where he couldn't find her, in case he dared to come inside. But since he'd likely heard from Philpot, he would already know she was here. Something compelled her to face him, to look him in the eye and let him know she was strong enough to stand up to him.

She moved forward again, next to the glass.

He stepped from the street onto the curb and came across the sidewalk to stand under the scant shelter of the overhang. They were face to face now, separated only by the glass. She looked into those cold blue eyes and felt the paralyzing fear that flowed down into her limbs. She willed her features to freeze, betraying nothing.

Without breaking eye contact, he reached up with his gloved hands and pulled back the poncho and hoodie that covered his head. Emma stifled a gasp as she saw the blistered, hairless patch that ran down the left side from crown to jaw, barely missing his eye.

This was her doing.

Slowly, the same way he'd unmasked himself, Boone covered his head again. With the same cold smile on his face, he turned away and walked into the storm. He had wanted to show himself. And he'd wanted her to know that because of what she'd done to him, he would make her suffer. If he had to chase her to the ends of the earth, he would never let her go.

* * *

John had made stops at Wrangell, Petersburg, and a couple of tiny settlements between. He was twenty minutes from Sitka, cruising at seven hundred feet, when the storm front hit with force that rocked the Beaver like a child's paper toy. Sleet splattered the windows. Clouds swept in around him, cutting off his vision. Even with the wipers working, he was flying almost blind.

John swore, knowing he'd pressed his luck too far. Trying to climb over the storm now would be an almost suicidal risk. There was no place to go but down.

He knew he was over water. But the convolutions of the coast, with its inlets, islands and reefs, could be treacherous. The simplest miscalculation might be enough to crash the plane into a mountainside, a rock, or even a tree.

He radioed his position and plan to anybody who might be listening. Then, with an eye on the altimeter, he began a careful descent. Howling wind battered the Beaver, shaking it back and forth like an animal with prey in its jaws. As the plane dropped, John struggled to see through the roiling clouds. His eyes strained for the slightest glimpse of the landscape below.

At two hundred feet he broke out below the clouds. A sleety rain was falling, drops splattering the plane like machine gun fire. Near the ground the wind was even stronger. But at least he could see. He was flying low over a narrow channel dotted with rocky islands. Landing the plane would be tricky, but he'd been in tighter spots—like the lake he'd landed on to rescue Emma.

Engine slowed to idle, flaps down, nose slightly up to slow the descent, he picked an open passage and glided in for a landing. The storm was beating the waves to a froth, which was likely why he failed to see the massive rock looming just below the surface. The left float shattered as the plane skidded across it, careened partway onto its side and crashed to a stop.

Dazed and shaken, John opened his eyes. His head felt like somebody had broken a brick over it. Reaching up, he felt a swollen, tender bruise, so sore he could barely touch it. The headset he'd been wearing was nowhere to be seen. What the hell had happened?

In a flash, it all came back—the storm, the descent through the clouds, and the landing he'd expected to go fine—except that it hadn't. His head must've struck something when the plane crashed to a stop. Whatever it was, it had hit hard. He felt dizzy and mildly nauseous. Probably had a concussion. Never mind, he needed to see about the plane, which was undoubtedly in even worse shape than he was.

After unfastening his safety harness, he pushed open the door, and jumped to the ground. The jar to his head as he landed elicited a grunt of pain.

The storm howled around him, wet and icy cold, as he inspected his plane. It had come to a stop on a stretch of rocky beach. The float on the pilot's side was destroyed, the struts holding it bent out of shape. The tip of the wing, where the plane had scraped along the beach and come to rest was crumpled. With time, money, and spare parts, the Beaver could be towed back to civilization and repaired. But there was no way he could take off and fly it out—especially in this godforsaken place.

Damn!

When he didn't show up in Sitka, the mail flight would be reported missing. Rescuers who'd received his last radio message would be out looking for him. But nothing was going to happen until the storm cleared. If the wind and rain hung around, he could be stuck here for days—and if he had a concussion, the one thing he mustn't do was sleep. If he did, there was a danger he might not wake up.

Still cursing himself for taking a chance on the weather, he climbed back into the cockpit and assessed his situation. He had a thermos of coffee, a couple of water bottles, and a few snacks. There was no telling how long they would have to last. The thing to do now was get on the radio and let his colleagues know that he'd survived a crash landing and was waiting to be picked up.

But when he tried to use the radio, there was nothing but silence. From the shock of the crash, or for whatever reason, the radio was dead.

When Emma came down for her shift at eleven o'clock, she had the loaded pistol John had given her tucked into the pocket of her uniform. Small as it was, the gun had enough weight to bump against her leg and bulge slightly beneath her apron. If a customer noticed it, she might be in trouble. But after Boone's visit that morning, she would not be leaving her room without it.

By noon the wind had let up. Gray clouds, drizzling cold rain, hung over the town. But the weather wasn't harsh enough to keep people from donning their rain gear and coming out to socialize over lunch.

"We get a lot of rain here," Pearl explained. "If we let it keep us indoors, we'd all turn into hermits."

Pearl hadn't been here earlier when Boone had stopped by the window. Emma hadn't told her about the brief visit. Pearl already knew that Boone was a threat. And after the fuss when Philpot had shown up, Emma had made a resolution—no more drama in the workplace.

The TV above the bar had been on all day with news of the storm. But there'd been no word from John. She could only hope he'd found a safe place to wait out the storm, and that he'd be home tonight. His text had mentioned that he wanted to talk. Did that mean he wanted to move forward together, or was he preparing her for good-bye? Either way, she would have to be ready. John was not an easy man to read.

David came in at his usual time. His mother let him out of the Escalade and drove away without so much as a wave. It was easy to understand why the boy wanted a job and a car. John's son was growing up. What he craved was independence.

It was about four o'clock, and Emma was helping David set the tables for dinner when the breaking news screen flashed onto the TV. Emma stood stunned, the forks in her hand clattering to the floor as the newscaster read the bulletin.

"A mail plane has been reported missing and is presumed to have gone down in the storm, somewhere between Petersburg and Sitka. Earlier today, the pilot, John Wolf, flying out of Ketchikan, radioed his position and indicated that he was trying to land. Nothing further has been heard from him. Attempts to contact him by radio have received no response. Search planes will be going out as soon as the weather clears."

Emma glanced at David. Like her, he was frozen to the spot, staring up at the TV as the broadcast continued. Pearl had come out of the kitchen, and she stood beside them, listening.

"We go now to our reporter in Sitka, speaking with Saul Mazursky, a former bush pilot and now mail supervisor. What's your take on this, Mr. Mazursky?"

An older man, weathered and graying, spoke into the microphone. *"If you know anything about bush pilots, you know two things—that they're tough and that they're like family to each other. The men in the air looking for John Wolf will be his friends and brothers. And they won't rest until they find him, because they know that John would do the same for them. He's one of the best pilots and finest men I've ever known—honest, dedicated, selfless, and as tough as they come. John, I know you can't hear me. But if you could, I would tell you, hang in there. Somebody's . . . coming."* Mazursky blinked and shoved the microphone back at the reporter.

Emma looked at David again. Tears were trickling down his face. He was hearing about his father, the man he hadn't been allowed to know.

See, your mother was wrong. People do change. Or maybe he was the same man all along. That was what she wanted to say to him. But those weren't the words the boy needed to hear. Instead, what she said was, "Pray for him, David. That's what he needs from you now."

John walked along the beach doing his best to stay alert. The wind had eased, and the rain was letting up some. But clouds lay like a thick gray blanket as far as the eye could see. He had spent much of the afternoon trying to fix the radio, with no success. He'd even tried his cell phone, but, as he should have known, there was no service here.

In an hour it would be dark. Not that it mattered. No pilot would be searching for him in this weather.

Even once the sky cleared, John knew that finding him wouldn't be easy. He had landed in a narrow inlet, with high cliffs on either side. A pilot in a plane would only be able to see him from directly overhead. Before then, he could pass out from the concussion or die of hunger and thirst—but he mustn't think of that now. He had set out anything that might hold water to collect the rain, saving the two precious quart bottles for as long as he could. Drinking the seawater in the inlet would only dehydrate him faster.

The night would be long and cold. Wrapped in his sheepskin coat, John had walked the length and breadth of the island looking for something that would make a fire. But this small pile of rock had no trees on it. And the few sticks of driftwood he'd collected were too waterlogged to burn. If he was to have any hope of rescue, when the time came, he would need to light a signal fire. For that he would need enough fuel to attract attention. Maybe something from the plane would work. But he would have to worry about that tomorrow.

He had planned to be home tonight, to pick up Emma after her work and drive someplace where they could be alone and talk. It was too soon for anything like a proposal, but he needed to know whether she could be happy in a place like Ketchikan, or whether she'd be walking out of his life as soon as she was able to leave.

If he could find the courage to say the words, he might even tell her he loved her.

Did she know he was missing? Had it been on the news, or was she waiting, expecting the call that wasn't going to happen?

Whatever it took, John vowed, he would survive to return to her and have that talk.

After a sleepless night, Emma was up at the crack of dawn. She dressed hurriedly, splashed her face, and hurried downstairs to the bar to turn on the TV.

It was too soon to expect good news, she told herself. But the clouds were breaking up. Search planes would be in the air. She could only pray that John would be found soon, and that he would be safe.

When the regional broadcast came on, there were no surprises. The search had begun, but it was too soon to ex-

pect results. The news program moved on to other stories—the cleanup after the storm, a robbery in Wasilla,
and a bear attack at a fishing resort. Still, until the time
came to change for her shift, Emma stayed in front of the
TV in the hope of hearing that John had been rescued. But
there was no more word of the search.

Pearl came in a few minutes before the lunch shift. One
look at Emma's face told her she was still waiting for
news. "Don't worry, honey," she said, giving Emma a hug.
"With so much territory to cover, these searches can take
time. They'll find him. You'll see."

But will he be alive? Refusing to voice the thought,
Emma fixed her face in a smile and finished setting the last
table.

"Oh, I meant to tell you," Pearl said. "David won't be
in today. His mother called to say he wasn't feeling well."
She moved closer to Emma, lowering her voice. "Between
you and me, I heard from Carl that David and Marlena
had a blowup over David's wanting to spend time with
John. Things got pretty emotional. I'm guessing Marlena
didn't want him coming in today. I hope she doesn't make
him quit. David has a mind of his own and he's becoming
a man. She can't control him forever."

"You're right, I'm sure," Emma said. "But I know John
wouldn't want to cause trouble between them."

Pearl shook her head. "Maybe not. But sometimes things
happen for a reason. People change. They grow up. And
there are worse things than David's learning that his father is
a good man after all."

Around three o'clock in the afternoon, four noisy male
hotel guests came into the bar to drink beer, eat snacks,
and watch a pro football game on TV. That put an end to
Emma's news tracking—perhaps a good thing, she told

herself. Each hour with no word about John only sank her deeper into despair. If he'd been found, and he was all right, he would likely call her. But if the news was bad, she wasn't family. Nobody would let her know. She could only wait to hear the worst.

As she worked, she felt the weight of the pistol in her pocket. All day she'd kept an eye out the window for Boone. He hadn't appeared, but she was still nervous. As long as she could stay in the hotel with people around her or lock herself in her room, she felt safe. But she couldn't hide from Boone forever. Sooner or later, something would have to change—and she would have to be ready for it.

Dinnertime was even busier than usual. With David gone, Emma, Pearl, and the other workers had to do his job along with their own. By closing time, when all the diners had paid and left, Emma felt dead on her feet. She cleared the last table, sank onto a bar stool, and clicked the remote through the channels in the hope of finding some news about John. But there was nothing on at this hour but sports, shopping shows, and old sitcom reruns. Giving in to strain and exhaustion, she laid her head on the bar and closed her eyes.

"Emma." It was the voice of Andy, the night manager at the hotel desk. "Two men in the lobby want to talk to you."

Two men. Emma's heart dropped. Was this like the military, where they sent two uniformed men to tell families their loved one had died? Had John told them where to find her before—

Never mind. Whatever the news was, she had to face it the way John would want her to. Taking a deep breath, and feeling slightly dizzy, she forced herself to walk through the door.

Two men stood at the foot of the stairs. The shorter one was a stranger, stubble-faced and wearing a down parka.

The other man, wrapped in a survival blanket, wearing a bandage on his head, and looking like a refugee from a war zone, was John.

With a little cry, she ran to him, almost knocking him backward with her joy. He winced as her arms went around him.

"Careful," the shorter man said. "The doc thinks he might have a cracked rib. He's got a concussion, too. They wanted to keep him at the hospital in Sitka but he insisted on coming back here. I live here in Ketchikan, and I was flying home, so it wasn't any trouble to bring him along. But he'll need somebody to keep an eye on him tonight."

"I can do that. He can stay in my room," Emma said without a second thought. She never wanted to let this man out of her sight again.

"Clive, here, was the one who found me." John spoke with effort. "I'd about given up when he flew over and saw me."

"He made a signal fire by pouring gasoline over his old sheepskin coat and one of the seats from the plane," Clive said. "If I hadn't spotted the smoke, I never would've seen where he was. And that landing was a doozy! I almost cracked up myself."

"I'd do the same for you any day," John said. "Pray to God I'll never have to. Meanwhile, I'll take you and your family out for a steak dinner after I'm on my feet again."

"I'd better help him up the stairs," Clive said. "The doctor gave him something for the pain. He's a little shaky."

Emma glanced at Andy behind the desk. "No problem," he said. "Go ahead."

Pearl was standing in the doorway to the restaurant.

Their gazes met. *Call David.* Emma mouthed the words and saw Pearl nod. Then she followed Clive as he steadied John on his way up the stairs.

Her mind swarmed with unasked questions. But the answers could wait. Right now nothing mattered except that John was safe and alive, and that he'd come back to her.

CHAPTER 12

Clive helped Emma ease John onto the double bed and get him out of his boots, socks, shirt, and trousers, leaving on his long, insulating underwear to help keep him warm while he rested.

"Hey, I'm not a patient," John protested as they finished undressing him and tucked him into bed with pillows to prop him into a semi-reclining position. "I can do this by myself."

"But *will* you do it, or will you get up and be off on some cockeyed errand? Knowing you, I'd advise Emma, here, to hide your clothes." Clive laid John's holstered pistol on the bedside table. "You heard the doctor. Warmth and bed rest, at least until tomorrow. And with that concussion, no sleeping too long at one time."

"Are you hungry?" Emma asked John. "I can warm up some chowder in the kitchen."

"They fed me in Sitka. I'm fine."

"My wife and kids will be wondering what became of me." Clive gave Emma a card he'd taken from his wallet. "Here's my cell number. If he gets too rambunctious, give me a call. I'll come over and set him straight."

Emma seized his hand at the door. "Thank you from the bottom of my heart," she said.

"Think nothing of it. John would've done the same for me. Maybe someday he will. Meanwhile, take good care of him. He said some nice things about you. I can see they're all true." Before Emma could thank him again, he was gone.

When she turned back to look at John, he was sitting up in the bed, a tired smile on his face. "Lock the door," he said. "All three locks."

Emma did as she was told. "Anything else?" she asked, not knowing quite what to expect.

"Yes. Take off that godawful outfit, get into something comfortable, and come keep me company. We've got a lot to talk about."

"Yes, we do." She untied her apron, lifted the little Kel-Tec pistol out of her pocket, and laid it next to his big .44.

Her fingers hesitated on the top button of her uniform. "Don't look," she said.

He turned his head away, "Good Lord, Emma, haven't you ever undressed in front of a man?"

"Sorry, I was raised by my grandma, with her old-fashioned rules. They sank in deep." She let the baggy pink uniform dress fall around her ankles, shed her bra, and reached for the top half of the thermal set she'd been using for pajamas.

"I suppose you could change in the bathroom."

"Yes, I know . . . but that seems almost . . . cowardly. Besides, it's cold in there." She kicked off her sneakers and pulled on the thermal bottoms. "All right, you can look," she said.

He was laughing, which was probably hurting his cracked rib. "Emma Hunter, you're one in in a million," he said. "Damn it, I love you."

Her hand shook as she tightened the drawstring around her waist. "I love you, too," she said, the confession wrung from her by profound relief. "I would have stopped living if you hadn't come back. Not that it makes anything less complicated."

He shifted against the pillows to make room for her, resting an arm along the top. "Come here," he said.

She did, snuggling up alongside him, her head nesting in the hollow of his shoulder. Nothing in her life had ever felt more right. They had so many things to say to each other, and all night to say them. The only question was where to begin.

She raised her face. He bent his head and gave her a lop-sided kiss that lingered long enough to send warm tingles through her body. "Tell me about the accident," she said. So he told her the story—the storm, the crash landing, the damage to the plane, and having to wait more than twenty-four hours in the damp cold before hearing the sound of an approaching Beaver. "By then I had the fire ready—a pile of junk from the plane, including one of the seats, even my coat. I poured gasoline over everything, tossed a match, and prayed that whoever was up there would see the smoke."

"And Clive found you. What about the plane?"

"It's still there. I'll have to pay somebody with a boat to get to it and fix it or tow it out. It won't be easy or cheap, but that plane is like an old friend. I can't leave it there to rust." His arm tightened around her. "Now, how about you? I was glad to see you were packing that pistol."

"Boone knows I'm here," she said, and felt his body tense against her. "When Philpot came by and recognized me, I knew it would only be a matter of time before he told Boone. Then, during the storm, I was in the bar. Boone walked up to the window and just stood there. He was wearing a hoodie, and when he pulled it back, I saw the burns. I've stayed inside and carried that pistol ever since."

"Don't take any chances, Emma." His voice had taken

on a serious tone. "Boone could be more dangerous than you know. Remember when you were speculating that he might have done to other women what he did to you?"

"Yes, I made a sick joke about bodies buried out behind that trailer." She looked up at him and read his expression. "Oh, no . . ." she murmured.

"A lot of things have happened since we last had time to talk," he said. "Philpot told me he'd performed an earlier fake wedding for Boone last spring. He saw it as a prank—a way for Boone to get reluctant women into his bed."

"So what happened to the woman? Does anybody know?"

"Philpot said she was older and plain, with big, thick glasses. When I drove to the trailer, I found a pair of women's glasses with thick lenses under a bush. I've been trying to get Traverton to send a team out there to search. So far he's been dragging his feet. He doesn't want to waste time and resources on what could be a wild-goose chase. But whatever happened, that woman wouldn't have left without her glasses."

Emma felt a chill, as if cold hands had tightened around her throat. "You think he *murdered* her?"

"Without a body, there's no way to tell. I took photos of the glasses and left them in place for evidence. Traverton showed the photos to Philpot for identification. But Philpot had a convenient memory block."

"By now he will have passed the word to Boone," Emma said. "If Boone knows he's liable to be charged, he could run—maybe across the border to Canada. At least, then, we'd be rid of him."

"Don't count on it. Boone could hide in the bush forever and still be a danger to you. He needs to be put away." His arm tightened, pulling her closer. "On a more cheerful note, I found evidence that Boone may have finished burning the trailer himself, after you got away from him. So you're off the hook for that."

"But not for his burns."

"Not likely. Boone wouldn't be stupid enough to burn himself on his own fire. Either way, he blames you for everything that happened. That's how his mind works. But I'm here now, and I swear, whatever it takes, I'll stop him from hurting you."

His arm tightened around her, making her feel precious and protected. Emma closed her eyes and nestled closer to him, feeling his warmth flood her senses with the clean aroma of his body, the sound of his breathing, and the slow, steady beat of his heart. She could stay right here forever, safe from the outside world, she thought. But that world was their world, and there were things that needed to be set right before they could move on together.

She stirred, rubbing her hair against his chin. "When the news of your crash came on TV, I was with David," she said. "We listened to an interview with a man they said was a mail supervisor. Older, silver hair."

"That would be Mazursky. Good man."

"He told the reporter you were the best pilot and the finest man he'd ever known."

"That's the sort of thing you'd say at a man's funeral."

"Your opinion, not mine. I'd be inclined to agree with him. But that's not why I'm telling you. David was listening to that broadcast. I could tell how moved he was. He even shed a few tears."

John didn't answer. She felt his throat move against her forehead.

"He didn't come in today," Emma said. "His mother said he was sick. But Pearl told me that Marlena and David had a big blowup because he told her he wanted to spend time with you."

John exhaled slowly. After a beat of silence, he spoke. "Nothing would make me happier than to be with David. But I won't put his life in turmoil by coming between him and his family. Marlena raised him when I wasn't there. She's done a fine job. And Carl's been a decent dad. As far as I know, he's treated David like his own. David's at a point in his life when he needs stability. I won't take that away by starting a family war."

"He'll be eighteen on his next birthday, old enough to make his own decisions."

"I know. His birthday's in March. I'll be open to whatever he chooses, but I can't choose for him."

Emma raised her face and kissed the corner of his mouth. She had a lot to learn about love. John was already teaching her. "How did you get to be so wise?" she asked.

"Wisdom is overrated," he said. "So is closing your eyes when a beautiful woman is undressing in front of you. Be warned, the next time it happens, I just might steal a peek."

"You might not have to." She turned in his arms for a long, deep kiss that left her warm and tingling. Nothing beyond that was going to happen tonight. When the time was right, they would both know it. Now was too soon. Their love was too new and still too tender. But she could hold him in her arms while he rested and make sure his sleep was safe. That was enough to fill her heart.

By crack of dawn the next morning John's energy had rebounded. Except for a lingering headache, he felt much like his usual self. Leaving Emma to sleep off her wakeful night, he went into the bathroom, eased the bandage off his head, and washed his hair in the shower.

He was nearly dressed when she opened her eyes with a startled look. "You're leaving? Are you all right?"

"I'm fine," he said. "But I have a lady's reputation to protect, a Jeep to pick up at Refuge Cove, and a cabin to check. Get some sleep before work. I'll be in touch." Bending over, he kissed her gently, then strapped on his gun in its shoulder holster and, after making sure the door would lock behind him, stepped out into the hall.

The hotel was quiet. The upstairs workmen had Saturday off and weren't coming in. The night clerk was dozing at the desk. Outside, the sky was clearing. The air was fresh and brisk, with a chill that made him miss the sheepskin jacket he'd sacrificed to the signal fire.

He walked to the little drive-up on the far side of the tunnel, enjoyed a cup of coffee there, and hailed a cab to take him to Refuge Cove. On the way, he clicked through a mental list of things he needed to do. He'd only missed yesterday, but it was as if the world had shifted while he was waiting to be rescued.

His Jeep was waiting in the marina parking lot, just as he'd left it. One worry out of the way. He'd planned to stop by the air marina to get a recommendation for someone with a boat who could help him salvage the Beaver, or better yet, help him repair it on the spot. But the office was closed, so that would have to wait.

He'd tried not to worry about the cabin, but there was always a chance that Boone had stopped by and left him more ugly surprises. At least, with the storm, the bastard shouldn't have been able to burn the place down. But John wouldn't breathe easy until he knew that everything was all right.

Damn it, he was sick of the way Boone had taken over his life and Emma's. He wanted to move forward, to plan a future with the woman he loved. But the threat from Boone had made her a virtual prisoner. With the discovery that Boone might have caused his first bride's death, the situation had become even more frightening. Boone wasn't just a con man. He was a psychopath. And now the target of his obsessive rage was Emma.

He had to be stopped.

Dealing with Traverton's cautious approach had been an exercise in teeth-grinding frustration. But there was a state trooper post just off the highway. He had nothing to lose by stopping in to find out what the detective had told them, and to ask about any plans for a search.

Minutes later he pulled into their parking lot, went inside the station, and told the desk officer what he wanted. "Your timing's perfect, Mr. Wolf," she said. "Sergeant Packard was just about to have me call you. I'll tell him you're here."

When she buzzed him, Packard came out front. Like John, he was Tlingit. But he was in his fifties and wore his hair short. The two were casual acquaintances, on good terms.

"John!" He extended his hand. "I heard about your crash on the news. Glad you made it out in one piece."

"Thank you." John accepted the handshake. "I wish I could say the same for my plane. You were going to call me?"

"That's right." Packard led the way back to his office. "I was on the phone with Detective Traverton yesterday. He told me about your friend's trouble with Boone Swenson and sent me photos of the evidence you found at the trailer site." Packard perched on the edge of his desk. "I'll cut to the chase. Given what we've seen and heard, we think an investigation is justified. We're putting together a search team, with a dog, to check out the site tomorrow. Since you're familiar with the place, it would be helpful if you'd agree to go along."

John's pulse skipped. Finally something was happening. "I'll do whatever it takes to help," he said.

"Then be here at six tomorrow morning, ready to go. Can you manage that?"

"I'll be here."

John felt a surge of optimism as he turned off the highway onto Revilla Road. At last there was a chance of finding enough evidence against Boone to put him away. He thought about sharing the news with Emma while he still had phone service. But it was early yet. She'd stayed awake much of the night watching over him. Let her rest. He would call her later, after he'd been to the cabin.

He was thinking about her, remembering how she'd felt in his arms, when his cell phone rang. For an instant he thought it might be Emma. But he was wrong. When he saw the caller ID, he braked and pulled off onto the side of the road before he answered.

"What is it, Marlena? Is David all right?"

"Why don't you tell me?" John couldn't remember the last time he'd spoken with her, but the desperate fury in her voice was unmistakable. "Last night he sneaked out of the house and went to a party. The police brought him home. He was . . ." She choked on the word. "He was *drunk!*"

John stifled a groan. "Where is he now? Is he safe?"

"He's still in bed, sleeping it off. This is all your doing!"

"Marlena, I didn't see him or talk to him last night. And even if I had, you know I'd never let him touch alcohol."

"That's not what I meant. I was always afraid he'd grow up to be like you. That's why I've kept you away from him all these years. But it didn't make any difference. He's your son. He's got your blood. He's going to be a drunk just like his father!"

John remembered what Emma had told him, about the blowup between David and his mother. "Is that what you told him? That he had my blood and was going to grow up like me? What did he say to that?"

"He said that was fine with him. Then he went in his room and slammed the door. He went to school the next day, but I kept him home from work. I didn't think it was a good place for him to be. He went to his room after dinner, to do his homework and play computer games, he said. The next thing I knew, it was after midnight and the police had him at the door. Carl's in denial, says it's up to me to deal with this, and I don't know what to do. . . ."

Her voice broke. John could tell she was crying. Marlena was a good woman. She'd struggled to move past a horrific family background and a bad marriage. He couldn't fault her need for total control. But it was a given that David would rebel at some point. He could only wish it hadn't been in such a self-destructive way, and that his own troubled past hadn't been partly to blame.

"What do you want me to do, Marlena?" he asked.

There was a beat of silence. "I want you to *hurt!*" she said. "I want you to hurt like I'm hurting. I want you to blame yourself and know that there's nothing you can do."

John had been thinking. "There's something that might make a difference. If you'll let me spend some time with him tonight, I can try it."

She hesitated. "After so many years of keeping him away from you, I don't know if I can. . . ."

"You can't go back and make things like they were before," John said. "If you close your eyes and pretend this didn't happen, he'll do it again. You know he will."

"Tell me, and then I'll decide," she said.

"All right, here's what I have in mind. . . ."

After he and Marlena had agreed on a plan—the first thing they'd agreed on in more than fifteen years—John drove on up the road to the cabin. To his relief, he found the place untouched, with no sign that Boone had come by. Now that Boone knew Emma was in the hotel, it appeared he'd lost interest in looking for her here.

He could only hope Emma would be safe inside the Gateway, with locks on her door, people around her when she went downstairs, and the pistol in her pocket. And he could only hope that tomorrow, at the site of the burned trailer, the team would find enough evidence to put Boone behind bars and end this nightmare for her.

With his pistol drawn, he checked the garage, the carving shed, and every room in the house. After assuring himself that everything was all right, he washed up, changed into clean clothes, and chose a spare wool jacket from the closet. It wasn't worth making a fire, since he didn't plan to be here that long. But he was hungry. There was cereal in the cupboard and milk in the fridge. He filled a bowl and made do with that for now.

Looking around the cabin, he found himself wondering if he would ever bring his son here. Until today he'd had little hope of that, but now he found himself imagining David in this room, looking at the photos of his ancestors on the wall and seeing the unfinished totem pole in the shed. Perhaps they could even work on finishing it together.

But maybe he was expecting too much. Maybe this intervention with his boy would only end in disappointment. He would have to be prepared for that.

A small cedar box, a size that might have held card decks or cigars, was tucked between the books on his shelf. John hadn't opened it in years. Now, remembering what was inside, he slipped it out of its place, sat down at the table, and raised the hinged lid.

He didn't have many pictures of his family. In years

past, seeing their faces had only brought him pain. But now, the prospect of showing them to David renewed his interest.

Handling them with care, he spread the photographs and newspaper clippings on the table, arranging them by age. He had never known his father's parents. A faded, grainy news photo, published after they'd died in a boating accident, gave only a dim impression of how they'd looked and who they'd been.

It was his widowed maternal grandfather who'd taken a lost and grieving boy under his wing and helped him grow to young manhood before leaving this earth at the age of eighty. The old man had always hated having his picture taken. He appeared in some of the ceremonial photos on the wall, as did his pretty young wife, who'd died before John was born. But in the only photograph he'd allowed to be taken as an old man, he was standing on the dock at Refuge Cove, holding a huge salmon. John, a boy of twelve, was in the picture, standing beside him. They had caught the fish together, or so his grandfather had always said. It was one of the best memories of John's life. Four years later, when John was just sixteen, his grandfather had passed away peacefully in his sleep.

The only formal photo was a portrait of his parents on their wedding day—so happy and in love, and so unaware of how sadly their lives were fated to end.

He'd forgotten how beautiful they were—his mother in traditional dress with her long black hair flowing around her shoulders, and his father, a fierce young warrior, born into the wrong century. Two hundred years ago he would have been the hero of his tribe. But when his time came, the only enemy left to fight was the white men's oil pipeline, pushing its way through pristine land that had belonged to his people, like a great silver snake with black blood running through its body.

The battle had been lost from the beginning. The death of the pipeline worker had been little more than an accident. But it had put Benton Wolf behind bars for manslaughter. Sentenced to ten years, he had barely served half his time when he died in a prison brawl. By then his young wife was already drowning her sorrow in alcohol.

There were a few school pictures of John growing up— a scrawny kid with hand-me-down down clothes, long hair, and a lonely look in his eyes. Bigger boys, like Boone Swenson, had picked on him at first, but they'd soon learned that he was tough for his size and would fight back. After the first few times, they'd found easier prey.

No photos had been taken at his shotgun wedding to Marlena. It had been a tense, hurried affair, performed at the county offices. David had been born at the Swenson homestead with Marlena's mother, Lillian, acting as mid-wife. The only photograph John had of his son was the one he'd framed and put in his bedroom.

John gathered up the pictures, put them back in the box, and replaced it on the bookshelf. He would show them to Emma the next time she came here. He hoped to show them to David someday, too. The boy's bloodline on his mother's side was nothing to brag about. But John wanted his son to know that he came from good, proud people.

After closing the cabin, he drove back to the highway. At Refuge Cove he parked the Jeep and walked down the beach to a quiet spot where he could look out across the water. He checked his watch before making a call to Emma. It was close to ten-thirty. Since her shift started at eleven, he calculated, she should be awake and getting ready to go downstairs.

She answered his call on the first ring. "Are you feeling all right?" she asked.

"Fine, just a little headache. I'm at Refuge Cove now, and I wanted to pass on some news." He told her about the planned investigation of the trailer site by the state troopers. "They've asked me to go along," he said. "I don't know what we'll find, so try not to get your hopes up."

"It's hard *not* to get my hopes up," she said. "I'm beginning to feel like a prisoner."

"I know. But this can't last forever. Something's got to break, and this may be it. For now, just be careful. Don't leave the hotel."

"You be careful, too. You know Boone. He could be anywhere. Will I see you tonight?"

"I'll be staying at the cabin. But I'll be coming by to pick David up at seven. It's a long story. I'll tell you later, okay?"

"Okay. This sounds interesting. But don't worry. I'll play it cool when you come to get him."

"I love you," he said.

"And I love you. Stay safe." She ended the call.

John walked back to the marina, borrowed a spare computer, and checked out some leads on getting the Beaver back in operation. He couldn't afford to wait. The plane was part of his contract with the mail service. They might arrange the short-term loan of another aircraft, but it wasn't a practical arrangement. Bottom line, if he couldn't fly, he couldn't earn a living.

If a boat could haul him to the inlet with a new float and replacements for the bent metal struts, he could put them on the plane and taxi, or be towed, out of the inlet to someplace where the wing could be mended or replaced. So far it sounded like the best plan. But he was still weighing the options.

After making calls and getting some estimates, he drove back into town and had a late lunch at the drive-up. The afternoon stretched ahead of him, with time to kill before picking David up at seven o'clock. Emma was working, and he had no reason to drive back to the cabin. But he hadn't spoken to Traverton lately. Something had finally compelled the detective to call the state troopers, send the photos, and recommend a search. Before he returned to the site tomorrow, John needed to know what it was.

He caught Traverton in the parking lot, coming back from lunch. The detective greeted John affably. "I was glad to hear you'd been rescued," he said. "Just goes to show you can't keep a good man down. Come on in. I had a feeling you'd be showing up today."

John followed him into his office. "I talked to Packard," he said. "I'll be going with the search team tomorrow."

"I know. Packard called me after you left him. He's grateful that you'll be there to guide the team."

"So what made you finally call them?" John asked.

"Come around by the computer, and I'll show you," Traverton said. "Remember when I told you I was going to search the missing persons database? Take a look at what I found."

He brought up a screen with a school-type photo of a woman. "I sent this to Packard," he said. "But I asked him not to show it to you. I wanted to see your face when you recognized it."

John read the text below the photo:

Bethany Ann Proctor, teacher, 39. Reported missing from Boise, Idaho, June 16, 2017.

John studied the woman in the picture—dark hair drawn back from a pale, narrow face, little or no makeup, as if she'd long since given up trying to look attractive. But her mouth was smiling, and her gentle brown eyes were magnified by her thick-lensed glasses—the same glasses

John had discovered at the trailer site. A tiny gold locket, the old-fashioned kind that opened, hung around her neck on a chain so thin it was barely visible.

She looked like a good woman, a kind woman. "I hope you haven't shown this to Philpot," John said. "Anything he learns will go straight to Boone."

"I know better than that," Traverton said. "We're going to keep quiet about this, at least until the team has searched the site. If Boone's guilty of a crime, we don't want to spook him."

"If Bethany Ann is out there, we'll find her." John was surprised at the surge of emotion when he spoke. Before, he'd only been interested in a reason to arrest Boone and get him out of the way. Now there was this woman with a face and a name—a woman needing love, who'd trusted Boone Swenson and been betrayed even more cruelly than Emma. She deserved justice. And she deserved to go home.

CHAPTER 13

As John drove to pick up David at the restaurant, he tried not to feel like a nervous teenager going on a first date. Hope battled trepidation. He looked forward to being with his son. But there was so much more at stake here than a pleasant evening.

Would his intervention help keep David from trying alcohol again and open the door to a new relationship between them? Or would the boy shrug it off and go his own way?

John tried to remember what he'd been like at that age—already drinking heavily and angry at the world. Would he have listened if some well-meaning adult had stepped in and tried to help? Probably not. He was already set in his ways. And he hadn't been much older than David when he became a father.

But it was different with David. He had a secure home with caring parents. The only disruptive influence in his young life was the father he'd barely known—the father who was trying to help him now.

Maybe this was a bad idea. Maybe he was about to make matters worse. But at least Marlena had been willing to give him a chance—maybe his only chance. He had to take it.

He pulled the Jeep up to the hotel and entered through the lobby. The restaurant was busy with Saturday night customers. He caught sight of Emma, bustling among tables. She gave him a quick smile and moved on.

Pearl, who was in on the plan, gave him a nod and disappeared down the back hallway. A few minutes later, David appeared, dressed in jeans and a down jacket. "Hi," he said. "Mom didn't tell me where we were going."

"She wasn't supposed to." John could feel his heart pounding as he ushered his son outside. A heavy weight of awkwardness hung between them as they climbed into the Jeep.

"I don't know what to call you." David fastened his seat belt.

"You can call me John." It was far too soon for *Dad.* He wouldn't expect that. Not yet. Maybe never. But that was all right.

"Why did Mom say I could go with you tonight?" David asked as John pulled away from the curb.

"I think you know. After last night, she's afraid you'll grow up to be a drunk like your father. She wants me to show you a thing or two."

"You're not a drunk. I found that out on the TV after you crashed. The man said you were the best pilot he ever knew. You couldn't do that if you were a drunk."

"You're right. I'm not a drunk. But I was, for a long time. It cost me my marriage—and it cost me my son." At least they were having an honest conversation. "So tell me. What was it you had to drink last night?"

"My friend said it was gin. He got it from his dad's liquor cabinet and brought it to the party."

"How did it taste? Did you like it?"

"Not really. It tasted like medicine. But after I had some, it made me feel good. I wanted more."

"So when did you stop?"

"When it was all gone."

"So why did you do it?"

He shrugged. "Because I could. Because I was curious. Because I was mad at my mom. I don't know, I just did it."

John drove in silence, taking the long way around to where he was going. For now he'd said enough. He wanted David to do the talking.

"Is it true what my mom says, that being an alcoholic is passed down in families—like your mother drank, and so did you?"

"I don't know. I started drinking when I was thirteen because my mother kept liquor around, and because it helped me forget things that made me feel bad, like remembering my father in prison."

"Yeah, Mom told me about him. She said he killed a man. Is that true?"

"Yes, but he didn't mean to. That's a story for another time." John could only hope there might be another time. "I don't drink anymore, but I'm still an alcoholic. That means the craving will always be there. If I took one drink, it would be like I'd never stopped. That's why I don't drink at all. Not even beer."

"And that craving's passed down in families? Is that what my mother meant?"

"It could be."

"So I could be an alcoholic, too?"

"Maybe. And if you are, that's a good reason not to start drinking at all." John pulled into the church parking lot.

"Hey!" David jerked upright in the seat. "Don't tell me you're taking me to church!"

"Only to the basement. I'm taking you to a meeting of the people who saved my life."

David hesitated. "What will I have to do? Will I have to talk to people?"

"Not unless you want to. Just sit in the back with me and listen. It won't be long—about as long as one of your classes at school. Then, unless you want to hang around, we can go get pizza and sodas."

"Can't we just get pizza and sodas?"

"Not this time. Come on."

They climbed out of the Jeep and walked around to the basement entrance of the church. David dragged his feet but didn't argue. John stopped him at the top of the stairs. "There's one rule I forgot to mention," he said. "You might see a few folks you know tonight, but nothing about who you saw or what they might have said can leave the meeting. You can't tell anybody about this except that you went. Understand?"

"Yeah. Is it sort of like a secret club?"

"Sort of. That's why it's called Alcoholics Anonymous."

"So everybody here is an alcoholic?"

"Right. And they're all either trying to get sober or stay sober. I haven't had a drink in seven years, but I still go."

Downstairs, the meeting had just started. They sat in the back, David slumping in his chair as if wanting to make himself invisible. He cast furtive glances around the small room. There were about twenty people in the meeting, sitting in rows with their backs toward him.

"Holy shit!" he whispered to John. "That bald guy is the soccer coach at school. And the woman over there with the red scarf is my friend's mom. I didn't know they were alcoholics."

"You never saw them here. And they never saw you." John shushed his son.

They listened while people stood and talked about their struggles with alcohol in their lives. Some looked well off.

Others looked like they'd slept on the street. Some were still summoning the strength to quit drinking. Others had been sober for years but still needed the support that came from sharing. John chose not to stand tonight. He didn't want to call attention to David or embarrass him. He could only hope his son was taking in what he heard and thinking about it.

After the meeting, John might have stayed for coffee and cookies, but he knew David would be more comfortable leaving. The boy was quiet as they walked to the Jeep. John waited for him to speak as they drove to the nearby pizza parlor, went inside, and ordered a large combo and Cokes.

"So how often do you go to those meetings?" David asked after the server had taken their order.

"Every couple of weeks, at least. It helps. And it gives me a chance to help other people."

"Do you get up and say, 'My name is John, and I'm an alcoholic'?"

"I do. That's part of the recovery process, letting people know you have a problem."

"My name is David and I'm an alcoholic." He spoke the words as if trying them on, then laughed and shook his head. "No way. I'm not ready for that."

"I'm hoping you'll never need to say that. So is your mother." John looked at him across the booth, filling his eyes with the sight of his son, filling his memory with the sound of his laughter. There was nothing on God's green earth he wouldn't do for the boy. But he knew better than to voice the thought.

The server set their pizza on the table. David wolfed down two big slices before he spoke again.

"What made you decide to stop drinking?"

"I hoped that if I was sober, I could go back to court

and get to have you with me part-time. It didn't work. The judge ruled against me. When it happened I almost started drinking again."

"I'm sorry. My mom has said some awful things about you."

"I know. And a lot of them are true. I gave her a bad time, and I was never there when she needed me."

"I don't know when I can be with you again." David slurped his Coke through the ice in the bottom of his glass. "My mom says that tonight is just for one time. After that, it's back to the old rules."

John's heart sank. He should have expected this. Still, it was hard to hear. "Your mother's the boss," he said. "We've got to respect her wishes. Promise me you'll do what she says and not argue or try anything behind her back. Otherwise you'll get us both in trouble."

"I'll be eighteen in the spring. Then I can do whatever I want. Maybe you can even take me flying."

"We'll cross that bridge when we come to it," John said. "Don't worry, we'll have plenty of time. All the time we want."

Even as he spoke, John felt a strange chill of foreboding. What if he was wrong? What if this was all the time they would ever have?

He had promised to have David home by nine-thirty. After they finished the pizza, and they'd exchanged phone numbers, he drove to the trim white house on the hillside and stopped in front. He'd hoped Marlena wouldn't come outside. She didn't. But he could see her silhouette against the front window sheers where she watched for her son.

"Thanks." David unbuckled his seat belt and unlatched the door. "Tonight was good. I learned a lot. I mean it."

"Can you promise me you'll think long and hard before you take another drink?" John asked.

David climbed out of the Jeep and stood at attention

next to the open door. "My name is David, and I'm an alcoholic!" he intoned in a somber voice.

John had to laugh. "Get going, you mutt!" he said.

David closed the door and walked up the porch steps. The door opened, framing Marlena in the light. Then the boy stepped inside and was gone.

All the way down the winding street and into town, John struggled to control a rush of churning emotions. He had waited more than half his son's lifetime for tonight. Though it was a simple outing, it had been all he could've hoped for. He would be counting the months until the next time.

But with so many uncertainties in life, how could he be sure the next time would ever come?

Acting on impulse, he parked the Jeep across from the hotel. There was one thing he needed right now—Emma in his arms. She should be getting off work any minute. He wouldn't stay long, but he couldn't go home to his lonely cabin tonight without seeing her.

The front door to the restaurant was already locked. He could see the dinner crew finishing the last of the cleanup. Emma glanced around and spotted him through the glass door. She smiled and turned the lock to let him in.

"So how did it go?" Pearl asked.

"Not too bad. He's a great kid."

"He is," Pearl said. "Emma, you two run along. We're almost done here."

He walked her into the lobby, where three people were standing by the desk. He ached to take her in his arms and kiss her till they both ached with need for each other, but he couldn't do it here. He hesitated, thinking it might be best to say good night and leave.

"Come on up." Emma nodded toward the stairs. Grateful, he followed her.

*   *   *

Emma's hand trembled as she turned the key in the lock. Last night, when she'd held John in her arms, he'd been weak and injured. But he appeared to have made a good recovery. It was a very different John who followed her into the room and locked the door behind them. The room was dark. Neither of them turned on the light.

She wasn't sure what to expect. She only knew that she felt safe with him, and that she loved him.

"Come here." He caught the ties of her apron, turned her around, and gathered her close. His kiss was deep and hungry, his mouth devouring hers. She went molten in his arms, loving the feel of him, the taste of him, wanting his hands in all the places her grandmother had warned her she should never let a man touch. She could feel the hard ridge of his maleness against her hips. She knew what it was, and she wasn't afraid.

She offered no resistance as he lowered her to the bed, then stretched out on his side, next to her. His kisses became gentle and tender as he cradled her close. "You know what I want, Emma," he said, brushing her hair back from her face.

"I know." She reached down and skimmed the fastening of his jeans with a fingertip that trembled slightly. What did she know about lovemaking? Her experience was limited to what she'd read in books and a few bouts of awkward groping from college boys that had left her feeling vaguely dirty. This shimmering, burning ache that surged through her body was like awakening to magic. She wanted to go where it was taking her—where *he* was taking her.

"What are you thinking?" He had propped himself on one elbow and was looking down at her in the darkness. "Are you afraid?"

"Only afraid that I'll do something stupid to spoil it for you."

He kissed her, his fingers fumbling with the buttons on her uniform. "Silly woman, nothing you could do would be stupid. But I really would like to get you out of this godawful outfit."

Feeling bolder, she asked, "Remember the last time I undressed and made you look away?"

He laughed. "Are you offering to let me look this time?"

"Do you want to?"

"I want a front row seat." He sat up, took her hands, and helped her off the bed. The room was dark, but enough moonlight filtered through the blinds for them to see each other.

She started on the buttons; but then he stood up, clasped her in his arms, and kissed her long and hard. "I have a better idea," he murmured huskily. "Let's undress each other."

They started gently, Emma shy at first. But as the urgency caught like flame to tinder, they were soon tearing at each other's clothes, hungry to caress each other skin to skin.

John's naked body was like sculpted bronze, smooth, solid and strong. She couldn't get enough of touching him, *all of him*. He moaned as she stroked him, stunned by her own boldness. When he broke away for a moment she wondered why, then realized it was to protect her.

He sat on the edge of the bed and pulled her between his knees. She pressed his head against her as he kissed her breasts, burying his face in the cleft between them. For the space of a long breath they clung like that. Then he pulled her into the bed. She was ready for him, all fear and hesitation gone. John was making love to her, her body responding to his, soaring in a world of beautiful sensations.

It was, perhaps, the best moment of her whole life.

Afterward, as she lay curled in contentment, he slipped out of bed and began pulling on his clothes.

"Can't you stay?" She looked up at him, wondering how it could be possible to love someone so much.

"I need to go now," he said. "I'll be meeting the troopers at first light. But the next time we make love, I don't want to have to get up and leave you. I want to lie all night with you in my arms, then wake up and do it all over again."

"I think I'd like that," she whispered.

"I'll make sure you like it." He leaned over and feathered a kiss across her lips. "I'll call you when I get back from the trailer site," he said. "If you don't hear from me, you'll know that I'm still with the troopers, and we're still looking for evidence."

"Be careful," she said.

"And you be careful, too. Stay in the hotel. Don't go out alone for any reason. Someday soon, this will all be over, Emma. It's got to be."

He leaned down for a last, lingering kiss. Then he turned, crossed the room, and stepped out into the dimly lit hall. The door clicked shut behind him, leaving Emma alone.

At first light John arrived at the state trooper post and met the investigation team—two troopers named Reuben and Pete, along with a dog handler named Ted and a golden Labrador named Daisy, both on loan from Juneau. The heavy-duty van was loaded and ready to go. Glancing into the open back, John saw an assortment of shovels, cameras, gloves and evidence-collecting kits, a stack of Kevlar vests, a stretcher, a carton of body bags, a cooler, and Daisy's travel crate, with the friendly dog already settled inside.

"Does she mind getting hauled on these outings?" John

asked, making conversation with Ted, a young Tlingit with long hair braided and wrapped like his own.

"Are you kidding?" Ted grinned. "She loves it. Getting out there, sniffing for stuff she's trained to find, and getting treats when she does good. It's like a game to her."

Pete, the graying trooper, was in charge. "You, up front with me." He pointed to John. "You two in the back. Let's get going."

They climbed into the vehicle. All three of the troopers were armed. On Pete's orders John had left his .44 locked in the Jeep. It made sense that the troopers wouldn't want to be responsible for an armed civilian firing a weapon. Still, John found himself wishing for the heavy pistol. No doubt Philpot had told Boone about the glasses. It would be like Boone to lurk around the area, anticipating that there would be a search. If damning evidence was found— or was about to be found—it was anybody's guess what he might do.

There wasn't much small talk on the way. John briefed the others on the location of the site and what he'd found on his previous visit. They'd all seen the photos, including the picture of Bethany Ann. According to the report, the woman had been reported missing by her fellow teachers, who'd been promised letters and photos from Alaska and had heard nothing. At least someone had cared enough about her to be concerned.

It was mid-morning when the van stopped at the edge of the clearing. The blackened frame of the trailer was still there. But even from a distance John could see that the site had been cleaned up. The gasoline cans were gone, as was some of the unburned debris. And he didn't have to guess that, when they looked under the blackberry thicket, the glasses would be gone. At least he'd taken photos. But for solid evidence, pictures couldn't compare to an actual object, which could contain invaluable DNA and finger-prints.

John swore. "Looks like the bastard got back here ahead of us."

"We'll find what we can," Pete said. "Sometimes it doesn't take much. Put on a vest. We'll do the technical stuff, but you'll be out there to answer any questions. Stay out of the way and don't touch anything. Got it?"

"Got it." John would stay out of the way, but he planned to keep his eyes and ears open for any sign of Boone.

He fastened on his Kevlar vest, along with the rest of the team. There was even a vest for Daisy. The dog stood still, her chocolate eyes bright with anticipation as Ted buckled it on her. Anybody could tell she was a pro.

"I paid for this vest myself after another dog got shot at a crime scene," Ted said. "It cost me almost a month's pay. The guys thought I was crazy, but she's family—besides, she's worth a lot more money than I am." He snapped the leash through a ring on her harness.

"Boone's a hunter," John said. "There must be plenty of animal remains around here."

Ted grinned. "Don't worry. Daisy's got that covered. Let's go, girl. Do your thing. *Find it.*"

When he gave her the command, the dog started sniffing around the edge of the clearing. Pete and Reuben had begun walking an imaginary grid, carrying their kits, their eyes on the ground. Every small thing they found was photographed and bagged for the crime lab. The glasses, as John had feared, were nowhere to be found.

John had expected to find boot prints, but Boone—assuming it *was* Boone—had wrapped his feet so that the soles would leave no pattern. Reuben took photos of the tracks and did a casting, mostly for size. They were fresh, laid down in the past couple of days. And they were big. John hadn't realized that Boone had such huge feet.

After circling the trailer, Daisy led Ted off into the woods. John followed them, wishing he'd brought his pistol. He didn't have a good feeling about this.

Daisy was onto something. She was tugging at her leash, pulling her handler deeper into the trees. John followed a few steps behind, his eyes scanning the forest, seeing nothing. A squirrel scolded from its perch in a tall cedar. Deeper in the forest, a jay squawked a warning. A flock of small, brown birds exploded, twittering, from the crown of the forest.

Through the trees, about thirty yards ahead, lay an open patch of ground, overgrown with skunk cabbage. The dog surged toward it, tugging at the leash. John's eyes caught a faint movement in the trees on the far side. "Get down—" he shouted, dropping low.

A shot rang out. The dog yelped and fell sideways. Ted crawled past John to cover the dog with his body. Acting on instinct, John grabbed the 9 mm Glock out of the trooper's hip holster, rose to his knees, and fired two shots after a fleeing figure, barely glimpsed through the shadowy forest. Long hair, hulking shoulders—it wasn't Boone. It was his older brother, Ezra.

The shots John fired had missed, as he'd expected they would. Ezra was already out of sight hidden by thick stands of spruce, cedar, and hemlock. Moments later the distant rumble of a vehicle confirmed that Ezra was gone—leaving a question that made John's blood run cold.

If Ezra was here, where was Boone?

Dressed for work, Emma checked her appearance in the mirror before leaving her room. Not that it mattered. In her baggy dress and sneakers, with her hair pulled back and no makeup, she didn't exactly look like a movie star. But as long as she showed up and did her job, what did it matter?

Although her hourly wage barely covered room and food, she was making good money in tips. Another week and she'd have enough for a cheap flight home—wherever home was these days. Her heart's desire was to stay here with John. But if there was anything life had taught her, it was that things tended not to work out—and having a Plan B was never a bad idea.

But she was getting tired. When she'd taken the job, she'd agreed to work double shifts, seven days a week. Desperate for money, she'd figured she could stand anything for two weeks. But the heavy work schedule, along with being cooped up in the hotel, was getting to her. Right now, for two cents and a day outside with John, she would bag the whole arrangement.

Through the walls, she could hear the work crew getting ready to update the next room with new paint, carpet, and bath fixtures. Her room would be next, so she would soon have to switch. Not that she minded. She'd grown used to the noise. And the workers were nice men, friendly and courteous. It was almost like having neighbors.

She'd slipped John's pistol into her pocket and was about to leave the room when she heard a knock. John had warned her not to answer to anyone, but the work crew was right next door. It was probably one of them, needing to tell her when she'd have to move her things. And she was about to leave anyway.

Without a second thought, she unfastened the three locks and opened the door. Boone's looming figure filled the frame. Before Emma could react, he shoved his way inside and closed the door behind him. He was dressed like the workmen, in paint-spattered coveralls and a baseball cap, which was probably how he'd gotten into the hotel and past the desk.

Emma had backed away from the door. As she shrank

against the dresser, a slow smile spread across his face. "Well, how about that," he said. "Just you and me."

She drew the pistol and clicked off the safety, holding it with both hands the way John had taught her. "Don't come a step closer," she said. "The gun's loaded and I know how to use it."

For an instant he looked surprised. Then he smiled, that charming old Boone smile that didn't work with her anymore. The burns on the side of his face were beginning to heal but he would never lose the scar.

"I'm not here to hurt you, honey," he said. "I just want to talk."

"Don't call me that," she said. "I've heard enough of your talk. If you want me to listen, you can give me back my money." Emma's hands were cramping around the pistol grip. Could she really shoot him?

He laughed. "That money was a wedding present, from you to me. It's mine now."

"That wasn't even a real wedding. Neither was the last one, with that other woman, was it? What happened to her, Boone?"

He shrugged. "She got mad, packed her bags, and left. At least, since it wasn't a real wedding, we didn't have to get a divorce."

"You're lying. John found her glasses and took the pictures to the police. But you already know that. And you know she's dead. I think you killed her, Boone."

What was she saying? Even if Boone hadn't come here to kill her, he was probably thinking about it now. If he came at her, could she shoot him? What if she wasn't fast enough? What if she missed?

Through the wall she could hear the sound of the machine that sprayed paint. It was loud enough to drown out a scream, but maybe not a gunshot.

His hands came up in a "calm down" gesture. "All right. I know she's dead. But it wasn't me who killed her. I swear to God. It was Ezra. He came by the trailer when I wasn't there. He wanted to share his brother's woman, and she wouldn't cooperate. Ezra's not all right in the head. That's all it took."

"Why did you come here, Boone?" She willed herself to hold the gun steady.

"To see you. To talk to you."

Liar, she thought.

"You've seen me. You've talked to me. Now get out of here before I pull this trigger." Summoning her courage she took a step toward him. "On the count of three," she said. "One . . . two . . ."

He was out the door, striding down the long hallway toward the stairs. Shaking, Emma locked the door, laid the gun on the bed, and called the police—even though she knew it would be useless. By the time they got here, Boone would be gone.

At the sound of shots, Pete and Reuben came pounding through the trees with their pistols drawn. When they saw John standing with Ted's pistol, and Ted crouched over the dog, they lowered their weapons.

Ted pulled back the vest to check Daisy for injuries. The gunshot, from a small-caliber weapon, had given her a nasty welt, but the vest had saved her life. She licked his hand, thumped her tail, and struggled to her feet, eager to finish the job she'd been trained for since puppyhood.

John returned the Glock to Ted's holster and gave the others a quick rundown on what had happened. Pete responded with a nod and a few choice curses, a subtle sign that there'd likely be no inquiry into the gunplay. Right now they had more important concerns.

Daisy was straining toward the patch of open ground. Ted gave her the lead. Moving with some pain, she reached the patch of skunk cabbage, sat down on her haunches, and gave three sharp barks.

"Good girl." Ted praised her and gave her a treat. "You heard the lady. She says there's something here."

John, Pete, and Reuben went back to the van and returned with a plastic tarp, picks and shovels, coveralls, gloves, boot covers, disposable filter masks, and a body bag, as well as Daisy's crate and water bowl. Ted had removed Daisy's vest to make her more comfortable. When the open crate was placed in the shade, she walked into it, drank some water, and lay down to rest.

John had done some digging in his time, but never like this. Every new cut of the pick or shovel was done with care, and every shovelful of earth was checked before being piled on the tarp. The fall weather was cool, but the direct sun on the open ground was hot. John's clothes were soaked with sweat under the protective coveralls. The men dug in teams of two, one pair working, the other pair guzzling water and Gatorade as they helped check the growing pile of earth.

About an hour into the dig, Reuben said, "There's something down here."

The digging became more careful. The sickly odor of decomposition rose from the soil as they dug around the buried mass. Slowly they uncovered bones, hooves, and a hide.

"Oh, hell," Pete swore. "It's a damn deer!"

Amid curses, the digging paused. Had this whole outing been a waste of time?

"No! Hang on!" Ted said as Pete and Reuben started to climb out of the hole. "I've never known Daisy to be wrong. Besides, why would anybody bury a deer out here in the woods except to hide something else? We've got to keep digging."

Pete nodded. Working together, they managed to lift the deer carcass out of the hole and lay it to one side. Under another two feet of earth, their probing shovels encountered a long, slender form bundled in a stained quilt.

Knowing what it was from the shape, they photographed it where it lay, then spread out the body bag. Gently they eased the bundle out of the earth and laid it, quilt and all, in the open bag. Before closing the zipper, Pete peeled back a fold of the quilt for a final photo. Looking down, John saw brutally smashed bones, dark hair, and the tiny gold locket he remembered from the missing persons file photo.

He couldn't hold back the moisture that blurred his eyes. "Hello at last, Bethany Ann," he said.

CHAPTER 14

By the time they'd shed their gear and finished reloading the van, everyone on the team was sweaty, smelly, and exhausted. They'd brought sandwiches in the cooler, but nobody felt like eating.

Ted and Reuben promptly fell asleep in the backseat, leaving Pete and John awake in the front. It was slow going over the network of rutted logging roads. They drove with the windows down, the cool, fresh air flowing into the cab.

"So what's next?" John asked, though he pretty much knew.

"We'll process the evidence here. The body will go to the lab in Juneau to establish the official cause of death."

"You saw the skull. Wouldn't you assume blunt force trauma?"

"Probably," Pete said. "But at this point, we can't rule out anything."

"So how soon can you arrest Boone for murder?"

As soon as the words were out of John's mouth, he knew he'd asked a useless question. The team had found Bethany Ann's body, but it had yet to be determined how she'd died, let alone that Boone had killed her. They'd found no fingerprints and no murder weapon at the scene.

He checked the urge to grind his teeth in frustration. All he wanted was for this to be over so that he and Emma could get on with their lives.

"If we had a reliable witness come forward, like maybe a family member, we could issue an arrest warrant," Pete said. "Otherwise, we'll have to sift through the evidence, which may or may not tell us anything."

"Hell, he married her in that fake ceremony. He took her to the trailer and probably took all her money. He was there—and as far as we know, he was the only one there."

"It's all circumstantial. Not enough for a conviction." Pete braked the van as two deer bounded across the road. "Traverton said you knew the family. What about the brother, the one who shot the dog? He was hanging around today, like he knew where the grave was and was trying to keep Daisy from finding it. He's the one we need to talk to."

"You could try. I could show you the family homestead on a map. But Ezra was born mentally disabled. Talking to him is like talking to a nine-year-old."

"Probably not a great bet on the witness stand. But we need to interview him all the same." Pete swung the van onto the asphalt highway and hit the gas pedal. The van shot ahead at a speed that would guarantee a record time back to the station.

John called Emma from the Jeep, parked next to the trooper station. He knew she'd be working, but he was about to head home to the cabin and would soon lose cell service.

"John?" She sounded shaken.

"Are you all right?" he asked. "Can you talk now?"

"Yes to both. The place isn't busy now. Let me step back into the hall." There was a pause. He could hear her ragged breathing. Something was wrong. "Did you find anything?" she asked.

"We found what was left of Boone's other bride. But not enough evidence to charge Boone. Not yet, at least. What is it, Emma? What's the matter?"

There was another pause. Maybe she was checking to make sure she wasn't needed in the restaurant. "Boone came into my room," she said. "He was dressed like one of the workmen, pushed his way in. I held him off with the pistol."

John's pulse lurched. "Did he hurt you?"

"No. He didn't touch me. I made him leave. But here's the thing. I told him I knew he'd murdered that woman. He swore he didn't do it. He said it was Ezra who killed her because she tried to fight him off." She took a deep breath, like someone gasping for air. "I called the police as soon as he left. Detective Traverton was there. I told him."

"But they didn't catch Boone?"

"I don't think so. Otherwise I'd have heard. I'm not sure anybody can catch Boone. He's like a ghost."

"That's what he wants you to believe. Don't let him reel you in."

After warning her to switch rooms, and promising to see her soon, John ended the call. For what seemed like a long time, he sat staring out the window of the Jeep, watching the play of low sunlight through the trees.

Ezra.

That didn't make sense. Boone's brother was strong enough to kill with his bare hands. But John had been around him enough to know that he had the simple mind of a child. True, he'd been raised as a hunter, and might shoot a dog, especially if someone told him to. But the idea that he would come on to a woman and bash her head in when she resisted didn't fit the picture.

Tired, sore, and just wanting to go home, he hesitated. Maybe he should leave well enough alone. But no, he knew what he had to do. With a weary sigh, he climbed out of the Jeep, and went into the station. Pete and Reuben would be in the garage, unloading the van and getting ready to go off duty. Ted would be headed for the airport and his flight back to Juneau with Daisy and the remains. But Sergeant Packard was still in his office. He looked up when John tapped on the open door.

"Come in and sit down," he said, pushing aside some papers on his desk. "I hear you hit pay dirt."

"We did, so to speak." John took the chair that faced the desk. "But I wanted to bring up something else. Did Traverton call you about Ezra Swenson?"

"He did. Evidently Boone named Ezra as the woman's killer. Besides that, Pete just told me that Ezra showed up at the crime scene, tried to shoot the dog, and ran off. It looks like we've got our man."

"That's why I'm here," John said. "I know how it looks. But I also know the family. They were my in-laws back in the day. Ezra's a scary-looking man. But he's mentally handicapped. And he's shy, especially around women. I can't imagine him killing one, not even if somebody like Boone told him to. Something here doesn't feel right."

Packard leaned back in his chair. "I appreciate your telling me this, but it's too late to make much difference. I got Traverton's call around eleven-thirty. By noon I'd located the homestead and sent a SWAT team out there to pick Ezra up. There was nobody home when the team arrived, but they were waiting when Ezra and his mother drove up in the truck. He surrendered without a fight. He's being booked into the county jail as we speak."

"And Boone? What about him?"

Packard shrugged. "As the only witness, he'll need to be questioned. But so far, he hasn't turned up."

"You know this case won't likely go before a jury," John said. "Innocent or guilty, Ezra won't be found competent to stand trial."

"Maybe not," Packard said. "But our job isn't to prosecute the bastards. Our job is just to catch them."

Dog tired, John drove back to the cabin. By the time he'd showered and downed a peanut butter and jelly sandwich with milk, he was ready for a good book and an early bedtime. But he remembered the strain in Emma's voice, and he knew she needed him. He needed her, too. He needed to hold her close and forget the things he'd seen, touched, and smelled today. And he needed to know that, for now at least, she was safe.

Leaving his damp hair loose, he dressed, closed the cabin, and drove back to town. From the docks, he could see her through the front window, finishing the nightly cleanup. If Boone were out here, there'd be nothing to stop him from shooting her, he thought. But that wasn't what Boone wanted. He wanted to have her, to possess her, to make her suffer in ways too awful to imagine. And now, with Ezra in jail for the murder that Boone had almost certainly committed, he would be bolder than ever.

He watched her a moment longer before he crossed the street. He'd hoped to see David, too, but his son was nowhere in sight. Maybe Marlena had put a stop to his working.

He stepped close to the window and waved. When she saw him, her face lit in a smile that made him glad he'd driven back to town. She was stunning when she smiled. It was hard to believe that he'd thought her ordinary-looking when they'd first met. There was nothing ordinary about the woman.

She unlocked the door to let him in. He held up the spare jacket he'd brought. "I thought you'd like to get out and go for a ride," he said.

"I'd love that," she said. "Just let me finish here."

Pearl came out of the kitchen and gave him a friendly greeting. "If you're looking for David, he went home early," she said. "He has a test tomorrow."

"How's he doing?" John asked. "Does he seem all right?"

"He's fine. I think you did him a lot of good." Pearl glanced toward Emma. "Go on. We're almost done here. I can finish."

"Thanks." She let him slip the jacket around her shoulders and usher her outside. As was getting to be a habit, he looked up and down the street for any sign of Boone. This excess caution was getting tiresome, but it was still necessary—now more than ever.

"Did you switch rooms?" he asked as he helped her into the Jeep.

"Yes. The new one's nicer, and the workers have promised not to let Boone onto the floor. Such kind men. Now that they know he's a danger, they've become protective of me."

"Good, but we've got a problem." He started the Jeep and headed south along the highway. "Ezra's been arrested for the murder of that woman."

"But isn't that a good thing? Boone said he killed her."

"Boone was lying. Ezra's no murderer. He may look dangerous, but he's a gentle giant, with the mind of a child. He's shy around strangers, especially women."

"Oh, no!" Emma cried. "John, this is terrible! I was the

one who called the police and reported him. This is all my fault!"

"It's not your fault, Emma. Boone played you. He knew that you'd never met Ezra, and that you'd report whatever he told you. Now Ezra's in jail for his crime, and Boone is pretty much free to come and go as he likes, which makes him all the more dangerous. Until we find a way to trip him up, you'll need to be very, very careful."

"I'm already being careful. Oh, John, that poor man! He must be so scared in jail—and I'm the one who put him there. Can you go with me to the police in the morning and tell them I made a mistake?" She was on the verge of tears.

"Not you. I'll go by myself. Maybe I can convince Traverton that Boone's the real murderer." John tried to sound encouraging, but something told him he'd have no better luck convincing Traverton than he'd had convincing Packard. Neither lawman liked being wrong.

He took the road to the boat ramp where they'd been once before, stopping the Jeep at the narrow beach. The stars cast shimmering reflections in the water. "Come here, Emma," he said, and pulled her close.

For a few quiet moments she nestled against him, quivering like a frightened animal. He wrapped her in his arms, wanting her to feel protected. His lips grazed her face, brushing her eyelids, her cheeks, and coming to rest on her sweet mouth. She was his woman, to love, keep, and protect. He wanted to build a life with her, to raise their children and grow old together.

But until he could promise to keep her safe, he had no right to speak of those things.

"This nightmare won't last forever, love," he murmured against her hair. "It will end, I promise, even if I have to end it myself."

And maybe that was the key to it all, he thought. He'd depended on the law to take Boone out of action and put him where he'd never harm Emma, or any other woman, again. But the law had failed him. It had failed Emma, and it had failed to get justice for poor Bethany Ann. Maybe it was time to take matters into his own hands.

The next day John paid a visit to Traverton to express his doubts about charging Ezra. "All you have to go on is Boone's word," he said. "And you know Boone's a liar. He tricked at least two women into fake marriages and took their money. Now he's pinning a murder he committed on his handicapped brother. That's pretty low, if you ask me."

Traverton gave him a cold look. "Just because Boone's a con artist, that doesn't mean he's a killer. As far as I'm concerned we've got our man. Ezra Swenson has been processed, arraigned, and assigned a public defender. The judge denied bail, on the grounds that he was a flight risk. My job is done. If you have anything more to say, you can say it to his lawyer. Here's the young man's card."

Robert Falconi. The name on the card had a familiar ring to it, John thought as he walked out to the Jeep. What were the odds that Ezra's public defender was related to a certain retired judge?

The law office was located above a travel agency on Grant Street. The building was nothing grand, but the law office, at the top of the stairs, was freshly remodeled with a neutral color scheme, high-end leather furniture, and original artwork on the walls. "Nice digs," John commented as the young lawyer strode into the reception area to meet him.

"Thanks." He looked about twenty-four, with thick, dark hair and an aquiline nose. "My mother has elegant taste and the money to go with it. Otherwise you'd be looking at folding chairs and a card table in here. "

"Your mother's the judge." It wasn't even a question. "You know her?"

"Some. But I'm here to talk about Ezra Swenson." He spent the next fifteen minutes filling the lawyer in on the background of the story.

"I talked to Ezra for just a few minutes," Falconi said. "But I got the impression he was a few pints short of a gallon, as they say. Until you showed up, my plan was to get him evaluated and declared incompetent to stand trial."

"That's exactly what Boone wants. His brother gets blamed for the murder, the case never goes to trial, and Boone gets off without ever having to show up."

"Are you saying that Ezra should be tried because he's innocent?"

"It would be better than shipping him off to some hospital for the criminally insane, where he'd pine away and die. What I'm saying is, before you seek a ruling on this case, you need to learn the truth. Talk to the mother, at least. Talk to Emma, too. She doesn't know Ezra but she can tell you plenty about Boone and the hellhole where he brought her."

"What about you? If this goes to trial, would you be willing to testify to what you just told me?"

"Absolutely. But that's not what you should be shooting for. Bring up enough evidence to get the case dismissed. That's what a good lawyer does."

"I'll do my best." Falconi looked young and sounded uncertain. John could only hope that the judge's son knew his job.

John had planned three errands today. The first two had ended in frustration—with a stubborn lawman and an irresolute public defender.

The third errand was different. He was about to cross the line to the dark side.

After a quick lunch, he drove to the house with the peeling blue paint—the house where Sherman Philpot lived. When he knocked on the door, it barely creaked open. Philpot's bloodshot eye glared at him through the narrow crack.

"What the hell d'you want, you sonofabitch?" he demanded. "Have you got that cop with you again?"

John shook his head. "Take it easy, man. I didn't mean for that to happen. And I'm not here to rat you out. I don't even need to come in."

"Good, 'cause I ain't invitin' you. Anything you got to say, you can say it right there."

"Fine," John said. "I know you're in touch with Boone, wherever he is. I just want you to give him a message."

"Okay. Let's have it."

"Since he's got a way of hearing things, he probably knows that I was with the state troopers when they found the body of his so-called bride. She was buried with a deer on top of her body to hide her remains."

"So?"

"The troopers combed the place for evidence, but there was one thing they missed—something that can tie Boone to the murder. The deer was mostly hide and bones, but there was a bullet in it, plain as day. When the troopers were packing up, I went back, took a picture, and put the bullet in my pocket. If I turn it over to the police, they'll run ballistics and match it to Boone's gun—or if not that, they can match it to other bullets they found in the dirt around the trailer. That'll nail him right to the wall."

"So what do you want from Boone?"

"A trade. That bullet for his promise to leave Emma in peace. He can call me. He knows my number."

"Hell, he'll laugh in your face."

"If he does, he'll end up sorry. Just tell him. Got it?"

"Got it." The door closed with a click.

John walked down the steps and back to the Jeep. He had lied. There might have been a bullet in the deer, but nobody had thought to check for it. John hadn't come up with the idea until last night, after he'd taken Emma back to the hotel.

Finding a similar bullet to pass off to Boone wouldn't be hard. There were probably some around the cabin from the game John had shot for meat.

Of course, he knew better than to think Boone would keep his promise to leave Emma alone. But that wasn't the idea. The plan was to click the recorder on his phone and get Boone talking. With luck, by the time the exchange was made, he'd have a recorded confession.

Now that he thought about it, it struck him as a crazy idea, like something out of a bad TV crime show. He couldn't begin to count the number of things that could go wrong. For all he knew, he could end up dead. But he had taken the first step. Now he had to see it through. He wouldn't tell Emma about the plan until it was over. She would only worry.

He was halfway home when his phone signaled an incoming text. He pulled off the road to read it.

Mr. Wolf, please contact me about the recovery of your airplane. If you're available for the next few days, I might be able to help you.

There was a phone number. John's pulse leaped. The problem of getting the Beaver repaired had kept him awake nights. If this was a solution, he would have to go for it.

If need be, his plan to trap Boone would have to wait a few days. Getting his plane back had to come first.

* * *

Emma cleaned up after the lunch rush and took her break, such as it was. Since she'd promised John that she wouldn't go out alone, she picked up the chicken sandwich the kitchen staff had made her, along with a cold soda, and took it upstairs to her room. Here, at least, she could eat in peace and quiet, put her feet up, and maybe do a little reading.

Part of her was counting the days until this work marathon was done. But with so many uncertainties hanging over her, she had no solid plan for what to do next. Should she look for a cheap apartment and another job, maybe as a substitute teacher or aide? Should she cut her strings here and fly back to the life she'd left behind? Could she count on staying with John, even though he had yet to mention that possibility?

Until Boone was out of the picture, there was no way she could make a decision.

John had called her last night. He'd gotten a text from a salvage dealer with a boat who could get him to his damaged plane with replacement parts and tools to do the work. The price was better than expected, but the man had other business and would only be available for the next couple of days, which meant John would need to leave first thing in the morning. He would be gone for at least two days, maybe longer. Again, he'd cautioned Emma to be careful and stay inside the hotel.

It was hard, having him gone at such a critical time. But Emma understood how much John depended on the Beaver for his work, and more. The plane was his lifeline to the sky and the freedom he loved. Without it, he was an eagle with broken wings. She couldn't begrudge him the time it took to recover it.

A glance at the clock told her the break was over. David would be coming in soon to start his shift. She'd grown genuinely fond of John's bright, cheerful son, but except for work chatter, they'd never had a chance to talk. She found herself wishing for a chance to know him better.

After washing her hands, she gathered up her plate, left the room locked, and went back downstairs.

The restaurant tended to be quiet at this time of day, between late lunch and early dinner. But as she crossed the lobby, she heard the sound of voices. One of them, a woman's, was shrill with anger.

"You get on that phone and call her, Pearl! Get my daughter here right now! This is family business, and, damn it, she's family!"

Emma's first impulse was to stay where she was. But that wasn't her job. Pushing aside a dark premonition, she walked through the connecting door.

Besides Pearl, there were two people in the restaurant. One, an elderly man with a nervous look, was getting up to leave. He slunk out with his meal unfinished and his cash on the table. The other, a woman, was standing in the middle of the room, surrounded by empty tables. Emma recognized her at once. Although she'd only seen her from a distance, there could be no mistaking Lillian, the matriarch of the Swenson clan.

Emma walked back to stand next to Pearl, as if in support. She wondered if Boone had shown his mother the school photo she'd given him, but to her relief, Lillian only glanced at her, with no sign of recognition.

"All right, Lillian," Pearl said. "I'll call Marlena, but only if you'll sit down and be still. Would you like some coffee? Maybe a doughnut or some pie, on the house?"

Lillian sank onto a chair with a weary sigh. Dressed in jeans, boots, and a man's lumberjack-style coat, she was a portly woman, but powerfully built, as if she'd spent a lifetime doing heavy work. Her thin, gray hair was pulled into a knot at the back of her head.

"I'll take some black coffee and a slice of your apple pie with ice cream," she said. At a nod from Pearl, Emma scurried off to get her what she'd asked for.

Moments later, when Emma came out of the kitchen, Pearl was still on the portable landline phone. Bending close, she placed the coffee and pie, along with a napkin and utensils, on the table. "Here you are," she said, getting her first good luck at the woman.

Weathered by wind, sun, and time, Lillian's creased face told a story of hard work, rough living, and disappointment. Her husband had either died or run off. Of the three children she'd raised alone, one son was weak in his mind, the other son was a lying sociopath, and her daughter had cut all ties to the family. Now the one child who'd stayed with her, maybe even loved her, was in jail for an awful crime he hadn't committed.

Looking into Lillian's bloodshot blue eyes, Emma caught a glint of tears.

I'm sorry, she wanted to say. *This is all my fault.* But she knew that would only make matters worse.

Without thanking her, Lillian took a forkful of pie and shoveled it into her mouth. Her hands were chapped and callused, another testament to the rough life she'd led.

Pearl was still on the phone. Placing her hand over the receiver, she turned to Lillian. "Marlena's not coming. She says that you're no longer family to her, and your problems are none of her business."

Lillian rose to her feet, upsetting the coffee cup. "Give me the damn phone!" She snatched it out of Pearl's hands. "Listen, you ungrateful little bitch, your brother Ezra's in jail for something he didn't do! They think he murdered a woman, out at Boone's trailer. You're still our blood. If that means anything to you—"

She went silent. The phone dropped to the table as she stared.

David had just walked into the restaurant.

CHAPTER 15

Pearl picked up the phone. "Marlena, you might want to get down here," she said, and hung up.

David glanced from Lillian to Pearl as if to ask, *What's going on here?* From the stories she'd heard, Emma guessed that the boy hadn't seen his mother's family since he was small. He didn't appear to recognize the woman standing at the table, staring at him.

Lillian spoke. "I know you. Ain't you Marlena and John's boy? David. Ain't that your name?"

David still looked puzzled, but he was a polite young man. "Yes," he said. "But my parents aren't married anymore. They're—"

"Don't you know me, boy?" she demanded. "I'm your grandma!"

Emma had moved to a spot near the front door to intercept any customers who might walk in on the drama. From where she stood, she could see the emotions warring in David's young face as he tried to make sense of what he'd just been told. She saw surprise, then denial, then at least a measure of acceptance.

"Well?" At least Lillian wasn't holding out her arms for a hug. "Don't you remember me at all? Hell, boy, when you was born, I was the one who delivered you. I was the first one to hold you. You was the cutest little black-haired thing. When I gave you to your dad, he was shaking so hard I was afraid he was gonna drop you. You don't remember me at all?"

David shook his head. "I was pretty little back then."

"And your mother never told you about me?"

"Mom never talked about you much. So I don't really feel like I know you." He managed a smile. "But maybe we can start over from here."

He held out his hand. Lillian seized it, clasping it hard. It wasn't a hug, but it was something, at least.

Emma felt a surge of emotion. *Well played, David,* she thought. *John would be proud of you.*

Moments later, a familiar black Escalade screeched to a halt outside. Marlena flung herself out of the driver's seat and strode into the restaurant. "You, David, into the car," she said. "Now."

David stood his ground. "Sorry, Mom, but I can't leave. I'm at work."

"Then get to work. There's plenty of it waiting for you in here." Pearl steered him into the kitchen, disarming the standoff before it happened. Emma moved back to her place at the door. There'd be customers coming soon, and this wasn't her battle to fight.

Mother and daughter faced each other across the table. "Well, I see you ain't changed," Lillian said. "You're as bossy as ever."

"Stay away from my son!" Marlena snapped. "I mean it, Mother. I don't want you near him."

The defiance went out of Lilian. Her shoulders sagged. "I ain't here about your son," she said. "I'm here to beg for your help. For Ezra. You know he can't be locked up in that jail. He'll die. Please, Marlena. Ezra never hurt you like Boone did. He was always kind. And he's your own flesh and blood."

Marlena sighed. "What is it you need me to do?"

"Just go with me to talk to the police, and to his lawyer, if he's got one. They won't listen to an old woman like me. But they will if you're there to back me up. That's all I'm askin'."

Marlena sighed. "Oh, all right. Let me make some calls first."

Pearl stepped up. "We've got customers coming in. I'll let you two into the dining room. You can talk and make calls in there. I'll have Emma bring you something to drink. More coffee, Lillian?"

"Yes, and you can bring that pie for me to finish."

"Just coffee for me," Marlena said.

Pearl opened the unused dining room and they took a table near the door. Emma eavesdropped shamelessly while she served them, finding excuses to wipe the tables and straighten the chairs nearby. Marlena usually treated her as if she were invisible. Today that was an advantage.

A call to the police station got Marlena the phone number of Robert Falconi, Ezra's court-appointed lawyer. She called him, and they talked for a few minutes while Lillian finished her pie and ice cream. After Marlena had ended the call, she turned to her mother.

"We're going to see the lawyer in a few minutes," she said. "He's going to ask you some questions. He told me what they'd be. I want you to be ready. No surprises. So let's practice. Pretend I'm him, asking you. First, did Ezra know where the trailer was?"

"We both knew," Lillian said. "It was Boone's private place. He didn't want us snoopin' around there, so we stayed away."

"Did Ezra ever go there alone?" Marlena asked.

Lillian shook her head. "The trailer and the homestead are about twenty miles apart. You know that Ezra couldn't ever learn to drive. When we go to town or anywhere else, I always take him. That's how I know he couldn't have gone to Boone's trailer and killed that poor woman."

"Could he have walked that far?"

"He's got bad knees. Rheumatism. I think it came on young from him bein' so big."

"All right, another question. When the state troopers were at the trailer site, Ezra was seen running away after he shot a search dog. How do you explain that?"

Lillian sighed and sipped the coffee Emma had poured to refill her cup. "Boone came by the day before. He said the lawmen would be nosin' around his property, and there was things he didn't want them to find. Lord, I was thinkin' maybe drugs, not a body. Anyway, he said that if they had a dog, Ezra was supposed to shoot it. I drove us there and waited in the truck while Ezra went in through the trees. He cried after he had to shoot that dog."

"Well, for what it's worth, Mr. Falconi mentioned that the dog was all right."

"Thank goodness. Ezra will be glad for that."

"Do you and Ezra always do what Boone tells you to?"

"Boone was born mean, and he's growed up meaner. You know that, Marlene. It don't pay to rile him. It's easier to just do like he says."

"So if Ezra didn't kill that woman and bury her, who do you think did it?"

Lillian didn't answer. She was quietly weeping.

Emma was clearing the table in the dining room after the two women left, putting the cups and saucers on a tray, when David wandered in. He stood for a moment, watching her. "Sorry, I guess that's my job you're doing," he said.

"Don't worry, it's almost done." Emma sprayed the table, wiped it clean, and looked up at him. "Are you all right, David?"

He shrugged, looking vaguely troubled. "I guess so. I was just thinking, a few weeks ago everything was normal. I was starting school, hanging out with my friends, wanting a car, and needing a job to pay for it. Then I came here to work, and it's like my whole life's gone a little crazy."

"Crazy how?" Emma asked, pleased that he was opening up to her.

He frowned, as if groping for words. "It's mostly family, I guess. My mother's life before she married Carl—my dad—has always been like this . . . this brick wall. She never talks about the family she grew up with. And she only mentions John because he's how I got here. All she's ever said about him was that he was a no-good drunk and an unfit father, and that's why she got custody of me. Oh—and that he was an Indian. That's why I'm so dark. I guess her family never liked Indians much. I knew who he was, but that's about all."

"So how's that crazy?" She knew but she wanted to hear it from him.

"Just . . . you know. Finding out that my real father isn't such a jerk after all. And finding out that I can choose not to be an alcoholic like he was. He taught me that. It's been crazy, but it's been good crazy. It's helped me understand myself better."

"He really loves you, you know," Emma said. "All these years, he's wanted to be in your life, but he's stayed away because he didn't want to stir up trouble with your family. You know that little bike that I have in the storage closet? It's really yours. He bought it for your twelfth birthday, and then he wasn't allowed to give it to you." She looked him up and down. "I'd offer it to you now, but I think you've outgrown it."

He grinned. "He must like you a lot, or he wouldn't have let you take it. I get the feeling you like him, too. If there's a chance you could end up being my stepmom, I want you to know that it's cool with me."

Emma felt the heat rise in her face. "Thanks, but it's way too soon to talk about that," she said. "What about today? I thought you handled the surprise really well. Are you all right with that?"

"You mean with having a redneck grandma I don't even remember? I could get used to that, I guess. She didn't seem too bad. Not that my mom's about to let me spend any time with her. And I guess I've got two uncles. I don't know much about them."

Emma wondered how much he'd heard after Pearl hustled him off to the kitchen. He might have been listening. But it wasn't her place to tell him about Boone and Ezra, she decided. That should be left to Marlena.

"Hey, you two." Pearl stood in the doorway to the dining room. "We've got customers coming in. Time to get back to work."

Emma hurried back into the restaurant. David had stopped and was talking to Pearl. Emma was close enough to hear their conversation. "Aunt Pearl, there's a big football game at school tomorrow afternoon. I'd really like to go with my friends. Would it be okay if I took tomorrow off? There's a party after, but I don't need to go. I could come in when the game's over."

Pearl looked displeased. "You really need to take this job more seriously, David. But all right, just this once. And don't worry about coming in after the game. You can work extra hours on the weekend if you want the time. Now get busy!"

David went off to the kitchen. Emma grabbed a handful of menus, fixed her face in a welcoming smile, and hurried to the door to greet her customers.

The dinner hour was even busier than usual, with a private wedding party in the dining room. Emma, David, and an extra server hired for the night had worn themselves out running between the tables, the bar, and the kitchen.

By the time Marlena picked up David at ten o'clock, Emma was dead on her feet. The pistol in her pocket felt as heavy as a sledgehammer as she carted the last load of dishes to the kitchen, crossed the lobby, and climbed the stairs to the third floor. A hot soak in the tub and a night between clean sheets would be pure heaven.

She unlocked the door, and, as was her habit, drew her pistol and scanned the room before stepping over the threshold. What she saw made her gasp. There on the dresser, resplendent in a cut glass vase, was a lavish bouquet of two dozen red roses.

Her heart slammed. Such a romantic gesture didn't seem typical of John, but the man was full of surprises. Emma checked the closet and the bathroom before locking the door. The scent of the flowers, almost dizzying in its sweetness, filled the room.

A small white envelope with her name on it was attached to the bouquet with a plastic clip. Heart pounding, Emma opened it and read the card inside—a single line.

Soon, my love.

Very romantic. Yes, the flowers could be from John, but how did they get into her room? She had to find out.

Locking her door, she hurried back downstairs to the lobby. "There are flowers in my room," she said.

The girl, one of several who worked the late shift, smiled. "Yes, I know. Aren't they lovely?"

"Were you here when they came? Can you tell me who delivered them?"

"Yes," the girl said. "It was the woman who runs the flower shop. I know her. They came about six. Since you were working, and I was afraid they'd wilt, I took the liberty of putting them in a vase we had here and taking them up to your room. I hope that was okay."

"Yes, it was fine. Thanks." Emma went back upstairs to her room. The scent of roses washed over her as she stepped inside and locked the door. She picked up the card, which she'd tossed on the bed to go downstairs. The message on the card was hand-printed, probably by the florist, which meant they would have been ordered by phone or online— something John could have done, even from Sitka. And they were truly beautiful, every flower perfect. They must have been very expensive.

Soon, my love . . .

So why was she feeling troubled?

She was in love with John. The giddy, pulse-pounding magic she felt when she was with him was all too familiar. She recognized it because she'd felt the same sensations when she was with Boone, and he had all but destroyed her.

She'd been head over heels in love with Boone without ever knowing who he really was. Now, less than two weeks later, she was in love with John. Could she trust her inexperienced heart? Did she even know what real love was?

Could she love John unconditionally? After what had happened the last time, could she give herself to him with complete trust, holding back nothing, for the rest of her life? If the answer was yes, why was she saving her restaurant tips for that "Plan B" airline ticket?

Was she afraid that he'd turn out to be like Boone?

Soon, my love . . .

After laying her gun on the nightstand, she walked into the bathroom, stripped down, and washed the aromas of fish, burger grease, and French fries from her skin and hair. Then she pulled on John's thermals, laid the card on the nightstand, and crawled into bed. Usually she enjoyed an hour of reading before she fell asleep. Tonight she was exhausted. With her senses awash in the fragrance of roses, she drifted into sleep.

She'd just begun to dream when her cell phone rang. The sound startled her awake. She sat bolt upright, her heart pounding as the phone rang again, then again. Reminding herself that only John and Judge Falconi had the number of her disposable phone, she picked up the call.

It was John, sounding upbeat. "Good news," he said. "We put the new float on the plane and towed it to Sitka. The repair work on the wing will be done tomorrow morning. The engine started up fine. Unless we find problems on the test flight tomorrow, I should be back in Refuge Cove in time to kiss you good night."

"That's great to hear," she said, wondering if he was waiting for her to mention the roses. "I have good news for you, too. Thanks to Marlena and her mother, Ezra's likely going to be cleared of the murder charge. I'll find out for sure tomorrow."

"Marlena and her mother? I never thought I'd live to see that." He chuckled, then his voice grew serious. "If Ezra's cleared, there won't be anybody for the law to go after except Boone. It's about time they put that murderer behind bars. Has there been any sign of him?"

"None that I know of. If Ezra goes free and Boone gets word of it, he could be on the run."

"Don't count on it. He could be anywhere. Stay in the hotel and keep your gun close by until you know for sure he's been arrested."

"I'll be careful," Emma promised. "And by the way, thank you for the roses. They're beautiful."

"Roses?"

Her heart seemed to stop. She knew. "Roses and a note."

"Emma, I didn't send you roses. I didn't send you anything."

Her body had gone cold. "He's playing with me, isn't he? Like a cat playing with a mouse!" She was shaking, as much from anger as from fear. How could she not have realized, as soon as she saw those roses, that Boone had sent them?

Soon, my love. He was taunting her.

"He's planning something, Emma," John said. "Don't do anything until I get back tomorrow. You might even want to call in sick and stay in your room. If he's not in jail by the time I get there, I'll deal with him myself. He'll never hurt you again, I promise. Now double-check your door and get some rest."

Get some rest.

That was a joke, Emma thought as she ended the call with yet another promise to be careful. As long as Boone was stalking her, there would be no rest. She would be hunted prey.

After placing the phone on the nightstand, she went to the door and made sure all three locks were securely fastened. The flowers sat in the vase on the dresser—their color bloodred, their cloying scent reminding her of the funerals she'd sat through, the loved ones she'd lost—her parents, who'd died in a car crash when she was in her early teens, and later, her grandmother, who'd slipped away at eighty-seven.

The single window in Emma's room was on the back of the building, overlooking an alley. The window appeared to be painted shut, but when she unlatched the top and pushed upward on the sash, it moved easily. A cold night wind blew into the room as she carried the vase to the open window, leaned over the sill, and dumped the flowers into the alley below. Then she snatched up the note and envelope, ripped them into tiny pieces, and tossed them after the roses.

For several minutes she left the window open, letting the fresh air flow into the room. But even after she closed it, crawled back into bed, and huddled shivering under the covers, the fragrance lingered to haunt her memory.

Soon, my love . . .

John had never been more anxious to get home. As he followed the jagged coastline south, with the Beaver performing well, his thoughts turned again and again to Emma.

The call he'd made to Sergeant Packard early that afternoon confirmed that Ezra Swenson had been released to go home with his mother, and that the troopers and local police had put out a dragnet for Boone. But so far, Bethany Ann's killer was nowhere to be found.

It made sense that, with Ezra cleared of the murder, Boone would either be running for the Canadian border, hiding out in the remote bush, or maybe on a boat, bound for some faraway part of Alaska. But as of last night it appeared he was still close by, and still intent on tormenting Emma.

Boon was obsessed with her—an obsession that made him reckless, vindictive, and as dangerous as a rabid wolf. If he was determined enough to get to her, even the hotel would no longer be safe.

John had phoned her that morning after a sleepless night. The strain in her voice had told him that her nerves were frayed to the breaking point. She needed him. And the need to be there to protect her was like a cry inside him.

He thought of the ruse he'd put in place two days ago, passing word through Philpot that he had vital evidence to trade. He could have saved himself the trouble. By now, the police and troopers knew that Boone was the killer they were looking for. Boone wouldn't care about getting the bullet, and any confession from him would be superfluous.

It didn't matter, as long as they caught the bastard and put him away for the rest of his life.

The sun was low in the sky, its fading light touching the clouds with flame. Each day seemed shorter than the last. Now he could see scattered lights along the coast, growing brighter. He slowed the engine and lowered the flaps for a smooth descent to the water.

By the time he taxied into Refuge Cove, docked the Beaver, and climbed into the Jeep, it was nightfall. Unless she'd decided to stay in her room, Emma would be working. Wherever she was, he didn't want to let her out of his sight until Boone was caught.

Without taking time to check the cabin, he drove into town. He could have called Emma from Refuge Cove, but if she was working or resting in her room, it would be best not to disturb her with a call. Either way, he wouldn't relax until he set eyes on her.

Relief swept over him as he parked across the street and spotted her through the window of the restaurant. She was working. She was all right.

As he opened the door and stepped inside, she gave him a passing smile. But he could see the weary shadows around her eyes. She looked ready to drop.

John found an out-of-the-way table. He took a seat to wait for Emma to get a free moment. He couldn't see David. Maybe the boy was in the kitchen.

Pearl crossed the room to his table. "That girl's about to collapse," she said. "You need to get her out of here and see that she gets some rest. Tell her I said it was fine. We're not that busy tonight."

"Thanks, I'll do that. Where's David, by the way?"

"He begged off for a ball game at school. Something tells me his heart isn't in this job. If he wasn't my nephew, I'd fire his little butt." She smiled as she said it, assuring John that David's job was in no danger.

Emma stopped by the table on her way back to the kitchen. "I just told this man to get you out of here," Pearl said to her. "Go on. You're a wreck. I can close."

"You're sure?"

"Just go."

"Thanks. I could use a break." Emma glanced down at her uniform, then at John. "Can you wait while I change? I got splattered with spaghetti sauce earlier."

"I can go up with you," he said, thinking of her safety.

"Don't bother. I'll only be a minute. Then I want to get out of here." She hurried off toward the lobby and vanished up the stairs.

Pearl brought John a Coke while he waited. He sipped it, feeling a vague uneasiness. Maybe he should have insisted on going upstairs with her. Boone had shown himself capable of reaching her almost anywhere. What if he'd found his way into the hotel and was waiting for her in the hallway outside her door?

Maybe he should call and make sure she was all right. He took his phone out of his pocket and scrolled to her number. But before he could make the call, he saw her come into the lobby, wearing jeans, a sweater, and her quilted jacket.

He joined her, and they walked outside, into the chilly night. He checked the street as they crossed. He even checked around and inside the Jeep before he let her in. But there was no sign of Boone anywhere. Maybe he was being overly cautious. Maybe Boone was on the run, after all.

"Hungry?" he asked her, starting the Jeep.

"Not really, unless you are. Just drive. That would be fine."

He turned onto Grant Street, planning to circle up and around the park, maybe stop for a while if she wanted, and then come back. He'd gone just a few blocks when his phone rang. David's name came up on the caller ID.

Alarms went off in his head as he took the call. He'd given David his number the night they went out. But why would the boy be calling him?

"David? Are you all right?"

There was a beat of silence.

"Howdy there, brother." Boone's voice triggered a chill that passed like an icy blade through his body. "I hear you want to make a trade."

CHAPTER 16

"What do you want, Boone?" John's pulse slammed as he pulled the Jeep to the side of the street. He willed himself to speak calmly. Emma was staring at him, frozen in horror.

Boone's laugh was pure, cold evil. "I'll give you one guess. You've got something I want. I've got something you want. We get together, we make a trade. Your son for my woman. Everybody wins."

Shock and denial struck John like a blast. This had to be some kind of hideous joke, he tried to tell himself. Any minute now, Boone would laugh, admit that it was all a prank, and end the call, just like he might have done in the old days.

But the situation was all too real. Boone had his son, and his only hope of saving the boy was to accept it and act calmly and deliberately.

"How do I know you've got David?" he demanded. "How do I know he's alive?"

"He's alive, all right. And it's up to you to keep him that way. Here, take a listen, brother." There was the sound of fumbling and a noise like ripping tape, a pause, and a voice.

"Let me go, you filthy piece of—"

The rest of the words were cut off by what sounded like a blow. But the voice was unmistakably David's. Hearing it was like a knot of barbed wire twisting tight around John's heart. He pictured his son bound and taped, maybe in pain, surely scared, but still defiant. In spite of everything he felt proud of the boy.

Boone laughed again. "Satisfied?"

"Where are you?"

"Remember the fun we used to have with those old paintball games? Wait about fifteen minutes. Then come alone, just you and the woman, and we'll make the trade. No weapon. If the cops show up, I'll kill the boy. You know I can do it. I've already killed once. I don't have a damned thing to lose."

"So why did you kill Bethany Ann?" *Keep him talking. Stall any way you can while you look for his vehicle. He has to be somewhere close in order to know you're out here with Emma. He might even be watching you.*

John pulled the Jeep away from the curb, turned around, and drove slowly back toward the docks, looking up and down the streets. He was aware of Emma, leaning close to hear the conversation. She was shaking.

"I got tired of the bitch," Boone said. "Always whining and wanting to go home. She couldn't cook worth a damn, and she was like cold mashed potatoes in bed. I couldn't let her leave. She'd seen too much of my business, and I'd pretty much spent her money, so there wasn't much use keeping her around."

"How did you do it?"

"Waited till her back was turned and whacked her in the head with a log splitter's maul. The bitch went down like she didn't feel a thing. Pretty smart the way I buried her with that deer, don't you think?"

The man was insane. And John could see no vehicle that might be his. If he could get a description, he could call the troopers and have them stop it on the highway. But Boone was probably aware of that, and he was too wily to let it happen. He knew every back road and shortcut in the county. If he didn't want to be seen, he wouldn't be.

"You're not that smart. You didn't fool the dog," John said.

"Well, I won't make that mistake again. I've said enough. You know the plan. Don't make me kill this boy." Boone ended the call.

Emma had heard the conversation, and she knew what John was facing. Still, she wasn't prepared when he pulled up in front of the hotel and stopped. "Get out and go inside, Emma," he said.

"No." Her answer came without hesitation.

"Go on. I'll find a way to rescue David. I'll do anything I have to, even if it means killing the bastard. But I can't ask you to go back to him."

"I'm the one Boone wants," she argued. "If I'm there, it will give us the best chance of getting David back. At least we'll have more options."

John didn't answer. She gazed at his grim profile in the darkness and understood the agonizing choice he faced. She couldn't allow him to make it. She would have to make it for him.

Maybe that's what love was.

"You have to take me with you," she said, knowing what that could mean for her. "We've got to do this together."

Without a word, John pulled the Jeep away from the curb and headed up the highway toward Ward Cove. Emma knew the place where Boone had said he'd be waiting with David. It was the old pulp mill site, closed down more than twenty years ago. John had mentioned breaking in there with a gang of teenagers to play paintball.

She tried to picture the place in her mind, the way John had pointed it out to her. She closed her eyes, struggling to bring back every detail. The largest warehouse was in use, but there were other buildings farther down the long, flat stretch of the dock, which extended past the water's edge.

She should have noticed more—doors, windows, fences, empty spaces, but at the time she'd seen the place, she'd barely given it a look. This was the best she could do.

Her pistol was in the zippered pocket of her jacket. The one thing she didn't have was her cell phone. She'd left it in the hotel room with her work clothes. That ruled out any chance she might have to call for help.

They'd gone about five miles up the highway when John's phone rang again. Without slowing the Jeep or checking the caller ID, John snatched the phone out of his pocket. "Boone?"

"What in heaven's name is going on?" Marlena's shrill voice carried to Emma's ears. "David hasn't come home yet. He's not answering his phone. I'm worried sick. Is he with you? Tell me the truth!"

"He's not with me. I can't talk now, Marlena. I'll call you later." He ended the call and dropped the phone into the cup holder.

She needs to know the truth, Emma thought. But she knew that John was in no position to tell her. And this was no time to argue with him. Marlena would call the police. But the police wouldn't know where to look or what to do. She and John were on their own.

John turned the Jeep into Ward Cove and headed for the gate to the pulp mill. The gate appeared padlocked, but when he got out of the Jeep, he saw that the lock had been cut and was simply hanging in place. Boone had been there ahead of him. It was easy to remove the lock and swing the gate open.

Back in the Jeep, he switched the headlights on high beam and drove through. The glaring lights would help him see ahead. They would also shine into Boone's eyes, making it hard to see what was directly in front of him. It was a small advantage, but right now everything counted.

Emma sat silent beside him, trusting him to do whatever was the right thing—trusting him to have a plan. But in this dark hour, his only plan lay in the certainty that he couldn't lose either of the two people he loved more than life.

He recognized the warehouse where he'd played as a teen, but the building, which stood next to the dock, was dark. Picking up his phone, he brought up David's number and called it. Boone answered. "I see you're here. Have you brought my lovely bride?"

"Emma's here. I want to see my son."

Something stirred in the shadows beyond the light. Someone—it had to be Boone—was standing outside, near the open doorway. John's pistol was under the seat but he couldn't risk using it. Not until he knew where David was.

"Leave the phone and get out of the vehicle, both of you," Boone ordered. "Put your hands up and walk into the light where I can have a look at you. If I see a weapon, the boy will be the first one to die."

John put down the phone and glanced at Emma. "Don't get out. No matter what he says, stay right where you are."

Leaving the pistol, he climbed out of the Jeep and walked into the circle of light. "Her, too," Boone said. "Get her out here."

"Not until I've seen David. Nothing's going to happen until you bring him out where I can see him."

He waited, refusing to move. Boone wouldn't really kill David, he told himself. Without his hostage he'd have nothing to bargain with. But then, Boone wasn't sane. It wasn't safe to assume anything.

When John got out of the Jeep, Emma was tempted to grab the phone and call Marlena, or call 911 to bring the police. But that would only make the situation more dangerous, and she was running out of time. John had left his .44 under the seat. Trying to use it could get David or John killed. But the little Kel-Tec was still zipped into her jacket, its shape barely visible inside the quilted pocket. Boone wouldn't expect her to have a gun, and even if he did, the small pistol might escape his notice.

John was unarmed, and Boone had nothing to lose by killing him. But Boone wouldn't kill her. If that was all he'd wanted, she'd be dead by now. Boone wanted her alive, so he could torment her. That, and the hidden gun, gave her advantages that John didn't have.

John had ordered her to stay in the Jeep no matter what. But if she wanted both John and David to live, she would have to act, and act decisively.

In the beam of the headlights, she could see that Boone had brought David out the door of the warehouse, holding him like a shield. David's mouth and wrists were bound with silver duct tape. His ankles were hobbled with rope so he could walk a little but couldn't run. The pistol in Boone's hand was pressed against his temple. David's eyes were wide with terror. Emma could imagine what the sight of him was doing to John.

She'd rolled down the window of the Jeep to hear what was being said. What she heard was Boone laughing. "See, your boy's just fine, bro. But he's a scrappy one. Put up a right good fight before I got him under control. It'd be a real shame to have to put a bullet through his head, wouldn't it?"

"The boy's your own flesh and blood, Boone. Doesn't that count for anything?" John was clearly stalling for time, waiting for an unguarded moment. But any move he made would be risky for both him and David. Emma knew what she had to do.

Boone laughed again. "Hell, that crap-assed sister of mine wouldn't spit on our family. She's no kin of mine in the way it counts, and neither is her boy. Now tell my woman to get out of that Jeep and get her butt over here before I get an itchy trigger finger."

Emma opened the door, climbed out of the Jeep, and strode into the headlights. "Let the boy go, honey," she said. "I'm here, and as soon these two no-accounts are on their way, I'll be ready for a real man. I'm all yours."

Even without seeing or touching him, she could feel John's tension. He'd ordered her to stay put. But it was as if they'd both known the truth—the only way to save David was for her to defy him. All he could do now was trust her.

Had she overdone her performance? But no, Boone was enough of a narcissist to lap up every word. He was even grinning.

"Come on," she said, walking toward him with a seductive sway of her hips. "We can't get the good stuff started while we've got company. Just let the boy go. Let his daddy drive him out of here before somebody sees that open gate and calls the police."

Boone's gaze narrowed. Maybe she'd overdone her act after all. "No tricks," he said, still holding the pistol to David's head. "You come over here and stand next to me. Then I'll think about turning the boy loose."

Knowing better than to take a false step, Emma walked to stand at his elbow. The door behind them was partway open. Emma's hand brushed its cold metal surface. "Here I am," she whispered in Boone's ear. "Now what do you say we get out of here?"

She felt him tense. Boone was strong, and he had the reflexes of a cougar. As long as he had his gun on David, there was no way she could outmaneuver him. Even with the pistol in her pocket, she could do nothing until John and his son were safe. She could only react to whatever move Boone chose to make.

When he made it, she had no time to prepare. In a single motion, he shoved David forward onto his face, yanked Emma through the door, and slammed it shut behind them. She was still fumbling to unzip her pocket and get to her pistol when he slid the heavy bolt and turned around with his gun pointed at her.

"Pretty good show out there, baby," he said. "But you didn't have me fooled. When we get to where we're headed, I'm going to make you scream."

The warehouse was a cavernous space, most of it empty. The only light, falling through high windows and two glass skylights in the roof, was cast by the waning moon. Emma could see her way, and she could see Boone, standing next to her, gripping her arm, but little else.

She imagined John outside the door, picking up his son and helping him to the Jeep. They would be all right, but there was no way he could get past the locked door to help her. It was time to fight for her life.

"Please, Boone." The fingers of her free hand had made it past the zipper to the gun in her pocket. Her fingertip disengaged the safety. She couldn't get the gun out without his seeing it, but maybe she wouldn't have to.

"Please let me go," she begged, trying to distract him.

"Without me along, you can make a clean getaway. You can start over somewhere, make a new life."

"Sorry, babe, but I can't leave you behind," he said. "You set the fire that burned me and turned me into a freak. No way am I letting you go. But I'll give you a choice. Either you come with me, or I shoot you right here. What's your answer?"

She'd found the trigger. Twisting the gun inside the pocket, she turned and forced herself to kiss him. But the kiss was awkward enough to make him suspicious. She was just squeezing the trigger when he shoved her arm. The shot went wild. The gun's recoil knocked her hand out of her pocket and sent her staggering backward. The weapon skittered across the floor, into the dark.

"You little bitch!" Boone slapped her so hard that she saw stars. "I could kill you now, but that would take the fun out of it. Come on, let's go."

Yanking her arm, he dragged her toward something she hadn't noticed until now. Framed by a low wooden rail was an opening in the floor with a stairway leading down to the water under the dock. At the foot of the stairway, barely visible in the dim, reflected light, was a boat.

As Boone dragged her down the stairway, Emma could see the boat more clearly. It was an open sport boat with an inboard motor, the kind of craft that might be used for water skiing or light fishing. It would make for a clever getaway. No one would see Boone leaving with her until it was too late to stop him.

Emma tried to keep fighting, but Boone was a powerful man, and by now she was exhausted. He dragged her down the last few steps and shoved her forward into the boat. As she fell, something struck her head. Stunned but still conscious, she lay still.

* * *

John had pulled the tape off David's mouth, freed his hands, and was about to help him up when he heard the gunshot from inside the warehouse. He recognized the report of a small pistol, most likely the Kel-Tec he'd given Emma. But he had no way of knowing what had happened.

David was sitting up, looking pale and shaken. "I'm fine," he said. "Go."

John ran to the jeep, grabbed his .44 from under the seat, and sprinted back to the door of the warehouse. That was when he discovered the door was made of painted sheet metal and securely bolted from the inside. From inside he could hear Boone's voice, fading with distance. So Boone was still alive, but did he still have Emma?

Mouthing something between a curse and a prayer, he raced around the corner of the building to look for another entrance. Then from underneath the far end of the dock, he heard a sound that made his heart drop. It was the starting roar of a powerful motor.

As John raced down the dock, a boat shot from between the pilings and headed out of the harbor, bound for open water. Boone was at the wheel. Emma, barely glimpsed, was lying across the rear seat. She was struggling to sit up.

By the time John reached the end of the dock, the boat was a hundred yards away. He could see it in the moonlight, headed for the mouth of the harbor, but the distance was too far for an accurate pistol shot. He might hit Emma or shoot a hole in the boat and sink it. All he could think to do was rush back to the Jeep and call the coast guard in the hope of intercepting the boat.

Then it happened. Boone glanced back and saw John, standing there. Whooping like a savage and revving the motor, he did something only a person as crazy as Boone would have done. He made a wide, circular turn and came back around on a course that would take him past the end of the dock at a distance of fifty yards. As he roared past, he shouted something and raised his hand, middle finger up, in an obscene gesture.

John shot him.

And Emma flung herself out of the boat.

The water felt like striking rough concrete as she hit. Then the icy cold closed around her. Such cold. The shock of it went clear through her.

Instinctively she kicked to the surface. She'd had a swimming class in college, but as a swimmer she was no better than average. And she'd never tried to swim in water this cold.

Her legs were stronger than her arms. She lay on her back, exposing as much of her body as possible to the air as she kicked with her legs. Maybe this was a mistake. Maybe she should have stayed in the boat with Boone. But drowning or freezing would be a kinder death than what he would do to her.

A memory flashed through her mind, the movie *Titanic,* with Jack clinging to the wreckage, slowly freezing to death in the icy water. Jack had taken a long time to die. Something told her that dying for real didn't take anywhere near that long.

How much distance had she covered? If she couldn't make it to shore, maybe she could at least reach one of the log rafts she'd seen floating in the cove. But she could feel the water sucking the heat from her limbs. She tried to kick harder but her legs were leaden. She was so cold, and so tired. . . .

Then she felt strong arms around her, supporting her in the water. "Hang on to this." John's voice rasped in her ear. He was out of breath, probably just as cold as she was, but when he pushed something in front of her, she managed to grab it. It was a floating log.

Ahead, in the moonlight, she could see one of the rafts, with some kind of shed on it. Then there were men, reaching down to pull them up. Somebody was wrapping her in a coat. In the near distance she could hear the wail of sirens.

John was holding her, his body shivering against hers. "It's all right, love," he murmured. "You're safe. It's over."

Emma spent the night in the hospital, being treated for moderate hypothermia. She woke the next morning with John sitting by her bed. No spooky roses, thank heaven. But he'd picked her up some good chocolates from the gift shop.

They held hands while he caught her up on all that had happened. It was David who'd made the call that brought the troopers and paramedics, followed by another call to his frantic mother. He and John had been checked over by the paramedics and released. Only Emma had needed treatment.

Boone had been shot in the shoulder. He'd blacked out from blood loss and wrecked the boat on one of the rocky islands outside Refuge Cove. Incredibly, he'd survived to be arrested by the state troopers. He was under guard in another part of the hospital, awaiting arraignment for murder and kidnapping as soon as he recovered. His lawyer would likely offer an insanity plea.

John lifted her hand and buried a kiss in her palm. "You did an incredibly brave thing, going with Boone, knowing what he could do to you. I would have given my life to free David, but I couldn't ask you to risk yours. I love you too much for that."

"I know. But I knew it had to be done, and that it had to be my decision. I couldn't lay that burden on you. I love you too much."

Freeing her hand from his, she reached up and laid it against his cheek. As he bent to kiss her, she felt, for the first time, the peace of knowing complete love and trust. There could be no room for doubt, for fear or even for a Plan B. They would always be there for each other.

EPILOGUE

Eleven months later

The raising of a new totem pole was always a grand occasion. Everyone who attended the ceremony—tribal members, family and friends—agreed that this totem, which would stand in a place of honor near the Clan House on the Totem Bight, was a masterpiece.

The few elders who remembered John's grandfather were happy to see his last totem pole finished and standing where it belonged. But of all the people there, no one was prouder than John, for the beautiful carving was the work of three generations. His grandfather had roughed out the design. John had done some work on it, but the gifted hand that had finished it and made it truly beautiful was David's.

The boy, who'd turned eighteen that spring had not been aware that he'd inherited the spirit of a master carver, but one day, when visiting at John's cabin, he had seen the unfinished totem pole in the shed and fallen in love. John had shown him the basic techniques of using his grandfather's tools, but the beauty of every detail had flowed from David as if it had been born in him.

Over his mother's objections, he had spent the entire summer after graduation working on the totem pole. Now that it was finished and in place, even Marlena, who was here today, had to concede that her son had a gift. David would be starting school at the University of Alaska's Southeast campus in Ketchikan, planning to become a teacher. But he already had plans to start another totem pole in his great-grandfather's old workshop.

As John stood at the edge of the crowd, he felt his wife's hand slip into his. "It's wonderful, isn't it?" Emma murmured. "He's done us all proud."

He slipped an arm around her waist, his hand resting on the rounded bulge beneath her sweater. Emma had enjoyed her job as a first grade teacher at a local elementary school. But she'd be taking maternity leave after Christmas. Knowing how much they both wanted children, John couldn't have been happier about the little girl who'd soon be joining their family.

With Emma beside him, he stood back from the crowd and looked up at the magnificent totem pole. It was as if all the generations were here—his grandfather, who'd taught him to value the old ways, John himself, who'd found his own, different path, and David, who seemed to have brought the family full circle.

Then there was John's father, the warrior, who'd died so young and so tragically. He, too, had possessed the gift of the master carver. Maybe, in spirit, he was here, too.

An eagle, circling overhead, swooped low, then soared again and vanished into the sunlight.